Isabelle shook her head. *Sorry, that's not going to work this time.*

Just as she had with Daniel Armand and his murderous accomplices, Isabelle turned the terrorist's ability against him. Before Jamie could even exhale, a ferocious wind whipped up behind him, blowing out the glass pane between him and the robots. A storm of broken glass pierced his body as he screamed in agony. He fell forward onto his face. Jagged shards jutted from his back. Blood spread across the tile floor. His body twitched spasmodically before falling still. She felt his heart stop beating. Jamie Skysinger was gone with the wind.

THE 4400®

THE VESUVIUS PROPHECY

GREG COX

THE 4400 created by
Scott Peters and Rene Echevarria

Pocket Star Books
New York   London   Toronto   Sydney

Pocket Star Books
A Division of Simon & Schuster, Inc.
1230 Avenue of the Americas
New York, NY 10020

This book is a work of fiction. Names, characters, places, and incidents either are products of the author's imagination or are used fictitiously. Any resemblance to actual events or locales or persons, living or dead, is entirely coincidental.

First Pocket Star Books paperback edition July 2008

POCKET STAR and colophon are registered trademarks of Simon & Schuster, Inc.

For information about special discounts for bulk purchases, please contact Simon & Schuster Special Sales at 1-800-456-6798 or business@simonandschuster.com.

Cover design: Alan Dingman/Art: CBS archive

Manufactured in the United States of America

10 9 8 7 6 5 4 3 2 1

ISBN-13: 978-1-4165-4317-6
ISBN-10:   1-4165-4317-1

The past is not dead. In fact, it's not even past.

—William Faulkner

NATIONAL THREAT ASSESSMENT

COMMAND INTELLIGENCE BRIEFING

To: Nina Jarvis, Director, Pacific Northwest Division
From: Archives (Classified.)
Re: Case File Chronology

Note: The events described in this dossier take place shortly after 4400 Incident E25, code-named "Graduation Day."

ONE

THE MAJESTIC WHITE peak of Mount Rainier was one of the first things Maia Skouris had seen when she'd Returned. The snowcapped mountain had loomed above her on that misty morning almost three years ago, when the eight-year-old girl had suddenly found herself standing on Highland Beach, alongside exactly 4,399 equally baffled souls. Maia remembered being scared and disoriented, not knowing where she was or what had become of her parents. Those feelings came back to her as the huge white glaciers grew steadily larger in the windshield of the chartered bus carrying her up the side of the mountain. She shuddered involuntarily in her seat. Maia was used to seeing the future, but sometimes the past sneaked up on her as well.

One minute I was picking flowers in California, she recalled. *The next minute there was a great big mountain on the horizon ...*

"All right, everyone," Alana Mareva addressed Maia and the other children from the front of the bus. A hint of a foreign accent colored the teacher's voice. Maia knew the elegant, dark-haired woman from outside school as well; Alana was Maia's mother's partner's girlfriend. "We're almost there."

The bus had left The 4400 Center over three hours ago, on a daylong field trip to Mount Rainier National Park. Towering green fir trees seemed to rush past outside as the bus full of kids climbed a steep mountain road toward the upper slopes of Rainier. A bright blue sky, dotted with fluffy white clouds, could be glimpsed above the treetops. The class had lucked out, weather-wise. It was a perfect day for an outdoor excursion.

Cheers greeted Alana's announcement. The hubbub of dozens of excited voices filled the interior of the air-conditioned bus. Ms. Tobey, the other teacher leading the field trip, clicked off the mounted TV set that had been entertaining the young passengers with a series of educational videos. Many of Maia's classmates had chosen to occupy themselves with their own books or computer games instead. Looking at the seemingly ordinary students and teachers, you would never guess that each and every one of them was, like Maia, one of the 4400—unless, of course, you noticed that Billy Hulquist was juggling marbles without actually touching them, or that Rory Plummer was drawing brightly colored designs in her notebook using only her fingertip. Duane Foxworth blinked repeatedly as he peered at the wilderness outside; Maia knew he was capturing snapshots of the scenery in his photographic memory. Sumi Price swayed in her seat, snapping her fingers to a rhythm only she could hear. Sumi's ears could pick up radio signals from as far away as Bucharest.

Pretty neat abilities, Maia thought enviously. *Too bad I can't trade mine for one of theirs.*

Precognition was seldom any fun.

Maia tucked her journal into the backpack resting at her feet. Despite her unpleasant associations with the mountain, she was looking forward to arriving at their destination. Her mother had insisted that Rainier was beautiful this time of year, and Maia had to admit that it would be kind of cool to see actual snow in the middle of May. Pushing her painful memories aside, she firmly resolved to have a good time. After all, she reminded herself, this sure beat being stuck inside a classroom all day.

"As we've discussed," Alana lectured, "Mount Rainier is the highest peak in the Cascades, rising to over fourteen thousand feet. That's almost three miles high. On a clear day, it can be seen from over one hundred and fifty miles away, all the way from Portland to Seattle. It is a dormant volcano, less than a million years old, and is part of the so-called Ring of Fire, a chain of seismic activity that stretches around the Pacific Ocean all the way to New Zealand."

Tyrell Hughes raised his hand to get the teacher's attention. "The volcano's not going to erupt while we're up there, is it?"

"I wouldn't worry about that." Alana gave the boy a reassuring smile. "Rainier hasn't had a major eruption for over five hundred years. It's bound to erupt someday, but there will probably be plenty of warning signs first. When Mount St. Helens erupted back in 1980, it was after months of preliminary tremors, bulges, and discharges of steam."

Even still, dozens of people got killed, Maia

thought. She had read about the 1980 eruption, which had taken place while she was still missing. Alana didn't seem to be in a hurry to mention that part.

"These days Mount Rainier is carefully monitored for any signs of increased volcanic activity," the teacher continued. "They wouldn't let us into the park if it wasn't safe."

"But it *could* go off today," Tyrell persisted. He seemed morbidly fascinated by the possibility. "Couldn't it?"

Alana sighed softly. "The odds are very much against it, Tyrell." The bus pulled into the parking lot outside the visitor center, and Alana looked grateful for the distraction. "Here we are, kids. Everyone ready to get off the bus?"

Another chorus of cheers testified to the children's eagerness to set foot on the mountain. Maia peered out the window at the breathtaking vista before her. A sign welcomed them to the Paradise area, elevation 5,400 feet. Acres of wildflowers carpeted the sloping green meadows ascending toward snowier slopes farther above. Granite boulders jutted from the verdant fields. Hiking trails led up and away from the visitor center, a futuristic structure that resembled a flying saucer.

Maia remembered Marco telling her that the very first modern UFO sighting had taken place near Mount Rainier in 1947, only a year after Maia had disappeared from California. Marco had speculated that many such UFO reports had been inspired by the glowing balls of light that had abducted the 4400 over the years. *Makes sense to me*, Maia thought, *although we'll probably never know for sure.*

Alana and Ms. Tobey herded the kids off the bus. "All right now, everybody stay together." Maia waited patiently for her turn to disembark. As she stepped down onto the pavement, the crisp mountain air carried the fragrance of heather and huckleberries. She took a deep breath, savoring the refreshing aroma. The sunlight, reflected off the icy glaciers above, was so bright that it made her eyes water. Lifting a hand to shield her eyes from the glare, she observed the winding paths leading up to the snow line. She wondered how high she would have to hike to reach all that frozen whiteness. It didn't seem that far away. Maybe there would be time to explore the trails after they checked out the exhibits at the visitor center?

Without warning, the future intruded on the present:

The snowy mountainside shakes. Hot steam vents from cracks in the earth. Maia's mother, Diana Skouris, confronts a nearby figure whose face Maia cannot see. Diana is wearing an NTAC vest over her snow gear. Tremors rock the ground beneath her feet, so that she can barely keep from falling. A deafening roar rises from below. The jets of steam smell like rotten eggs. "You have to stop this!" *Diana shouts urgently. Maia glimpses a masculine figure in a flannel shirt, his face turned away from hers. The man seems to be trembling in sync with the shuddering mountain.* "You don't want to be remembered this way. D. B. Cooper never hurt anybody!"

Melting snow starts to bubble and boil . . .

"Maia? Are you all right?"

The future faded from view, just like it always did, and Maia found herself looking into Alana's worried brown eyes. The teacher was crouched in front of Maia, examining her student with obvious concern. Maia saw her own face reflected in Alana's eyes. She looked pale and frightened. "What is it, Maia? Did you see something?"

Alana was very familiar with Maia's ability.

Maia nodded. She stared up at the crest of the mountain, half expecting to see an explosion of heated gases and lava blowing the peak apart.

Despite the warm sunlight, a familiar chill came over her as she spoke with utter certainty. "The mountain is going to wake up."

Alana gulped. Her dark eyes widened in alarm. She glanced around anxiously to see if any of the other children had overheard Maia, only to discover a circle of frightened kids surrounding them, obviously hanging on Maia's every word. Ms. Tobey tried to steer the onlookers away, but it was too late; some of the younger kids were already crying and begging to go home. Tyrell looked like he was about to throw up.

I'm sorry, Maia thought guiltily. The terrified expressions of her classmates tore her up inside. It wasn't fair; even in the company of her own kind, she still ended up feeling like a freak. *I didn't mean to spoil everything. I can't help what I see.*

"Are you sure?" Alana asked, loudly enough for the other kids to hear. She seemed to be trying to calm them as much as Maia. "It's impossible to predict exactly when Rainier might erupt."

"It's not impossible," Maia said. She had learned from experience that lying about her visions only made things worse. Like the time she hid her predictions from her mommy and all the 4400 got sick. "I just did it." The memory of what she had just seen was burned into her brain. "And I know who is responsible."

"Responsible?" Alana's brow furrowed in confusion. "Maia, people don't cause volcanoes to erupt."

"This one will." She remembered her mother shouting at a faceless figure in a flannel shirt. "His name is D. B. Cooper."

TWO

"THE SKYJACKER?"

Nina Jarvis, director of the National Threat Assessment Command, sat at the end of a long conference table at NTAC Headquarters in Seattle. A middle-aged brunette, she wore a tan dress suit and pearls. Metal blinds, pulled shut over the clear glass walls of the conference room, shielded those present from outside scrutiny. The low ceiling and overhead lights gave the chamber the feel of an underground bunker. A division of Homeland Security, NTAC had been tasked with monitoring the 4400 situation.

"That's what Maia said," Diana Skouris replied

to her boss. Diana was a slender woman in her mid-thirties, with auburn hair and green eyes. A black vest complemented a lightweight turtleneck sweater. She squirmed uncomfortably in her seat. As always, it felt odd reporting on her own adopted daughter, but NTAC had learned to take Maia's prophecies very seriously. She was *never* wrong.

"I always figured he was dead," Tom Baldwin commented. Diana's partner sat across from her, his rugged features illuminated by the glow of the computer screen in front of him. Sandy blond hair gave him a youthful look that was belied by his careworn face, which, even when relaxed, showed evidence of the strain he'd been under for the last few years. Pale blue eyes peered out from beneath his furrowed brow. He wore a blue serge jacket over a checked dress shirt that was open at the collar; Diana wasn't sure she'd ever seen him wear a tie. "That was, what, about thirty-five years ago?"

"Pretty much," Diana confirmed. Her own screen was occupied by a 1972 composite sketch of a middle-aged Caucasian male who looked vaguely like a young Ross Perot, with a narrow face, combed-back black hair, beady brown eyes, and a deeply tanned complexion. A narrow black tie was knotted around his collar. An alternative

sketch depicted him wearing the wraparound
Ray-Ban sunglasses he'd sported during part of the
flight. Although she had vague memories of hearing about the notorious hijacker when she was just
a kid, she had reviewed the case in preparation for
this meeting:

On the night before Thanksgiving, November
24, 1971, a man traveling under the name "Dan
Cooper" had hijacked a Northwest Orient flight
out of Portland, Oregon. Claiming to have a bomb
in his suitcase, Cooper quietly issued his demands
en route to Sea-Tac Airport, where he released
the passengers in exchange for $200,000 and four
parachutes. He then ordered the pilots and crew
to fly the jet toward Mexico at an unusually low
altitude and speed. Somewhere over southern
Washington state, he had exited the plane via the
rear stairway—and was never seen nor heard from
again. Despite an extensive FBI manhunt, neither
Cooper nor his body had ever been located. Over
the years, various names had been bruited about
as possible suspects, and there was no shortage of
theories regarding his fate, but the fact remained
that the true identity of "D. B. Cooper," as the
press mistakenly christened him, remained unknown to this day.

So how come Maia saw me confronting him on top of Mount Rainier?

"Even if he was still alive," Nina observed, "wouldn't he be in his eighties now?" In fact, Cooper's file contained an age-progressed version of the original FBI sketch. Scrolling down through the document, Diana found a color drawing of a wrinkled, white-haired old man. He looked rather too elderly to go mountaineering anytime soon.

"Not if he's one of the 4400," Marco Pacella pointed out. The floppy-haired head analyst looked like he should be working at Microsoft, not NTAC. Thick black glasses and a Hawaiian shirt gave him an endearingly nerdy appearance. He sat beside Diana at the table; they had been seeing each other for a while now. She wasn't quite sure where their relationship was going, but Marco was a sweet guy who was also one the smartest people she knew. "For all we know, he hasn't aged a day since he disappeared back in seventy-one."

Good point, Diana thought. All of the 4400 had returned to the present the same age they had been when they were first abducted by agents from the future. Technically, Maia herself was over seventy-eight years old, but, emotionally and physically, she was still just a ten-year-old girl. Diana tried not to think about the fact that her daughter was actually old enough to be her grandmother.

"So D. B. Cooper might be one of the 4400?" Tom shook his head at the notion. "Now there's one theory I've never heard before."

"It's possible," Marco said. Behind his glasses, his eyes gleamed with enthusiasm. "How cool would that be? Cooper's not just another hijacker; he's become a kind of cult hero, inspiring books, movies, pop songs, raps, et cetera. A New Wave band named D. B. Cooper released three albums back in the early eighties. Seth Green went looking for him in a recent comedy. There's even a yearly festival, 'D. B. Cooper Days,' held over in Cowlitz County, where some people believe Cooper touched down." He grinned infectiously. "I actually hit the festival a couple years ago. It was a blast."

Diana remembered Marco trying to talk her into attending the celebration the previous November. As it happened, she had been busy with a case at the time. "I suppose any unsolved mystery has its own fascination, but I can't say I approve of people romanticizing a wanted hijacker."

"Well, nobody actually got hurt in the D. B. Cooper incident," Marco pointed out. "The rest of the passengers didn't know there was a problem until

Cooper ordered them off the plane at Sea-Tac. We don't even know if the bomb in the briefcase was for real." He shrugged. "Besides, this was back before people were all stressed-out over terrorists. There weren't even metal detectors in the airports then."

Hard to imagine, Diana thought. The world had changed so much over the last few decades. She felt an extra twinge of sympathy for her daughter, who had suddenly jumped from 1946 to the present. *It's a wonder she's adapted as well as she has.*

"You say Cooper's been referenced in pop songs and raps?" Tom queried Marco.

A pop culture maven, Marco nodded in confirmation. "Oh yeah. Kid Rock cited him in one song. MF DOOM mentioned him in a rap just last year."

Diana had no idea who "MF DOOM" was. *Some sort of hip-hop artist,* she guessed.

"Could that be where Maia picked up the name?" Tom asked.

Diana shook her head. "I talked to her about that. The name means nothing to her, except that she heard me use it in her vision." She chuckled softly. "Maia's musical tastes lean more toward Frank Sinatra and the big band era."

"Beats Britney Spears," Tom said with a smirk.

Amen, Diana thought.

"Putting aside the Cooper issue for now," Nina said, all business, "I'm more concerned about another aspect of Maia's vision. She thought she saw Mount Rainier erupting?"

"She saw it 'waking up,' to be exact," Diana reported. "Earth tremors, jets of hot steam, and so on. It certainly sounds like brewing volcanic activity to me."

Marco's face took on a more serious expression. "That would be serious bad news. Mount Rainier is considered the most dangerous volcano on the continent, mostly due to its proximity to high population centers like Seattle and Tacoma. The main threat would be the lahars, volcanic mudflows composed of pulverized rock and ice. Resembling rivers of wet concrete, the lahars would obliterate everything in their path, including entire towns and forests, as they rushed downhill toward the lowlands. Geological surveys indicate that past lahars have stretched all the way to Seattle, burying everything along the way. You might also get tsunamis in Puget Sound and Lake Washington." He paused for emphasis. "We're talking a disaster of catastrophic proportions, way worse than when Mount St. Helens blew its top."

"I remember that," Tom said. "I was in junior high then. The eruption rattled all the doors and windows at our house, waking me up at eight-thirty in the morning, and we were over a hundred miles away from St. Helens. My grandparents' cabin up in the mountains was completely covered with ash."

"Right," Marco said. "Now imagine a large chunk of Rainier sliding downhill at top speed, only eighty miles away from where we're sitting right now. And the latest U.S. Geological Survey gives a one-in-seven chance of Rainier erupting in our lifetime."

Diana frowned. "According to Maia, the odds are a lot better than that. Or worse, depending on how you look at it."

A hush fell over the room as they all contemplated the disaster Marco had just described. *That's what I've got waiting for me?* Diana thought in chagrin. She briefly flirted with the idea of moving far away from Rainier to ensure that Maia's prediction never came true. Experience, however, had taught her that the future didn't work that way. If Maia said something was going to happen, it happened. Any attempts to circumvent her visions invariably led you right to where she predicted. *All I can do is trust my instincts and take my chances.*

Nina finally broke the silence. "Just to clarify, this isn't *the* Catastrophe that the 4400 are here to prevent?"

It had been Tom who first discovered that the 4400 had originally been abducted not by aliens, but by inhabitants of the future. In theory, these mysterious individuals had endowed the 4400 with special abilities and returned them to the present in order to change the future somehow, thereby averting some terrible future catastrophe. Diana had only recently met one of the future people in the flesh; "Sarah Rutledge" had posed as Maia's long-lost sister in an attempt to spirit Maia away to a previous century, as part of yet another stab at altering history. In theory, "Sarah" and her enigmatic cohorts had the best of intentions, but Diana sometimes had her doubts. It was difficult to feel well-disposed toward people who had tried to kidnap her daughter . . .

"Probably not," Marco said. "The master plan of our friends in the future is still a bit murky, but everything we've learned so far suggests that they're concerned with some sort of global apocalypse in the distant future, when time travel is actually an option. The eruption of Mount Rainier, as horrific as it would be, is probably not what they're worried about."

"I wish I could say the same," Nina groused. She looked over the agents assembled in the room. "So now what?"

Tom cracked his knuckles. "Doesn't Seattle already have a volcano emergency plan in place?"

"That's right," Marco declared. "A lahar detection system monitors Rainier's ground vibrations with sensors that transmit radio warnings to both Fort Lewis and Pierce County's 911 center, which is staffed around the clock. Unfortunately, there might not be much warning when the mountain blows. Once the lahars start moving, a lot of communities will have only forty-five minutes to evacuate before their homes and businesses are swept under. Maybe less."

There were over three million people in the Seattle metro area, Diana recalled, not counting all the small towns and suburbs between here and Tacoma. Was it even possible to evacuate that many people in a timely fashion? As a mother, she knew that the local schools held regular volcano emergency drills, but who knew whether all that practice would pay off if and when Rainier finally erupted. If nothing else, the property damage would be immeasurable. Entire communities could disappear beneath the gigantic mudflows. The very landscape of the Pacific Northwest would be changed forever.

"I see," Nina said grimly. "I'll quietly inform FEMA and Pierce County of our concerns, but the last thing we want to start is a panic. This stays between us, at least for the time being."

"Are we sure that's the right thing to do?" Marco asked. "Shouldn't we warn the public of Maia's prediction to give them a chance to evacuate? It seems to me that we've got the makings of a serious moral dilemma here. Do we have the right to withhold information regarding a potentially major disaster?"

Diana shuddered at the thought of an eruption catching the citizenry by surprise. "Marco may have a point here. Maia has never been wrong before."

"But that doesn't mean we don't have a chance to prevent the eruption," Tom argued. "Isn't the whole point of the 4400 that the future *can* be changed? That's why they were sent back to us in the first place."

"Tell me about it," Marco said. "We've spent hours down in the Theory Room trying to reconcile precognition with the concept of a mutable future. Predestination versus time travel. Let me tell you, it's enough to make your head spin."

Nina frowned. "I can't base my decisions on metaphysics. All I know is that I can't justify throwing the entire Pacific Northwest into crisis mode simply on the word of one admittedly gifted little girl. I'm going to need a lot more information before I push the panic button on this one." She lowered the screen on her computer and rose from her seat. "For now, follow up on the 'D. B. Cooper' angle. Maybe we can get a clearer picture of what we're dealing with once we've located that piece of the puzzle."

"In other words," Tom said dryly, "you just want us to track down a legendary fugitive who may or may not be alive, and who has eluded capture for nearly forty years?"

Nina cracked a tight smile as she exited the conference. "You got a problem with that, Baldwin?"

"Nope, just asking."

He shared a wry look with Diana, but she couldn't shake an ominous sense of dread. Maia had seen Rainier stir from its ancient slumber and Maia was never wrong. *And I'm going to be right on top of the mountain when it happens.* She knew better than to try to avoid that scenario; for all she knew, any attempts to circumvent Maia's prediction would lead directly to the very outcome she sought to avert. She could only hope that Maia and Tom and everyone else she cared about was far away from Rainier when the moment came. As far as they knew, only two people were destined to meet atop the quaking mountain.

Me . . . and D. B. Cooper.

A few blocks away, a woman sat alone at a Starbucks, sipping on an iced chai as she pretended to read a magazine. Stylish sunglasses concealed the woman's eyes, which were actually fixed on the meeting taking place in the NTAC conference room. The intervening walls and distance provided no obstacle to her surveillance. She could see through most anything these days, thanks to her singular ability. Her "spy-eyes," as she thought of them, were a gift from the future. Reading lips, on the other hand, was something she'd had to learn on her own.

She hadn't always seen her ability as a blessing. At first, before she learned to control it, her mutated eyes had nearly driven her insane. She had seen too much, too deeply. Human beings had turned into walking collections of bones and organs. She couldn't even judge where she was or how far away something was anymore. Physical obstacles and distances had no longer served to orient her. She had lost all sense of her location. Shocking, confusing images impinged on her from all directions, no matter what she did to block them out. Locking herself up in a pitch-black closet had brought her no relief. Not even squeezing her eyes shut had kept the maddening visual overload at bay. She had seen right through her own eyelids.

In retrospect, she mused, *it's a miracle that I never clawed my eyes out.*

And it was all NTAC's fault. Although she hadn't known it then, it was the promicin inhibitor in her bloodstream that had kept her from mastering her new ability. Once the scandal forced the government to stop illegally pumping their poison into her veins at every checkup, she'd discovered how to focus her eyes so that she saw only what she wanted to see. It hadn't been easy, but she'd done it.

Now it seemed that all her efforts had been rewarded. Despite a few frustrating moments, when the NTAC agents' faces had been turned away from her, she had managed to get the gist of the discussion. *Mount Rainier? Oh my God!* She fished a cell phone from her purse and hit the speed dial. This news was too big to keep to herself. Her foot tapped impatiently against the floor.

"It's me," she said tersely, once the call was picked up at the other end. "There's something you need to know. . . ."

THREE

THE FACES OF the 4400 blinked across the screen of Tom's laptop, until they threatened to blur into a meaningless montage of mug shots. Tom paused the search long enough to lift his reading glasses and rub his weary eyes. He had scoured this database so many times that sometimes the familiar faces flashed through his mind even when he was sleeping. Attrition had reduced the surviving returnees' numbers over the last few years, but there were still a hell of a lot of files to go through. He and Diana had been at this for a couple of hours now. They sat across from each other at a desk in their office, the lids of their laptops flipped up so that they looked like they were playing a game of Battleship together. Tom's jacket was draped over the back of his chair. A mug of cold coffee rested beside his keyboard.

"I think I have something," Diana said.

A jolt of adrenaline energized Tom. Getting up from his seat, he circled around to look over Diana's shoulder at the case file on her screen. NTAC mug shots offered front and side views of a middle-aged man with mussed black hair and a heavy tan. A caption identified the man as "De-Meers, Cooper."

"He fits the profile," Diana explained. "Right age, right race, right gender. Same general physique. Plus, he disappeared in 1971, about the same time that D. B. Cooper jumped out of that jet with two hundred thousand dollars." She rapidly scanned his bio. "He also served as paratrooper during the Korean War, which gives him skydiving experience."

Tom peered at the photo on the screen, taken when the man was first processed by Homeland Security, right after the 4400's return. "He kind of looks like the guy in the FBI sketch. Hard to tell for sure." Like most of the returnees back then, DeMeers had a dazed, befuddled expression on his face. Unlike the others, fresh scratch marks covered his face, and he was missing one of his front teeth. He looked as if he'd been in a fight or an accident right before he was abducted. "Where is he now?"

"According to his file, he works as a fish vendor down at Pike Place Market." She looked up at Tom. "Feel like a trip to the Market?"

Tom nodded. He reclaimed his jacket from the back of his chair. "Let's go."

Pike Place Market, which was built into a steep hill overlooking the waterfront, was Seattle's number one tourist attraction, something Diana was acutely reminded of as they made their way through a crowd of locals and tourists toward the front entrance of the Market. Giant red letters spelled out PUBLIC MARKET CENTER above the fresh fish and produce stalls facing the street. The glowing hands of a large neon clock confirmed that it was a little past noon, right in the middle of the midday rush. MEET THE PRODUCERS proclaimed a billboard atop one of the adjacent buildings, summing up the Market's original mission statement. Although the historic landmark had started out as simply a place where Seattleites could buy their fruits and vegetables directly from local farmers, its copious booths, stalls, and shops now hawked everything from crafts to magic tricks, as well as the freshest seafood in town. A distinctly fishy odor wafted past Diana's nostrils, reminding her that she hadn't had lunch yet.

Maybe I can grab a bite after we pick up DeMeers for questioning, she thought. A life-sized bronze piggy bank, the Market's official mascot, greeted her at the entrance. Diana rubbed its snout for luck. Hopefully, DeMeers would come with them willingly.

To avoid creating a scene, they had left their NTAC flak jackets in the car. The two agents blended in with the various shoppers and sightseers as they stepped beneath a wooden awning to approach the fish market. A generous assortment of crabs, clams, oysters, salmon, halibut, catfish, lobster tails, shrimp, squids, rainbow trout, and other aquatic foodstuffs were laid out atop sloping beds of crushed ice. Boxes of smoked salmon, decorated with Northwest Indian designs, packed the shelves behind the front counter, along with gift packs of specialty sauces and spices. Strips of smoked eel hung from a cord stretched up over the stall. CAUTION: LOW FLYING FISH, warned a handwritten sign pinned up over the front counter. Fishmongers, clad in orange rubber overalls, gleefully hurled slippery, silver salmon carcasses back and forth between one another, to the delight and amusement of the crowd, who oohed and aahed in appreciation every time a vendor caught one of the scaly missiles. Light applause greeted each successful toss. Diana remembered bringing Maia to see the fishmongers' performance not long after she had first adopted her. The wide-eyed girl had correctly predicted the one time a vendor missed a catch.

"You see him yet?" Tom asked her quietly.

Diana scanned the faces of the men behind the counter. At first she didn't spot anyone who looked like D. B. Cooper or Cooper DeMeers, but then her eyes zoomed in on a middle-aged fishmonger weighing a swordfish steak on an electronic scale. Unlike the conservative-looking returnee picked up at Highland Beach two years ago, this man had a shaved skull and a bushy, salt-and-pepper beard. Still, he looked to be the right general age and build: mid-forties, about 175 pounds, a little under six feet tall. A gold tooth glittered near the front of his smile, right where DeMeers had lost one of his upper incisors. She discreetly pointed the bald man out to Tom. "I think that might be him."

Tom nodded. "Kind of a new look."

"If I were D. B. Cooper," Diana observed, "I might change my appearance, too. Hijacking a commercial aircraft is a federal offense; there is no statute of limitations. Thirty-three years or not, 'Dan Cooper' is still wanted by the FBI."

"Good point." Tom surveyed his surroundings. "But if he got away with two hundred thousand dollars, what's he doing slinging salmon for a living? Could he really have blown through it all before he was abducted?"

Diana edged her way through the crowd surrounding the fish market. A busker played a harmonica nearby. A gaggle of chattering teenagers got in her way. "Let's find out."

She found herself wishing that DeMeers worked at a less popular attraction. "Excuse me," she murmured repeatedly as she and Tom tried to reach the counter. Captivated by the flying fish display, the crowd was reluctant to let her through. The two agents were still a couple of rows of people away from their suspect, however, when a stranger suddenly stepped up to the counter and thrust his face toward the bald-headed fishmonger. "Cooper DeMeers?" the man asked urgently. "Is that you?"

Who in the world? Diana wondered, caught

off guard by this unexpected development. The speaker was a chunky, bull-necked white man, whose reddish-blond crew cut and "Semper Fi" T-shirt hinted that he might be an ex-Marine. A youthful face placed him in his twenties. Narrow green eyes squinted at DeMeers. Diana thought the newcomer looked vaguely familiar, but she couldn't immediately place his face. She exchanged a puzzled look with Tom, who appeared equally baffled. Was this just a coincidence, or something else altogether? Her body tensed for action. Where the 4400 were concerned, she had learned not to take anything for granted.

"Who's asking?" the fishmonger replied warily. He had no discernible accent, just like D. B. Cooper. "Do I know you?"

"You've gotta come with me!" Crew Cut insisted. His gruff tone made it clear he wasn't kidding around. He acted as if it was a matter of life and death. "They're coming to get you. They know who you are!"

Uh-oh, Diana thought. *This isn't good.*

"That does it." Tom reached beneath his jacket and pulled out his badge, which he raised in the air. "NTAC!" he shouted over the hubbub. Abandoning subtlety, he and Diana began to elbow their way through the crowd. "Everybody stay right where they are!"

DeMeers's eyes widened in alarm. He started to back away, but Crew Cut reached across the counter and grabbed on to his arm. "Hurry! Come with me!" He tugged DeMeers toward a gap in the counter. "We can still get away!"

"Let go of me!" DeMeers shouted. Frightened brown eyes shifted back and forth between the stranger and the NTAC agents closing in on him. Scattered applause gave way to confused murmurs and exclamations as the milling crowd became aware of the disturbance. Nervous spectators backed away from the confrontation, getting in the way of Diana and Tom, who could only watch in frustration as the burly stranger refused to release his grip on DeMeers's arm. The fishmonger stared in confusion at the hand clutching his wrist. He flinched, as though jolted by static electricity. "Hey, what are you doing to me?" He tried to yank his arm free. "Let go, damnit!"

Diana felt the situation escalating out of control. "Both of you," she shouted. "Hands in the air where I can see them!"

Crew Cut ignored her, but DeMeers's face swung toward her. He was visibly agitated; his entire body was shaking uncontrollably. Swollen veins throbbed at his temples. His eyes were bloodshot. For a second, Diana feared he was having some sort of seizure.

What's wrong with him?

Without warning, the ground shook beneath Diana's feet. A grinding roar, which seemed to rise up from the very bowels of the earth, drowned out the sudden shouts and screams of the people around her. Diana stumbled unsteadily and grabbed a painted iron support column to steady herself. People tumbled onto the hard tile floor. An avalanche of crushed ice and frozen fish spilled across the floor of the Market, adding to the confusion. The cold ice engulfed Diana's shoes and ankles, chilling her feet. The slippery seafood didn't make staying upright any easier. Hanging lamps swung wildly above the fish stand. Crashing noises came from the adjacent stalls as produce and merchandise hit the ground. Glassware broke somewhere nearby. Dust rained down from the wooden awning overhead. A neon sign exploded in a shower of sparks.

Earthquake! Diana realized. She glanced anxiously at her partner and saw Tom lurching toward her, somehow managing to stay on his feet. He nodded at the fish market, not about to let their suspects get away from them. His jaw was clenched in determination as he waded clumsily through the spilled ice and seafood, his feet slipping on the wet tiles. The initial tremor only lasted for a few heartbeats, but seemed to go on forever. Is this the Big One?

Satisfied that her partner was okay, at least for the moment, Diana worried about her daughter, and prayed that Maia's school at The 4400 Center hadn't been hit too hard by the quake. She fought a temptation to try to reach Maia via cell phone; most likely, communications networks were already being flooded by frantic residents seeking loved ones and emergency services. Instead she turned her attention back to Cooper DeMeers and the anonymous leatherneck accosting him. The two men looked just as startled by the quake as everyone else, but DeMeers regained his bearings a little faster than the stranger. Taking advantage of the unexpected tremor, the fishmonger yanked his arm free of the other man's grip. Crew Cut fell forward against a half-empty bed of ice. He snatched again at DeMeers. "Don't give me any trouble," he snarled, still intent on his unknown mission despite the seismic shocks jolting the Market. "You're coming with me!"

"The hell I am!" Bracing himself against the other side of the counter, DeMeers grabbed a fresh halibut by the tail and swung it around, walloping the stranger in the face. The blow staggered the man, who fell backward into the reeling crowd. The initial tremor seemed to have subsided, but smaller aftershocks continued to rattle the Market. Was the worst over, Diana wondered, or was this just the beginning? DeMeers bolted from the stall and took off down the main arcade. Diana realized that she was closer to the fleeing fishmonger than her partner was.

"I'll take DeMeers!" she shouted at Tom. Letting go of the steel column, she stumbled after the suspected hijacker. Crew Cut, having managed to extract himself from a tangle of panicked civilians, glared angrily at Diana before dashing for the stairs leading to the lower levels of the market. Tom was already in hot pursuit of the stranger. Tom shoved a disoriented street performer out of his way.

"Got it," he called back to her. "Watch yourself."

You, too, Diana thought. She reached beneath her jacket and retrieved her Smith & Wesson semiautomatic pistol. As one of the 4400, DeMeers could very well be endowed with some

dangerous superhuman ability. Not every returnee
had developed an ability right away, but over the
last few years she and Tom had come up against
men and women who could shatter skulls with a
thought, emit lethal viruses from their pores, read
minds, and perform any number of other unnatural feats. Diana understood that she was taking a
serious risk chasing after DeMeers. Who knew
what he might be capable of? Hell, if he really was
D. B. Cooper, he had once threatened to blow up
an entire 727. *I could be dealing with a pretty ruthless
customer here.*

The tremors began to subside, but pandemo-
nium still filled the marketplace. Throngs of terrified people poured out of the Market into the open
streets. Spilled fruit and vegetables were trampled
beneath the crowd's feet. The air smelled of salt
water and salad. People were crying and squealing and thanking God that they were still alive.
Diana had to force her way through the disorderly
exodus; she felt like a salmon fighting her way up-
stream.

Covered by an awning, the arcade stretched
for blocks alongside Pike Place, a long boulevard
running parallel to the waterfront several stories
below. Stalls packed with fresh produce gradually

gave way to rows of long tables that were usually manned by a wide variety of local craftsmen and artists. Heaps of handmade sweaters, quilts, jewelry, scrimshaw, knickknacks, souvenirs, candles, snow globes, carved driftwood, and other merchandise littered the tables and floor, abandoned by dealers and customers alike. A miniature ceramic pig crunched beneath Diana's shoes as she hurried after DeMeers, who was keeping a few yards ahead of her. His orange rubber overalls made him easy to keep track of.

"Stop!" she called out to him. "There's no need to run. We just need to talk to you!"

The fishmonger glanced back at her over his shoulder, then kept on running. Because he was wanted by the FBI for hijacking, she wondered, or only because he was spooked? Unfortunately, relations between NTAC and the 4400 had hit an all-time low recently, after the former head of NTAC, Dennis Ryland, had been implicated in a plot to inject the 4400 with an untested promicin inhibitor that had nearly killed them all. Some twenty-three returnees had died from the injections, before an antidote was found. Tom and Diana had personally exposed the conspiracy, but that made little difference as far as most of the 4400 were concerned. These days the returnees regarded NTAC with suspicion if not outright hostility, which made things a good deal more complicated.

Thanks a lot, Dennis.

"NTAC! Coming through!" Diana hollered. Part of her wondered whether she should be pursuing a suspect in the middle of an earthquake, but what else was she supposed to do? She couldn't shoot or arrest a misbehaving geological fault line; she just had to hope that Seattle's Disaster Aid and Response Teams were already mobilizing to deal with the earthquake and its aftershocks. In the meantime, she had a job to do. "Give it up, DeMeers! You're just making things harder for yourself!"

He glanced back again to see Diana gaining on him. Gulping, he spied the gun in her hand. Bloodshot eyes widened in fear. Veins pulsed across his cranium. "Leave me alone!"

A powerful aftershock rocked the arcade. Chairs and tables toppled over. A section of awning crashed down between them, raising a cloud of dust and debris. Coughing on the haze, Diana hurdled a heap of splintered timbers in order to keep after DeMeers. Long hours at the gym paid off as her racing legs ate up the distance between her and her quarry. She was clearly in better shape than the fugitive, who was flushed and breathing hard. Her hand held on tightly to the grip of her pistol. She had no intention of firing, except in self-defense. The shaking ground and panicked crowd made it impossible to get a clear shot, but maybe she could bluff DeMeers into surrendering. "Stop or I'll shoot!"

"Mommy!"

A shrill cry yanked Diana's attention away from DeMeers. Looking to the right, she spied a lost child crawling out from beneath an overturned handicrafts stand. The toddler, who looked no more than two years old, had obviously gotten separated from her mother in the chaos; it was a miracle she hadn't already been trampled by the heedless crowd. Tears gushed from the little girl's eyes. She clutched a stuffed orca to her chest.

"Where's my mommy!"

To her alarm, Diana spotted a sparking electrical cable dangling from a shattered overhead lighting fixture. The live wire was sputtering dangerously close to the unsuspecting toddler, who was now tottering on two feet across the cracked tile floor. The cable hissed like a lurking serpent.

"Hold on, honey!" Diana called to the girl. "Stay right where you are!"

Tucking her pistol back into its holster, she rushed forward and swept the girl up into her arms and away from the lethal wire. "It's all right," she cooed reassuringly into the toddler's ear. Her eyes searched the wrecked arcade for some sign of a parent or guardian. "We'll find your mommy."

To her relief, a tearful young woman came running up to them. Diana thought she recognized her as one of the street musicians who performed at the Market for spare change. "Harmony!" the mother cried out, her voice hoarse with emotion. "Ohmigod . . . Harmony!" Moist blue eyes looked gratefully at Diana. "Thank you so much! I tried to hold on to her, but . . . everyone was running and screaming and pushing . . ."

"I understand," Diana said, relinquishing Harmony to her mother. She liked to think that some good Samaritan would look out for Maia in similar circumstances. "I'm glad I could help." Leaving mother and child to their tearful reunion, she turned to look for DeMeers, but, no surprise, the suspected skyjacker was long gone. Diana guessed that he had disappeared into the surrounding streets and alleys. For all she knew, he was halfway to the Space Needle by now.

She let out an exasperated sigh. At least the

earthquake seemed to be over for the moment. *That was a lucky break for DeMeers,* she thought, *or was it more than luck?* An ominous suspicion was already forming at the back of her mind. *First, Maia links D. B. Cooper to an eruption on Mount Rainier. Now a 4400 matching Cooper's profile gets away from us thanks to a convenient earthquake?* You didn't have to be a genius like Marco and his buddies to see a possible connection there. Diana felt a chill run down her spine. This case was getting scarier by the moment.

And who was that stranger who tried to get DeMeers away from us? Where does he fit into this picture?

Maybe Tom had succeeded in apprehending the other man. Resisting an urge to check immediately on her daughter, Diana wheeled around and headed for a nearby ramp leading down into the lower levels of the Market. She was desperate to know that Maia was safe, but right now her duty to her partner took priority. He was counting on her for backup.

Hang on, Tom, she thought. *I'm coming.*

DOWN UNDER. 3 FLOORS—OVER FIFTY SHOPS TO SERVE YOU! read the sign above the staircase leading down to the Market's lower levels. A large painted arrow indicated the way.

Tom took the steps two at a time, squeezing his muscular frame past the hordes of frenzied men and women racing up the stairs. Squealing patrons erupted from the subterranean complex like lava spewing from a volcanic fissure. He struggled to keep the hefty stranger in sight; thankfully, the frenzied crowd seemed to be impeding the leatherneck's escape as well. He and Tom appeared to be the only two people racing deeper into Down Under, instead of rushing madly toward the surface. Tom couldn't help thinking that the fleeing civilians probably had the right idea. This old building was no place to be during an earthquake; he doubted that the historic structure conformed to modern construction codes.

Just my luck, he thought. *Of all places for this perp to run.*

The wooden floor rolled beneath his feet as he hit the bottom of the steps. His memory instantly flashed back to that last big jolt in 2001. He had been at his desk at the FBI that morning, when the entire building had started shaking like Galloping Gertie. The 6.8-magnitude temblor had caused major property damage all the way from

Pioneer Square, just a few blocks south of here, to the capitol building in Olympia. It had even shifted all of Seattle five millimeters to the northeast. Miraculously, there had been only one fatality, a heart attack, and Tom had counted himself lucky that he and his family had come through the quake unscathed. Little had he known that less than two months later his son Kyle would be in a coma and his nephew Shawn would disappear from the face of the Earth. In a sense, that quake in '01—the so-called "Rattle in Seattle"—had marked the beginning of the turmoil he'd been living through for the last five years. This quake didn't seem quite as strong as that earlier disaster, but it set his nerves on edge nonetheless.

Can the self-pity, he scolded himself, shaking off the unsettling memories. *Keep your mind on the job.*

Down Under was a warren of underground shops lining a maze of winding corridors. Comic books, candy, used books, antique postcards, rare coins, natural foods, jewelry, carved bones, crystals, handbags, pipes, and tobacco were among the goods on sale in the varied small emporia. Chain stores were expressly forbidden, in order to preserve the unique, idiosyncratic nature of the Market. Ramps and stairwells led down to two more stories of shops and snack bars. Tom's girlfriend, Alana, often liked to browse the Market on weekends, so he knew the layout pretty well. Still, even with everyone else abandoning the lower levels in droves, he knew it would be all too easy to lose track of the stranger in this sprawling labyrinth. His footsteps echoed through the underground tunnel as he chased after the stranger. Jelly beans, shopping bags, and other discarded possessions littered the floor. A collectible action figure had been stomped to pieces, strewing tiny plastic limbs in his path. Tom held up his badge.

"NTAC! I'm ordering you to—"

An aftershock shook Down Under. Dust and plaster rained down from the ceiling, joining the random debris covering the floor. Tom glanced up apprehensively. He didn't want to get pancaked between collapsing floors.

"You there!" he shouted at the stranger. "It isn't safe down here. You need to come with me."

"That's what you think!" the man yelled back at him. He looked more irritated than anxious about being chased by a federal agent. His ruddy face showed no sign of surrender. "You don't know who you're messing with, g-man!"

Who the hell is this guy? Tom wondered. He felt

certain that he'd seen the man's face before . . .
maybe in the 4400 database? He reluctantly drew
his gun. He didn't want to fire at someone whose
identity and motives remained unknown, but the
fact that the other man had tried to snatch De-
Meers away from them suggested that he was up
to no good. Could he be a member of the Nova
Group? The radical terrorist organization, composed of renegade 4400 members out for revenge
against the government, was on its last legs since
NTAC had taken their leader, Daniel Armand,
into custody a few days ago, but there were probably still a few splinter groups out there looking for
trouble. Did Cooper DeMeers belong to a surviving Nova cell? Was that why he ran from them?
Tom wanted answers . . . pronto.

"Freeze!" he ordered, drawing a bead on the
stranger. He gripped the pistol with both hands to
steady his aim, despite the lingering aftershocks. A
dusty haze clouded the air between the two men.
Tom's finger tightened on the trigger of his sidearm. "This is your last warning!"

To his surprise, the stranger merely smirked at
the sight of the gun. "Don't waste your bullets,
flatfoot!" He darted to his left and Tom fired at
the man's leg. The gunshot reverberated through

the subterranean warren of shops. He thought it looked like a good hit, but it didn't even slow the stranger down. The man ducked into a jewelry shop only slightly larger than a cubbyhole, momentarily disappearing from sight. THE HOUSE OF JADE was painted on the shop's dusty window. Tom glimpsed toppled shelves and display cases inside.

Swearing under his breath, he hurried toward the open door of the emporium. He had his quarry trapped now; there was only one way out of the minuscule shop. He flattened himself against the wall next to the entrance, just in case the stranger was armed, but no bullets came flying out of the House of Jade. Holding his gun in the high-ready position, he spun around and charged through the door. "Hands up!" he ordered. "I want to see them!"

But there was nobody there. The tiny shop was indeed a dead end, but all Tom found inside was the mess the earthquake had made of the business. Polished green gemstones rolled across the floor. A cash register lay overturned atop a counter. Loose bills and coins were scattered about for the taking. Tom stepped over a shattered display case. Broken glass crunched beneath his soles. Looking around, he saw at once that the cramped shop offered no place to hide.

The nameless stranger had vanished into thin air.

Or had he? Tom had yet to encounter a 4400 who could turn himself invisible, but there was a first time for everything. Holding his gun out in front of him, he cautiously waved his arm through the seemingly empty air around him. It wasn't until he had meticulously swept the whole shop, encountering no unseen presences, that he finally dropped his guard and conceded that the stranger had gotten away somehow.

Well, that settles one thing, he thought. Either the stranger was the second coming of Harry Houdini or he was definitely one of the 4400. Tom tried to figure out what kind of unnatural talent the man might have used to make his amazing escape. Teleportation? The ability to walk through walls? Once he would have rejected both scenarios as absurd, but the last few years had drastically broadened his sense of what was truly possible in this brave new world of theirs. Since the 4400 had returned to the present, he had encountered a serial killer who could make other people murder for him, enjoyed eight years of domestic bliss in an alternate reality created by Alana, and discovered a future intelligence residing in the body of his son. He shook his head wearily. After all that, why not a disappearing Marine as well?

"Tom!"

Diana came rushing into the jewelry shop. A quick glance at the trashed store, and her partner's brooding expression, told her all she needed to know. "Your guy got away, too?"

"I'm afraid so." He thrust his sidearm back into its holster. "DeMeers?"

She shook her head. "I lost him in all the chaos upstairs." She let out a heavy sigh. "So now we've got *two* missing suspects?"

"That's about the size of it," he admitted. He glanced around at the scattered debris. "At least the Market is still standing." Given that this part of Seattle was largely built on loose, soggy soil, they were lucky that the ground hadn't liquefied beneath them.

A window at the rear of the shop offered a breathtaking view of Elliott Bay. In the distance, the immense snowy bulk of Mount Rainier hovered ominously above the scenery like a castle in the sky.

"Yeah," Diana said grimly. "For now."

FOUR

THE VIEW WAS impressive, Shawn Farrell admitted.

Like most native Seattleites, he hadn't visited the Space Needle in years. It was a place for tourists and for entertaining relatives from out of town. Over six hundred feet tall, the famous spire was left over from the 1962 World's Fair and had been hovering like a flying saucer over Seattle Center since before he was born. On a clear day like today, you could see all the way to Mount Rainier to the south, the Cascade Mountains to the east, Elliott Bay and the Olympic Peninsula to the west, and Puget Sound to the north. Closer to home, the Needle's circular observation deck looked out over downtown and the waterfront.

If he squinted, Shawn could spot the roof of The 4400 Center several blocks away. Directly below him were the myriad attractions of the Seattle Center, the old fairgrounds, which now hosted a variety of museums, concert halls, stadiums, and exhibitions. Carnival rides filled the Fun Forest across from the Needle. From atop the towering spire, even the giant Ferris wheel and roller coaster looked like kiddie rides. The psychedelic exterior of the Experience Music Project, its painted steel contours undulating across the street, glinted in the sunlight.

Yep, the view was nothing to sneeze at, Shawn conceded.

Too bad he was too tense to enjoy it.

The source of his discomfort clung to his arm as they strolled around the deck. "Thank you so much for the lunch," Isabelle Tyler chirped. The lovely young woman wore a light green sundress that showed off her supple figure. A mane of curly brown hair tumbled past her shoulders. Silver earrings matched the glittering chain necklace around her neck. "It was just as romantic as I imagined!"

"Well, I knew you wanted to check out the restaurant here," Shawn said with a shrug. Only nineteen years old, the neatly groomed young man had already become the head of The 4400 Center and the unofficial spokesman for the returnees. His short brown hair contrasted with Isabelle's billowing tresses. They were an attractive couple. Heads turned as they walked past the other sightseers upon the deck; Shawn suspected that most of the men were envying his drop-dead gorgeous girlfriend. *But they don't know her like I do,* he thought ruefully. *They don't know what she's capable of.*

Did anyone?

Technically, Isabelle was not one of the 4400. She was the child of two returnees, conceived in the future under mysterious circumstances. Only a few months ago, she had been a little baby who couldn't even walk or talk yet, but then she literally grew up overnight, going from gurgling infant to full-grown woman in the blink of an eye. No one, not even Isabelle, really knew why, or what her full potential was. Shawn only knew that her abilities were off the charts.

And that she had the emotional maturity of a two-year-old.

"You're so thoughtful to have remembered that!" She gave his arm an affectionate squeeze. "No wonder I love you so much."

Shawn winced. Not for the first time, he

regretted getting involved with Isabelle. He had tried to resist her seductive advances, but she hadn't taken no for an answer. When Isabelle wanted something, she went for it, full speed ahead. In the beginning, her impetuous, uninhibited nature had been exciting, but that was before he realized just how dangerous she was.

Only a week ago, Daniel Armand, the ruthless leader of Nova Group, had launched a psychic attack on Shawn, driving him out of his mind. Isabelle had personally tracked Armand down and forced him to restore Shawn's sanity, but she had left a trail of dead Nova Group members in her wake. Jane Nance had been fed to her own cats and dogs. Jorge Molina had been burned alive in his garage. There was no proof that Isabelle had actually killed anyone, but Shawn knew she was responsible. She had practically admitted as much to him, claiming that she would gladly kill a hundred people for his sake. He also had his suspicions regarding the recent death of Matthew Ross, a lobbyist for The 4400 Center, who had dropped dead of a stroke the very same day. Had Isabelle killed him, too? The one time Shawn had worked up the nerve to ask her, she had evaded the issue, but he wouldn't put it past her.

He felt a twinge of guilt as he recalled that Isabelle *had* saved his sanity after all; if not for her, he'd be gibbering in a padded cell somewhere, tormented by hallucinatory voices inside his head. If she did kill those people, she did it for his sake. *How can I turn on her because of that?* Isabelle was still learning how to be an adult; she didn't know any better. Perhaps he owed it to her to try to make this relationship work?

Today's lunch date atop the Space Needle had been an attempt to recapture the spark between them, but it wasn't working, at least as far as he was concerned. His skin crawled as she pressed herself against his side. He felt trapped. He wasn't sure he could get out of this relationship even if he wanted to. Breaking up with Isabelle could be hazardous to his health.

"You're awful quiet," she commented, a tad suspiciously. As far as Shawn knew, she couldn't actually read his mind, but she seemed to sense that he wasn't enjoying himself. She peered at his face. "Something wrong?"

"No," he lied. "Just enjoying the view." Avoiding her eyes, he paused and leaned against a guardrail. Float planes landed on Lake Union several miles away. Ferries, cruise lines, and cargo ships crossed

Elliott Bay. People strolling the grounds below looked like tiny toy soldiers. A cool breeze rustled his hair.

"Okay," Isabelle replied, sounding not entirely convinced. He could feel her probing gaze upon his face. "You're not still upset about what happened last week, are you? I told you before, you should forget all about that. You're well again, and we're together." She tossed her hair. "What else matters?"

Aside from the fact that you killed two, maybe three, people without a hint of remorse? The chill running down his spine had nothing to do with the wind blowing off the bay. He pictured Jane Nance's partially devoured body, imagined Jorge Molina trapped inside his burning garage, remembered Daniel Armand babbling like a lunatic. Matthew Ross's funeral had taken place only days ago. *What happens the next time someone crosses you?* Isabelle was growing more confident and comfortable with her abilities every day. Not even her father could control her anymore. Shawn wasn't sure anyone could.

"Shawn Farrell! Isabelle Tyler!"

A harsh voice assailed them. Shawn spun around to spot a young Native American man standing in the doorway to the observation deck. A fringed buckskin jacket and blue jeans clothed his lanky body. Glossy black hair was tied back in a ponytail. A bear-tooth necklace dangled around his neck. He looked only a few years younger than Shawn and Isabelle. Hate-filled eyes glared from his acne-scarred face.

It took Shawn a moment to place the newcomer: Jamie Skysinger, a 4400 who used to hang out at the Center. Shawn hadn't seen him around for a while; rumor had it he had joined the Nova Group.

Uh-oh, Shawn thought. Nova Group had never forgiven him for cooperating with NTAC against the terrorists. And Isabelle had single-handedly wreaked havoc among their ranks.

"Traitors! Backstabbers!" Jamie snarled, shaking his fist. "You don't deserve your abilities!"

"Oh, really?" Her expression darkening, Isabelle stepped toward their accuser. Her own fists clenched at her sides. Shawn laid a restraining hand upon her shoulder. Maybe there was still a way to avoid further bloodshed?

"Wait!" he pleaded, as much to Isabelle as Jamie. "Let's talk about this." He raised his open palms in a nonthreatening manner. "Too many people have been hurt already. If you're in trouble, maybe I can help."

Jamie snorted in contempt. "Are you serious? We trusted you once and you sold us out to NTAC, even after they tried to exterminate our kind! That makes you an accomplice to genocide." Alarmed by the confrontation, the other sightseers fled the scene, leaving Shawn and Isabelle alone with Jamie. "Hope you know how to fly!"

He took a deep breath and exhaled. A cyclonic wind suddenly buffeted Shawn and Isabelle, hurling them backward. Shawn frantically grabbed on to the guardrail, but the wind was too strong. His feet left the ground as he and Isabelle were flung from the observation deck out into the empty air above the Seattle Center. Within a heartbeat, they were carried past the safety grid installed to foil would-be jumpers. Some five hundred feet below, the fairgrounds spread out beneath him like a kid's diorama. Gravity seized Shawn and he realized he was about to die. Even if his healing powers worked on himself, which they didn't, there was no way anyone could survive a plunge like that. He spotted Isabelle tumbling through the air several yards away. Their eyes made contact. She reached out for him, but the unnatural gale had already blown them too far apart. Only their common peril united them, perhaps for the very last time. They seemed destined to die together.

Or maybe not.

To his surprise, an invisible force took hold of Shawn, halting his fall. *Isabelle,* he realized. It had to be her doing. The telekinetic surge propelled him back toward the observation deck, even as Isabelle herself plummeted from sight. "Shaaaawnnnn!" she called out as she fell, her voice trailing off before disappearing entirely.

She had saved him—again.

Shawn crashed back onto the deck, colliding with Jamie. The two men collapsed onto the narrow skyway circling the saucer. The startled assassin had the wind knocked out of him, but quickly recovered. Thrashing beneath Shawn's weight, flailing at him with his fists, Jamie sucked at the air, trying to take another deep breath.

No way, Shawn thought. *Not again.*

As a healer, he usually employed his ability to help people, to erase whatever injuries or diseases might be afflicting them, but he had discovered early on that he could also reverse the process. It wasn't something he liked to demonstrate, but Jamie had pushed him too far. A complicated mixture of rage and guilt churned inside Shawn at the thought of Isabelle's death. In the split second before they fell, she had chosen to save him instead of herself. Uncertain how he was going to live with that knowledge, he took out his anguish on Jamie.

"You killed her!" He grabbed hold of Jamie's wrists with both hands. Shawn's brow furrowed in concentration, and the strength instantly fled from the killer's arms. Unable to free themselves, the limbs drooped lifelessly in Shawn's grasp. Jamie stopped grappling with him, and started gasping for breath instead. Shawn shouted angrily at him. "She didn't deserve that. No matter what she did!"

"S-stop," Jamie croaked hoarsely, barely able to speak. His face acquired a bluish, cyanotic tint as Shawn mercilessly drained the life force from his body. Ugly purple shadows formed beneath sunken eyes. Waxy skin stretched tight over his skull. His jaw fell open, exposing a gaping black cavity. Failing lungs wheezed and whistled. His body twitched spasmodically. Brown eyes rolled up until only the whites could be seen. He looked more dead than alive. "P-please . . . stop . . ."

Shawn had never come so close to killing

someone before. In the past, bystanders had always intervened before he went too far. He was tempted to go all the way this time, to repay his debt to Isabelle by turning her killer into a corpse. But then he heard a horrified gasp coming from a nearby doorway. He looked up to see a uniformed security guard staring at him in horror. Sheer shock froze the guard in place. "Holy crap," the man whispered, visibly afraid to come any closer. "What in heaven's name are you doing to that guy?"

The guard wasn't the only spectator. Frightened faces gazed at the nightmarish tableau from behind the tinted windows of the saucer. All at once, Shawn realized that he was in danger of confirming the world's worst fears about the 4400. Tomorrow's headline flashed before his mind's eye:

4400 LEADER KILLS WITH TOUCH!

Coming to his senses, he let go of Jamie's wrists as though they were scalding him. The terrorist's arms dropped limply onto the floor. Jamie moaned, his chest heaving, as the color slowly began to return to his features. He sat up slowly.

"I . . . I didn't mean . . ." Shawn stood up and backed away from the fallen assassin. "He's part of the Nova Group," he stammered by way of explanation. His heart was still pounding a mile a minute. Perspiration glued his shirt to his back. "He tried to kill us . . . I thought we were going to die . . . both of us . . ."

Isabelle.

He staggered to the guardrail and looked over the edge. At first he couldn't find her, then his eyes zeroed in on a still, small form lying on the pavement at the base of the Needle. He couldn't believe how tiny she looked from this height. Blood pooled beneath her head like a halo.

She's gone, he realized. *She's really gone.*

An unexpected rush of relief caught him by surprise. As much as he hated to admit it, even to himself, part of him was glad she was dead.

It's finally over. I'm free.

He wondered how he was ever going to break the news to her father . . .

Then the earthquake hit.

A sudden tremor caused the Needle to sway like a willow in the wind. The lurch threw Shawn off balance and he slammed into the guardrail, bruising his shoulder. Inside the saucer, sightseers screamed and swore as they stumbled and fell. Cameras, binoculars, and other personal items crashed onto the deck.

"Hey!" the guard shouted behind him. "Don't make a move!"

For a second, Shawn thought the man was yelling at him, then he realized that Jamie had scrambled to his feet. Apparently the terrorist still had enough juice in him to make a break for it. Taking advantage of the confusion engendered by the quake, Jamie lunged for the nearest exit. The overwhelmed guard made a halfhearted attempt to detain Jamie, but an unnatural gust of wind knocked him aside, even as the momentary tremors subsided. The crowd inside the saucer scattered in fear as the killer bolted for the elevator, vaulting over the bodies of fallen tourists. Shawn let him go. Overcome with shock and emotion, he didn't have the strength to chase after Jamie. His legs felt like rubber as he sagged against the guardrail, letting the unyielding metal support his weight. The quake was over, but he was still shaking like a leaf. *I'll notify Uncle Tommy,* he promised himself. Jamie Skysinger was NTAC's problem now. *They know how to deal with terrorists.*

The Needle stopped swaying, and Shawn gazed mournfully at the lifeless figure five hundred feet below. Not even a freak earthquake could drive Isabelle's death from his thoughts. Now that she was gone, his memory perversely summoned up all the happy times they had shared together, before her more lethal tendencies asserted themselves. The whole world had been new to her, and she had sought out fresh experiences with boundless enthusiasm. Her restless curiosity had devoured entire encyclopedias. The ultimate prodigy, she had instantly mastered every skill she set out to learn. He remembered teaching her how to swim, how to drive, how to make love . . .

His throat tightened. *I'm so sorry, Isabelle.* He wished that he could truly regret her passing, but perhaps it was all for the best. That much power had never belonged in the hands of someone who grew up incredibly too fast. *Maybe the future made a mistake creating you . . .*

For a few moments, everything went black. The world, with all its puzzling contradictions and conflicting demands, went away. Isabelle savored the blissful oblivion.

Then her eyes snapped open.

She found herself lying on her back upon the pavement, staring up at the underside of the saucer hundreds of feet above. Capsule-shaped elevators carried passengers up and down the length of the tower. Startled gasps erupted from the awestruck bystanders surrounding her. Many of them seemed to be getting up off the ground, after apparently falling for some reason. They backed away nervously, unsure what to make of her apparent resurrection. "It's impossible!" someone blurted. "Nobody could survive a fall like that!"

Except me, she thought. *Or so it seems.*

She sat up, somewhat surprised to be alive. Granted, her survival was not totally without precedent. She had once jumped from the roof of The 4400 Center and walked away unharmed, but that had been a mere two or three stories, nothing compared to the dizzying plunge she had just taken. Isabelle had read that three people had jumped from Space Needle over the years. None had survived. Apparently, she was even more resilient than she'd imagined.

Good to know.

Her head was ringing, and an annoying pain throbbed at the back of her skull. Groaning, she probed the injury with her fingers. They came away bloody, but the wound already felt as if it was healing over. The throbbing gradually faded away. Isabelle wiped her fingers on the hem of her dress. The designer frock was torn, frayed, and barely hanging on. One of her high-heel shoes was lying a few yards away.

"Are you all right, miss?"

An older black man leaned over her. He reminded Isabelle of her father, but was a bit more heavyset. He appeared to work at the Seattle Center. A plastic name badge identified him as MAURICE. She appreciated his concern.

"I think so." She started to stand up, but Maurice placed his hand against her shoulder. "Don't move," he urged her. "You should wait until the paramedics get here."

"But I'm fine," she protested.

"What happened?" another bystander asked. She was a skinny white woman wearing the typical tourist attire: shorts, sneakers, souvenir T-shirt, and baseball cap. Her fingers nervously toyed with a copper bracelet. "Did you . . . jump?"

No, I was pushed. Anger flared inside her as she recalled being ambushed atop the Needle. A horrible thought struck her, momentarily shoving her outrage aside. *Shawn!* She had grabbed on to him with her mind as they were falling, but had that been enough to save him? She glanced around desperately, afraid of spotting another body upon the pavement. The intrusive crowd blocked her view, and she shoved them aside just by thinking about it. Alarmed men and women yelped as an invisible force drove them from her line of vision. She didn't see Shawn lying anywhere nearby, but maybe he had landed somewhere out of sight?

The freaked-out rubberneckers were making tracks away from her. She grabbed Maurice before he could run away, too. He regarded her with obvious apprehension. "You're one of them, aren't you?" He swallowed hard. "The 4400?"

Sort of.

She didn't have time to explain. "There was a man with me," she said urgently. "My boyfriend. Did he fall, too?"

Maurice shook his head. "No, miss. Just you!"

Her heart leapt at the news. Shawn wasn't dead. She had saved him after all, despite the best efforts of yet another Nova Group fanatic. A scowl marred her lovely features. *I should have tracked them* all *down before this,* she thought venomously. *Before they had a chance to come after us again.*

Screams and shouts came from the ground floor pavilion at the base of the Needle. "Out of my way!" a hoarse voice shouted as their assailant burst from the glass doors onto the sidewalk outside. Isabelle, whose encyclopedic memory had absorbed

the files of every single 4400, had already identified the terrorist as one Jamie Skysinger, abducted
September 15, 1987. Panting breathlessly, he
charged past the throng of tourists recovering from
the quake. He hurdled over a decorative flower
bed, not even trying to be subtle in his escape. He
couldn't have looked more guilty if he'd tried.

"You!" Isabelle leapt to her feet. She pointed
an accusing finger at her attacker. "You shouldn't
have done that." The fury in her voice was un-
mistakable. How dare this walking hurricane spoil
her romantic stroll atop the Needle. "I was on a
date!"

His face blanched as he spotted Isabelle, alive
and well and out for blood. She wondered how
much he'd heard about what she had done to
some of his fellow terrorists. It hadn't been pretty,
but Isabelle had no regrets; she'd do it all again if
that's what it took to keep Shawn safe. Smirking,
she hoped that Jamie knew every gory detail of his
comrades' deaths. If not, she'd be happy to share
them with him.

Something had certainly put the fear of God
into him; he looked a lot less confident than he
had been up on the observation deck only minutes ago. All his righteous fury had evaporated,

leaving only naked fear behind. "S-stay away from me!" Sweat ran down his face. His Adam's apple bobbed up and down. He ran from Isabelle as though the devil herself was after him.

Close enough, Isabelle thought.

She sprinted after him. She limped at first, as the lingering after effects of her meteoric fall slowed her down. Hairline fractures sent sharp pangs through her legs with every step, but the pain only heightened her hunger for revenge. A broken heel hobbled her, so she kicked off her remaining shoe. After only a few yards, her stride evened out. She chased after Jamie with all the speed and grace of a panther.

He looked about desperately for some place to hide. The elevated tracks of the Monorail ran overhead, but the train, another "futuristic" relic of the World's Fair, offered no chance of escape. The aging Monorail had been out of service for months. Ignoring the steps to the terminal, he dashed diagonally across Thomas Street toward the nearest shelter.

The Science Fiction Museum and Hall of Fame was nestled in the southwest corner of the Experience Music Project, a bizarre architectural experiment that looked more like an enormous piece of abstract art than a building. Purple, red, blue, silver, and gold glittered across twisting waves of painted aluminum and stainless-steel shingles. The amorphous contours of the edifice were a source of considerable local controversy; some people found the edifice, designed by eccentric architect Frank Gehry, revolutionary. Others thought it was just a big, garish blob. A metallic green robot perched above the entrance to the Sci-Fi Museum like an extraterrestrial gargoyle.

There was no line in front of the museum, so Jamie rushed inside. Gaining on him, Isabelle followed him into the lobby, where a life-sized replica of Gort, the giant robot from *The Day the Earth Stood Still*, stood by motionlessly as Jamie shamelessly bypassed the ticket counter and headed straight toward the doorway to the galleries beyond. A museum employee, who looked appropriately nerdy, tried to block him. "Wait a sec. You need a ticket!"

Jamie elbowed the poor guy in the gut. He raced through the doorway, briefly vanishing from Isabelle's sight. Doubled over in pain, the hapless ticket taker nevertheless looked up as Isabelle approached the gate. She shot him a warning glance.

"Don't even think about it."

He wisely backed off and let Isabelle enter free of charge.

A large floating sphere dominated the first of the museum's four main galleries. A kaleidoscopic montage of memorable images from movies, TV, books, and comics flashed across the curved surface of the globe. Martian invaders torched whole cities. Gorillas on horseback chased Charlton Heston through the brush. Flash Gordon rocketed toward Mongo. E.T. phoned home. Zippy sound effects and sound bites played softly in the background. Displays of sci-fi memorabilia, including Captain Kirk's chair and uniform, lined the walls. Posters, first editions, and movie props were mounted within glass display cases. Most of the artifacts came from the personal collection of a local Microsoft billionaire. Etched-glass portraits of celebrated writers and filmmakers adorned the Hall of Fame on the far right. Computer kiosks offered visitors an opportunity to explore various topics at greater depth.

Isabelle recognized every image projected onto the central globe. Given that she owed her very conception to time travelers from the future, she had naturally reviewed all the relevant literature on the subject, which had given her a pretty good familiarity with science fiction in all its forms. Alas, H. G. Wells and his progeny had not provided her with any concrete answers regarding the purpose of her existence, only lots of occasionally diverting fairy tales. She had since moved on to other interests, like sex and relationships, but she still recognized a clip from *Blade Runner* when she saw one.

A shimmering starfield ran along the top of the walls. It took Isabelle's eyes a second to adjust to the dim lighting, but she had no trouble picking up Jamie's trail. His headlong flight through the gallery was causing plenty of commotion.

"Hey, watch where you're going!" a bystander protested as Jamie barreled through a clump of visitors loitering in front of an enormous mural depicting the history of science fiction. Isabelle glimpsed the illustrated timeline out of the corner of her eye as she raced through the gap Jamie had carved through the crowd. "This is a museum, not a frakking race track," the aggrieved fan called after her. "Show some respect for other people!"

Don't blame me, Isabelle thought. *Talk to the guy who thought he could get away with blowing me off the Space Needle.*

The fleeing terrorist careened past an exhibit

on the planet Mars, in fact and fiction, to reach a stairwell leading down to the bottom floor of the museum. He stumbled on the steps, almost falling down the stairs, but managed to regain his balance. Isabelle was right behind him, her bare feet slapping against the steps as she chased after Jamie. She hit the bottom just as Jamie scrambled out of the stairwell.

"You can't get away from me!" she hollered. "You and your terrorist buddies should have learned that the last time you targeted Shawn." Her vengeful outbursts provoked anxious looks from the other museum goers coming down the stairs. The smart ones turned around and headed in the opposite direction. "You're going to pay for messing with me and my boyfriend!"

Just like Daniel Armand.

And Jane Nance.

And Jorge Molina.

And Matthew Ross . . .

Beyond the stairwell, the next gallery had been dressed out to resemble the interior of some imaginary spaceship, complete with curved archways, imitation steel fittings, and an extensive "armory" of science fictional weapons. Ray guns, phasers, *bat'leths*, lightsabers, disruptors, weirding modules, pulse pistols, crysknives, blasters, and other futuristic ordnance were mounted behind glass, alongside an assortment of lurid book and pulp magazine covers. A tarnished metal sign required visitors to "Secure All Weapons with Safety Locks Engaged." Impulsively, Isabelle smashed her fist through the glass and grabbed hold of Barbarella's crossbow.

She had liked that movie, especially the sexy parts.

An alarm went off as she wrenched the crossbow from the wall. The high-pitched wail hurt her ears and jolted the handful of other visitors exploring the gallery. Startled tourists gazed at her in alarm, then scattered for the exits. Blood dripped from her knuckles, but the superficial cuts were already healing. She spotted Jamie among the fleeing men and women. The back of his buckskin jacket presented a tempting target.

Hefting the loaded crossbow, she took aim at Jamie and squeezed the trigger, only to discover that the prop weapon was strictly decorative. *Of course,* she realized, kicking herself mentally. *I should have known it was just make-believe. After all, I'm not a little kid anymore.*

She hurled the prop away in disgust. The blaring alarm annoyed her. *That's a relief,* she thought, as the siren was cut off abruptly. With nothing more to distract her, she dived into the mob of evacuees between her and Jamie.

Across from the armory, a jumbo-sized video screen posed as a window to the "spacedock" outside. Famous interstellar vessels, from the *U.S.S. Enterprise* to Buck Rogers's art deco rocket ship, zipped past the supposed porthole as she chased Jamie into the next gallery. Frantic to get away from her, the shrieking crowd parted to let her through. Peering over the heads of the patrons in front of her, she spotted Jamie silhouetted against a wall-sized screen that offered eye-catching vistas of a series of futuristic skylines. The Jetsons' cheery cartoon universe contrasted sharply with Jamie's disheveled, sweaty-faced panic. His ponytail had come undone somehow and his straight black hair fell across his face. He looked dead on his feet.

"Help me, somebody!" he shrieked, but none of the escaping tourists came to his aid. "She's going to kill me!"

Isabelle smirked. She found she enjoyed playing cat and mouse with the would-be killer. "How about that?" she mocked him. "You can tell the future, too. I thought only that creepy little blond girl could do that."

She let him scramble away again. Unlike Jamie, she wasn't even tired yet. She glanced idly at the assorted memorabilia on display as she pursued Jamie as relentlessly as Yul Brynner in *Westworld*. An exhibit on doomsday scenarios looked interesting; she made a mental note to visit the museum again when she had more time. Did Shawn like sci-fi? It dawned on her that she had no idea. There was so much they still had to learn about each other . . .

If only the Nova Group would just leave them alone.

To her surprise and amusement, she discovered that the next gallery had been given over to a special exhibit on the 4400 themselves. THE 4400: HOPE FROM THE FUTURE? asked a large banner above a collection of magazine covers and newspaper headlines concerning the 4400's return and subsequent activities. A holographic ball of white light hovered above a miniature diorama of Highland Beach, with an enlarged color photo of Mount Rainier serving as a backdrop. Snippets of news bulletins from the day of the return were piped over the loudspeakers. "The comet is now heading straight for Earth!" an apprehensive anchorman announced. "Scientists predict destruction on a planetary scale. . . ."

Boy, did they have that wrong, Isabelle thought. In the end, the "comet" had merely delivered the 4400 back to the present. There had been no Earth-shattering collision. Only time would tell whether the advent of the 4400 constituted a different sort of catastrophe. Isabelle hadn't made up her mind about that yet. She cared about *some* of the returnees . . .

She frowned as she noted a portrait of the late Jordan Collier among the artifacts; even as an infant, she had never trusted Collier. As far as she was concerned, the charismatic tycoon's assassination had been a very good thing. If nothing else, it had left Shawn in charge of The 4400 Center, right where he belonged.

No thanks to Jamie Skysinger and his murderous comrades.

A fresh surge of anger flared inside her as she realized just how close Shawn had come to joining Collier in oblivion. Would the museum have updated their 4400 exhibit to include Shawn's obituary? Probably, although no one would have mourned Shawn as much as she would have. Her expression hardened as she ran out of patience.

"Time's up, Jamie," she announced. Her voice echoed down the dimly lit hallways. "This was fun for a while, but I'm getting bored now." She heard him panting up ahead. His footsteps were dragging. There was no way he was getting away from her. "Besides, I really need to get back to Shawn."

A feeble whimper drew her straight to him. Having taken a wrong turn, Jamie had run into a dead end. Isabelle had him cornered in an alcove devoted to the display of famous fictional robots and cyborgs. Robby, the Terminator, RoboCop, R2-D2, the robot from *Lost in Space,* an old-school Cylon, and other cybernetic celebrities looked on pitilessly as the trapped militant searched in vain for an escape route. Isabelle stood at the entrance to the alcove, blocking his path. Jamie's bloodshot eyes pleaded for mercy. "Please," he begged. "Don't do this. People like us, we shouldn't be fighting each other. That's just what NTAC wants!"

"I think you're confused," she replied. "I'm *nothing* like you." According to the late Matthew Ross, before she killed him, her ultimate destiny was to destroy the 4400. She still wasn't sure what she thought of that, but disposing of scum like Jamie definitely felt right, natural, like this really was what she was meant for. "You're what I'm here to exterminate."

Jamie gulped. His back was up against a row of robots, who posed behind a thick sheet of glass like a mechanical police lineup. METAL OR MORTAL? read the blocky inscription above the display. Isabelle smiled coldly. Jamie was definitely the latter.

Unwilling to go down without a fight, he tried to pull himself together. Wheezing, he sucked the cool air into his lungs. Isabelle shook her head. *Sorry, that's not going to work this time.* He had caught her off guard before, but she had his number now.

Just as she had with Daniel Armand and his murderous accomplices, she turned the terrorist's ability against him. Before Jamie could even exhale, a ferocious wind whipped up behind him, blowing out the glass pane between him and the robots. A storm of broken glass pierced his body as he screamed in agony. He fell forward onto his face. Jagged shards jutted from his back. Blood spread across the tile floor. His body twitched spasmodically before falling still. She felt his heart stop beating. Jamie Skysinger was gone with the wind.

Isabelle didn't give a damn. A crimson pool flowed toward her bare feet, and she stepped backward to avoid getting blood on her toes. Her own heartbeat and pulse were perfectly regular. Murder was nothing new to her; even as a baby, she had ruthlessly eliminated anyone who posed a threat to her. She contemplated the lifeless corpse, then glanced back over her shoulder as she heard footsteps approaching. A portly security guard came running around the corner, then skidded to a halt at the gory sight before him. "Ohmigod," he exclaimed. "What the hell happened?"

Isabelle shrugged. "I'm afraid there's been an accident." She nodded at the corpse. "Some of the 4400 just don't know how to control their abilities." She wasn't worried about being charged with Jamie's death; she could say in all honesty that she hadn't laid a hand on him. The evidence would back her up on that. Despite their suspicions, the authorities had never been able to prove she'd killed anyone. She just hoped Shawn wouldn't be too upset. He could be oddly squeamish about these things. *It's not my fault,* she thought petulantly. *That stupid terrorist shouldn't have ruined our day.*

Being careful to avoid stepping in the blood, she leaned over and yanked Jamie's bear-tooth necklace from his neck. She handed the necklace to the dumbfounded guard.

"For your exhibit," she explained.

She left him standing there among the robots. She was anxious to get back to the Space Needle and find Shawn.

He must be wondering where I am.

FIVE

ACCORDING TO HIS FILE, Cooper DeMeers lived in the University District, just up the bus line from the Pike Place Market. As Diana and Tom drove north on Aurora Avenue, she was relieved to see only minimal damage from the earthquake a few hours ago. Small heaps of rubble littered the streets. Dangling phone lines and electrical cables needed fixing. Yellow CAUTION tape fenced off damaged stretches of sidewalk. A few businesses had closed for repairs. Darkened store windows implied scattered power outages through downtown, but a quick phone call had assured Diana that Maia and other kids at The 4400 Center were okay. Still, the unsettling tremor had her nerves on edge. She felt all shook up, in more ways than one.

"Could have been a lot worse," Tom observed from behind the wheel of their blue Chrysler sedan. After three years as her partner, he didn't need to be a 4400 to know what she was thinking most of the time. Diana rode shotgun beside him. "No fatalities reported so far. They're saying the quake was only a 4.8."

"Yes, but the epicenter was right below the Market, and the quake struck just as we were closing in on DeMeers." She fretted over the suspicious timing. "That can't be a coincidence, can it?"

"I don't know," he hedged. "The whole region's an earthquake zone. Everybody knows that. There's a fault running right across downtown, parallel to I–90." That was only about three miles behind them right now. "Plus, I saw DeMeers's face when the Market started shaking. He looked just as startled as everyone else."

True enough, Diana thought. Her own memory confirmed Tom's observation; the sudden earthquake had seemed to take everyone by surprise. "But what if he didn't do it on purpose? Maybe his 4400 ability is only just now manifesting itself?" Not all of the 4400 had developed their

paranormal gifts right away. Some returnees hadn't
discovered their talents until years after their return. Hitherto unknown abilities were often acti-
vated by extreme emotional stress, as in the case
of Orson Bailey, whose destructive mental ability
only surfaced when he was extremely angry. "What
if DeMeers's anxiety this afternoon caused a latent
4400 ability to wake up? Today's earthquake could
be only the beginning."

"What are you saying?" His brow furrowed.
"That D. B. Cooper possesses some sort of . . . ?"

"Tectokinesis?" Diana supplied.

Tom gave her a bemused look. "You just made
that up."

"Guilty as charged," she confessed. Still, the
portmanteau term, melding tectonics with telekinesis, seemed to fit the ominous theory forming in her mind. "But is a man who can trigger
earthquakes with his mind any more fantastic than
some of the other phenomena we've encountered
since the 4400 came back?"

"You've got me there," Tom admitted. "So you
think he might be able to stir up a volcano, too?
Like in Maia's vision?"

Diana nodded. "That's what I'm afraid of."

Maybe moving to Seattle wasn't such a great

idea, she thought. Before joining NTAC, she had worked for the Centers for Disease Control in Atlanta. Georgia got pretty muggy in the summer, but at least it wasn't a ticking geological time bomb . . .

It was still a couple of hours until rush hour, so they made relatively good time through the dense downtown traffic. She and Tom had already alerted their respective families that they might be working late. Alana had graciously volunteered to look after Maia. Diana was grateful for one less thing to worry about.

"And then there's our *other* mystery," Tom reminded her. "Who was that guy who tried to get to DeMeers before us?"

Diana recalled the beefy leatherneck with the crew cut. "He looked ex-military to me. A Marine maybe." A disturbing idea troubled her. "You don't think our friends in Homeland Security or the NSA are behind this, do you?" It certainly wouldn't be the first time that another arm of the government went behind NTAC's back to deal with the 4400 on their own. Too often the Feds' right hand was deliberately kept in the dark as to what the left hand was up to. "Maybe some sort of black-ops attempt to liquidate DeMeers before he blows up Mount Rainier?"

"Or an attempt to recruit him," Tom suggested, "like they did with Gary Navarro." A ballplayer with an unwanted ability to read minds, Navarro had been unwillingly pressed into service by the NSA, who had employed him to track down and eliminate foreign-born returnees for the sake of national security. Tom scowled at the memory. "I'm sure there are folks in Langley or the Pentagon who could find uses for a genuine human earth-shaker."

Sadly, Diana couldn't put it past them. She still felt guilty over her role in exposing Gary's telepathy. Instead of helping him adjust to his new ability, the government had exploited him instead. Did the same fate await Cooper DeMeers?

"Well, that would explain how Mister Crew Cut knew we were coming for DeMeers," she pointed out. "Maybe one of Nina's bosses in HomeSec tipped him off?"

"Possible," Tom said. "But don't forget: she was also sharing our info with the higher-ups in charge of the state's emergency responses. The leak might have come from there."

Another explanation occurred to Diana. "What about the Nova Group? They've been in retreat ever since we apprehended Daniel Armand, but there are still some splinter groups out there. Look at that attack on Shawn and Isabelle Tyler this afternoon."

NTAC had briefed them on the events at the Seattle Center, which had taken place about the same time that she and Tom had been chasing their respective fugitives through the Pike Place Market. Tom had been tempted to check on his nephew firsthand, but Agent Garrity had assured him that NTAC already had a team on the scene. Glancing behind her, she saw the Space Needle a few blocks to the southwest. From this distance, you couldn't tell that the top of the tower was now a crime scene.

"I've got to admit," Tom said, "I don't like the idea of the Nova Group getting their hands on DeMeers, especially if they're still in the assassination business."

Diana knew he had to be worried about his nephew. Shawn's allegiance to The 4400 Center sometimes put him at odds with NTAC, but Tom still cared deeply about his sister's oldest son. This was twice in two weeks now that the Nova Group had targeted Shawn.

"Too bad we can't question Jamie Skysinger, but I guess Isabelle took care of that." Her acerbic tone conveyed her distrust of the arrogant young woman. Diana didn't consider herself prejudiced against the 4400, but Isabelle Tyler always gave her the creeps. It was the way Isabelle looked at you, she had once explained to Tom: like you were ant and she was deciding whether or not to pull your legs off. And then, of course, there was the way dead bodies kept turning up in Isabelle's wake. *This makes four so far.*

"Yeah, I guess," Tom said tersely.

Lately he looked uncomfortable whenever Isabelle's name came up. Diana wasn't sure what that was all about, unless perhaps he didn't approve of Shawn's affair with the woman. *Can't blame him there,* she thought. It was hard to forget that only weeks ago Isabelle had been a two-year-old. She doubted that Isabelle's father, Richard, was all that happy about the relationship, either.

"We're here," Tom said, changing the subject.

They cruised down University Way, better known as "the Ave." As usual, the funky neighborhood was abuzz with activity. College students, punks, hippies, panhandlers, buskers, teenage runaways, and other varieties of street people crowded the bustling sidewalks. Bookstores, coffee houses, newsstands, music stores, ethnic restaurants, art-house theaters, pubs, clubs, and vintage clothing stores faced the wide, two-way boulevard. Diana's bohemian sister, April, would have fit right in. Diana wondered briefly where her peripatetic sibling was right now. She hadn't seen April since their falling-out last year, after her sister had tried to take advantage of Maia's precognitive ability for her own personal gain. Diana caught herself instinctively scanning the faces of the pedestrians in search of April.

She'll turn up eventually. She always does.

Diana noted that the Neptune Theatre was showing a double bill of *Duck Soup* and *A Night at the Opera* and wondered if Maia would like to see the Marx Brothers on the big screen. Unlike most kids these days, Maia had no objections to black-and-white films. *Heck,* Diana thought, *she probably caught the movies on their original runs.*

Tom located a parking space on a side street intersecting the Ave. Posters for obscure bands were plastered over nearby walls and lampposts, alongside political handbills and manifestos. Diana didn't recognize the names of any of the bands, which made her feel terminally unhip. As they got out of the car, she noted a bumper sticker on the rusty VW Bug parked in front of them: JORDAN

COLLIER DIED FOR YOUR SINS. She had to wonder how many supporters the Nova Group had in this neighborhood.

DeMeers's address led them to the front door of a basement apartment located under an Indian restaurant. The spicy aroma of fresh curry wafted down the steps. Diana wondered if the suspect fishmonger would be careless enough to return to his home after evading them at the Market. She reminded herself that they still didn't know for sure that Cooper DeMeers and D. B. Cooper were one and the same. Maybe DeMeers was just another paranoid 4400 who had gotten spooked by the unexpected arrival of NTAC at his place of employment? If it was even she and Tom that he had fled from. For all they knew, DeMeers might have been trying to get away from Crew Cut instead.

We've got too many questions, she thought, *and not enough hard facts.*

Tom knocked on the door, but nobody answered. He glanced at Diana. "What now?"

She decided that they had probable cause that Cooper DeMeers was a legitimate threat to public safety, not to mention a wanted fugitive. The courts often granted NTAC plenty of latitude where the 4400 were concerned. Too much so, according to some. She nodded at Tom.

"Go for it."

The cheap lock was no match for Tom's brawny shoulders. They burst into a darkened room, guns drawn. Sunlight filtered through a dirty window, offering a glimpse of a cluttered living room. A startled mouse squeaked and scurried for the shadows. At first glance, the rodent seemed to be the only resident at home.

Diana located a light switch. An overhead lamp lit up the room, exposing a modest one-bedroom apartment furnished with thrift store relics. A dilapidated recliner, its imitation leather upholstery patched with swatches of duct tape, faced an unpainted, plasterboard entertainment center. Soiled dishes were piled in the sink of the attached kitchenette. A half-empty bottle of bourbon rested on the kitchen counter. A framed poster of a sleek red sportscar adorned one wall. A 2006 Seattle Seahawks calendar was pinned to a bulletin board in the kitchen. *Definitely a guy's place,* Diana decided. The stuffy apartment reeked of tobacco.

"All clear," Tom called out from the bedroom, while Diana checked out the bathroom. Working as a team, they quickly ascertained that DeMeers was not at home. Dirty laundry on the floor smelled of fish. A solitary toothbrush suggested that he lived alone, although, oddly enough, an abrasive metal file rested in a cup alongside the toothbrush. A perfumed bottle of hair conditioner, on the other hand, implied that he might have a girlfriend who slept over sometimes. The general lack of housekeeping gave Diana the idea that he wasn't expecting company right away.

"No wonder he lives in U. District," she commented. "This guy lives like a college student."

Tom emerged from the bedroom. "Reminds me of my old dorm room." He surveyed their shabby surroundings. "One thing's for sure. If DeMeers is D. B. Cooper, he blew through that two hundred grand pretty fast, if he hung on to it at all."

"I know what you mean," she agreed. The rundown apartment made her own condo look like Bill Gates's mega-mansion. "Let's snoop around and see if we can find any answers."

Putting away their sidearms, the agents proceeded to search the dwelling. Diana wasn't sure what they were looking for exactly, perhaps some clue as to DeMeers's current whereabouts or recent activities? She wrinkled her nose in disgust; the oppressive tobacco odor made staying in the apartment a chore. Dirty ashtrays, and cigarette burns on the carpet, also betrayed the fishmonger's unhealthy habit. Diana recalled that "Dan Cooper" had chain-smoked during that hijacking years ago, back when you could still smoke on planes. According to the FBI profile, Cooper had been a bourbon drinker, too.

Interesting, she thought

Playing a hunch, she fished through a waste basket until she found a crumpled cigarette carton bearing an engraved portrait of Sir Walter Raleigh.

Bingo.

"Check this out." She held up the wrapper. "D. B. Cooper smoked Raleigh's."

"That's what the stewardesses on Flight 305 said all right," Tom replied from the kitchen, where he was busy rifling through the junk drawers under the counter. He gestured at the partially drained bottle of Jim Beam. "You spot the bourbon?" He had clearly picked up on the possible significance of the booze as well.

"You bet." She continued to fish through the trash until she came across a wadded-up flyer at the bottom of the basket. *What have we here?* Her eyes widened as she unfolded the paper and perused its contents:

FIGHT FOR THE FUTURE!
OPPOSE THE GOVERNMENT'S FASCIST CAMPAIGN AGAINST THE 4400!

FACT: The 4400 represent the next step in human evolution—and humanity's only hope of averting a pending catastrophe.

FACT: The U.S. Government, via its NTAC storm troopers, has systematically harassed and persecuted the 4400, their loved ones, and their supporters. They have poisoned innocent citizens via THE INHIBITOR CONSPIRACY, incarcerated numerous returnees on bogus charges, and been implicated in the death of many others.

FACT: Kyle Baldwin, the "lone gunman" responsible for Jordan Collier's assassination, is the SON of a high-ranking NTAC agent with a history of brutalizing the 4400. Coincidence—or proof that Collier's death was ordered at the highest levels of the military-industrial establishment?

A NEW WORLD DAWNS!

The 4400 cannot save the future alone. Don't let paranoid government officials crush humanity's potential for the sake of "national security." Fight back against NTAC—BY ANY MEANS NECESSARY!

Ouch, Diana thought. The slanted take on Collier's assassination was particularly galling; she knew for a fact that Tom's son, Kyle, had been temporarily possessed by a hostile entity from the future when he'd shot Collier. Kyle had not wanted Collier dead, and neither had NTAC. *But try convincing people of that . . .*

She walked over and handed the flyer to Tom. "Take a look at this."

He quickly scanned the document, his jaw tightening when he got to the part about Kyle, then looked up at Diana. "Nova Group propaganda?"

"It sure looks like it," she agreed. Maybe De-Meers was into more than just tossing fish for tourists? His name hadn't showed up on any of the lists supplied by Daniel Armand, but that was no guarantee that he wasn't affiliated with the terrorist group in some way. The Nova Group's cells were set up so that no single individual could identify every member of the outlaw organization. "You think he's gone from skyjacker to terrorist?"

"Not such a big leap," Tom observed. He returned the flyer to Diana. "Then again, the FBI always regarded Cooper's crime as nonpolitical in nature. During the hijacking, he issued no political demands or statements, nor did any militant group ever claim responsibility for the incident. The conventional wisdom is that Cooper was just after the money."

Diana mulled it over. "On the other hand, De-Meers's experiences as a 4400 could have radicalized him. Lord knows the inhibitor scandal turned a lot of the previously law-abiding returnees against the federal government. And not without reason." She bagged the cigarette wrapper and flyer as evidence. "Even if Cooper was apolitical back in seventy-one, that doesn't mean he has no axes to grind in the twenty-first century."

"You've got a point there," Tom admitted. "What the 4400 have gone through would change anybody." He extracted a small black address book from a drawer by the phone. He flipped through its pages. "I'm not seeing Armand or any of his chief lieutenants listed here, but we can check this against a full list of Nova Group members and sympathizers when we get back to the office."

"Sounds good," Diana said.

She decided to give the bedroom another pass. The unmade double bed had room for two, but Diana found only masculine attire in the nearby chest of drawers, which supported the idea that any lady friends lived elsewhere. The ubiquitous stink of tobacco competed with the fishy odor emanating from an overflowing laundry hamper. A small bookcase held a couple of shelves of paperback books. Scanning the titles, she found mostly Westerns and spy thrillers. *Nothing too controversial there,* she conceded. Granted, DeMeers also had a hardcover copy of Jordan Collier's bestselling *4400 and Counting,* but who didn't these days? Most returnees had probably checked out Collier's tome at some point. She owned two copies herself, one for home and one for the office.

Not exactly a smoking gun.

A peek under the bed didn't reveal anything more incriminating than a stack of men's magazines. She rolled her eyes as she saw that the top magazine was the issue of *Playboy* featuring a special pictorial on "The Women of the 4400." Diana had been appalled when the issue first came out, even as she'd realized that it had probably been inevitable. Although most of the returnees wanted nothing more than to blend inconspicuously back into society, a few of them had invariably tried to cash in on their newfound notoriety. For instance, the magazine's cover model: Zora Lynn Zounek, a Bettie Page lookalike from 1961, who now possessed the ability to selectively vaporize items of clothing. Last Diana heard, Zora now had an act in Vegas and a highly profitable website. Diana shook her head. Sometimes she had to wonder what on earth the future had been thinking . . .

More promising was the locked foot locker she found tucked away in the bedroom closet. The corrugated steel trunk looked big enough to hold an encyclopedia or two. "Tom, over here." Joining her in the bedroom, he helped her drag the locker out of the closet. Ignoring the padlock, he used a Swiss army knife to unscrew the hinges connecting the locker to its lid. He looked like he'd done this before; Diana decided she needed to invite Tom over the next time she had some Ikea furniture to assemble.

As they flipped open the lid, Diana half expected to find stacks of unmarked twenties, left over from the $200,000 the hijacker had made off with over three decades ago. Instead they found a treasure trove of souvenirs relating to the incident: the original FBI "Wanted" poster bearing the sketch artist's portrait; scrapbooks bulging with news clippings and magazine articles; a VHS copy of *The Pursuit of D. B. Cooper*, starring Treat Williams as Cooper; a handful of true-crime books on the hijacking; a hardcover novel titled simply *D. B.*, videotaped episodes of *In Search of . . .*, *Barnaby Jones*, *NewsRadio*, and *Prison Break*; CDs, cassette tapes, and a few old vinyl records; a program for last year's "D. B. Cooper Days" festivities; a matchbook from the Ariel Store and Tavern in Cowlitz County, and hard copy printouts from various websites, including a complete listing of the serial numbers of all ten thousand of the twenty-dollar bills paid out to D. B. Cooper in 1971.

It was quite the collection.

Tom whistled appreciatively. "Looks like we've hit the mother lode."

"Tell me about it," Diana said. Suddenly, the theory that D. B. Cooper had been one of the 4400 was looking a lot more plausible. She sifted through the telltale memorabilia.

Marco was just going to love this . . .

SIX

"D. B. COOPER never hurt no one, but he sure did blow some minds. . . ."

Tom caught a snatch of a lyric from Diana's iPod. His partner was quietly humming to herself as she checked the names in DeMeers's address book against their lists of suspected Nova Group associates. He looked up from the screen of his laptop. After calling it quits last night, they were back on the case this morning. A photo of Cooper DeMeers was pinned to the bulletin board in their office, next to a schematic diagram of the Nova Group. DeMeers's extensive collection of hijacking memorabilia was currently on ice in an NTAC evidence locker.

"What's that you're listening to?" he asked.

"Wha—oh, sorry." She turned down the music and slid the headphones away from her ears. "Marco downloaded some Cooper-related songs for me." A rueful smile lifted the corners of her lips. "Now I can't get this silly ballad out of my head. Is it bothering you?"

He shrugged. "Nope. Just curious." Frankly, he had never quite figured out what a smart, attractive woman like Diana saw in a science geek like Marco, but, hey, his partner's personal life was none of his business. With one divorce to his name, and a 4400 girlfriend he'd first met in an imaginary reality, he was in no position to throw stones. "Any progress?"

"Not really," she confessed. "DeMeers doesn't seem to have associated with his fellow 4400s much. He's stayed in touch with a couple of returnees he met in quarantine, but nobody on any of our watch lists."

Tom glanced at the address book. "Who knows? It might be worth checking out some of those connections anyway, if nothing else pans out." In the meantime, he had been reviewing security camera footage from Pike Place Market in hopes of identifying the mystery man who had tried to intercept

DeMeers before them. As he stared at the grainy black-and-white footage, Tom wondered again just how the nameless leatherneck had managed to get away from him yesterday. The security footage confirmed that the man had seemingly vanished into thin air. *He* has *to be a 4400*, Tom concluded. *That's the only explanation.*

Working on that assumption, he ran a screen capture of the stranger's face against the 4400 photos in their electronic database. Tom watched the mug shots scroll across the screen until an electronic chirp announced that the computer had found a possible match. "Hold on," he told Diana. "We may have something here."

She circled around the desk to join him as he reviewed the file of one William Patrick Gorinsky, abducted February 28, 1947. According to the profile, "Bill" Gorinsky was an ex-Marine who had mysteriously disappeared after returning home from World War II. Twenty-six years old, biologically speaking, he had yet to display any paranormal abilities. *At least none that we know of,* Tom thought. He squinted at Gorinsky's mug shot, comparing it to the blurry screen capture occupying another corner of the screen, as well as to his own memories of the disappearing man at the

Market. "That *could* be him. And he's got the right military background."

"Problem is," Diana said, "he's also got an airtight alibi." She pointed at the screen. "Read a little further. William Gorinsky has been confined to a mental hospital for the last three years."

Abendson Psychiatric Hospital was a sprawling complex of imposing red-brick Victorian structures, each large enough to house several dozen inmates. A wrought-iron wind vane spun atop the shingled roof of the main building. A chain-link fence enclosed the hospital grounds, which were located, along with several other hospital and medical facilities, on "Pill Hill" in south Seattle. Tom and Diana had first visited Abendson last year while dealing with a mentally disturbed 4400 named Tess Doerner. They were met at the door by the director of the hospital, Doctor Nicholas Clayton.

"Good to see you again, agents." Clayton was a lean, middle-aged man with a neatly trimmed black beard and a somewhat hangdog expression. A long white jacket attested to his profession. As doctors go, he had always struck Tom as something of a cold fish. His bedside manner needed work, which probably explained why he had ended up as an administrator. "I trust Mister Farrell is still well?"

Shawn had been briefly confined at Abendson during his mental breakdown the previous week, before Isabelle forced Daniel Armand to restore Shawn's sanity. Tom hadn't really had an opportunity to talk much to his nephew since then, but his understanding was that Shawn was indeed back to normal. *Aside from the occasional attempt on his life, that is.*

"Shawn's fine," Tom said. "Thank you for assisting us today."

"We're always happy to cooperate with the authorities." The doctor handed them a pair of visitor's passes to affix to their jackets. "Especially where our 4400 patients are concerned."

He guided them past the reception area and down a long beige corridor. Shuffling figures, often escorted by nurses or orderlies, trundled past them, sometimes muttering to themselves. Bedroom slippers swished across the scuffed linoleum floors. The faces of the patients held haunted, dazed expressions. A nurse pushed a pill cart from room to room. Tom guessed that many of the inmates were highly medicated. Bursts of hysterical laughter or tearful cries occasionally came from behind closed doors. The smell of antiseptic pervaded the corridor.

Tom tensed involuntarily, the medicinal sights

and smells raising unpleasant associations. He had spent too much time in hospitals during the three long years that his son Kyle had lain in a coma, the victim of a botched attempt to yank him into the future. The mysterious cabal behind the 4400 disappearances had meant to abduct Kyle, but had snagged Shawn instead, while accidentally leaving Kyle in a vegetative state. Tom still hadn't entirely forgiven the manipulative time travelers for what they'd put his family through.

"William Gorinsky is in Ward fifty-nine," Clayton explained, "a facility specifically devoted to caring for 4400s who are having difficulty coping with the enormity of what happened to them." His voice took on a slightly pedantic tone as he expounded on the topic. "Although the vast majority of the returnees have adjusted to the twenty-first century, a small fraction of them have suffered nervous breakdowns, delusions, and other disorders."

They arrived at a pair of locked double doors. A sign on the door read:

WARD 59

A secure area.

Authorized personnel only.

All visitors must be approved at Reception.

A hospital employee manned a glass booth adjacent to the doors. Clayton signaled the guard who buzzed them in. Tom took note of the tight security measures; it would be tricky for Gorinsky to sneak out of the ward undetected.

They entered a spacious rec room furnished with an assortment of worn tables and couches. Handfuls of 4400 patients clustered throughout the room, engaged in various harmless activities. Jigsaw puzzles lay partially assembled atop card tables. Quiet games of solitaire and bridge were in progress. A chubby senior citizen played chess against himself; it took Tom a minute to realize that the pieces were changing colors at random. A TV set, set to a classic movie channel, droned softly in the background, but nobody seemed to be paying it much attention. Tom vaguely recognized the faces of the patients from the datafiles back at NTAC. At first he was surprised to see nearly a dozen returnees in the mental ward, but then he considered all that the 4400 had gone through. Each and every one of them had been abruptly plucked from their lives, then deposited in 2004 without any warning or explanation. Some of them, like Shawn, had only been missing for a few years, but others had found their old lives hopelessly lost in the past. Loved ones had grown older, moved on, or even died of old age. Homes and possessions had been consumed by time; jobs and careers had been rendered obsolete. And as if that weren't traumatic enough, they also found themselves endowed with bizarre new abilities beyond their comprehension, which caused them to be regarded as dangerous freaks by large segments of the population. Sometimes even their own friends and families rejected them, like poor Lily Moore, whose once-loving husband took out a restraining order against her. *When you think about it,* Tom reflected, *it's a wonder more of the 4400 aren't basket cases.*

A nurse was busy dispensing pills to the inmates, who washed them down with little paper cups of water. "Is the promicin inhibitor administered to your patients?" Diana asked. Carefully applied, the inhibitor could be used to suppress a returnee's paranormal gifts. The patient's blood work had to be rigorously monitored, though, to avoid the fatal side effects that had killed over twenty returnees.

"Only to those whose abilities pose a threat to themselves and others," Clayton stated. "For obvious reasons, we'd like to avoid a recurrence of what we went through last year." Tess Doerner, a paranoid schizophrenic with the ability to control people's minds, had taken over the entire hospital before Tom had figured out how to resolve the situation peacefully. "But many of our patients have not manifested any abilities at all, including William Gorinsky."

We'll see about that, Tom thought.

"Doctor Clayton! Doctor Clayton!" A young woman came running up to them. Bell bottoms, tie-dye, and love beads made her look like she had just stepped out of 1968. A peace sign was painted on her cheek with lipstick. Her radiant face was alight with excitement. "Have you heard the news? Neil Armstrong just walked on the moon!" She pointed at the TV set; there was a burst of static and an old Fred Astaire movie was suddenly replaced by grainy NASA footage of the first moon landing. The patients watching the movie protested meekly. "It's one small step for man, a giant step for mankind!"

"That's quite thrilling, Jessica," the doctor humored the woman. "But can you please put the television back the way it was? I think some of our friends were watching that other program."

Jessica blushed in embarrassment. "Oops! I'm so sorry." She snapped her fingers and the movie picked up where it had left off. "I guess I got carried away a little. But just think of it . . . man on the moon! Can you believe it? I'll bet we'll have lunar colonies by the year 2000. . . ."

"No doubt." Clayton signaled a nearby orderly, who gently led Jessica away. "My apologies for the interruption. A truly sad case. She literally refuses to accept that nearly forty years have passed since her abduction."

"I got that impression," Tom said. He wondered how many of the doctor's patients were caught in a similar time warp. Kyle had originally had trouble adjusting to the three-year gap in his memory, but at least he still knew what year it was. Thank goodness he hadn't ended up in a place like this.

Leaving the rec room behind, Clayton escorted them down another hallway. Open doors offered glimpses of various patients' private rooms. They looked relatively cozy, at least compared to the detention cells back at NTAC headquarters. A hefty Samoan orderly waited outside a closed door near the end of the hall. An embossed label identified it as Room F-19. Gorinsky's name was scribbled on a slip of paper affixed to the door. Tom remembered the orderly from previous visits to Abendson. Matt, wasn't it, or maybe Mike?

"Good afternoon, Matt," Clayton greeted the orderly. He paused before the door to deliver another lecture. "Mister Gorinsky is one of our most severe cases. He's confined here because he kept compulsively returning to Highland Beach, where the returnees first appeared, in hopes of finding a way back to his own time. He nearly died of exposure a couple of times, waiting for a glowing ball of light that never came. Now he swings between angry rages and near-catatonic depression." He nodded at the orderly. "Matt's here in the event that Mister Gorinsky gets violent, although I doubt that will be a problem today. Alas, he's been particularly withdrawn lately."

Except when he's on the run through Pike Place Market, Tom thought. *Assuming we've got the right guy.*

His hand upon the doorknob, Clayton hesitated before admitting them. "Might I ask the nature of your interest in Mister Gorinsky?"

"Just routine," Diana assured him. "His name came up in the course of an ongoing investigation."

"Well, I doubt you'll get much out of him," Clayton said, "but you're welcome to try." Accompanied by the massive orderly, he led them into a small, tidy bedroom. Barred windows offered a view of the landscaped grounds outside. Lace curtains, drawn back to admit the afternoon sunlight, tried to mitigate the intimidating effect of the sturdy iron bars. A hunched figure, wearing a ratty white bathrobe, sat in a wheelchair by the window, staring silently at the shrubbery outside. He did not react to the visitors' arrival. "Bill?" the doctor addressed Gorinsky. "You have company."

His face turned away from them, Gorinsky did not respond. Tom could only see the back of the man's head, but the close-cropped red hair and thick neck matched his memories of the fugitive at the Market. Broad shoulders drooped forward. Mottled scarring on the man's neck suggested that he had been seriously burned sometime in the past. The discolored flesh resembled melted wax. *Funny,* Tom thought. *I don't remember noticing that before.*

"Bill? Mister Gorinsky?" Clayton tried again, but to no avail. He might as well have been speaking to a marble bust instead of a real live human being. The doctor sighed and shook his head. "I'm afraid you're wasting your time. When he gets like this, nobody can get through to him. We've even tried electroconvulsive therapy to jolt him out of these depressions, but without much success."

"Electroshock?" Tom reacted in surprise. *Doctors still used that?* He'd thought that shock treatment was a barbaric practice that had been abandoned years ago, along with leeches and prefrontal lobotomies. "You serious?"

"Actually," Diana enlightened him, "ECT is making something of a comeback. Granted, the technique was abused back in the bad old days, but a more refined version has shown impressive results when it comes to treating clinical depression."

"You don't say." Tom took her word for it, but the idea still sounded like something out of a Frankenstein movie. As far as he recalled, none of Kyle's doctors had ever suggested shocking Kyle with hundreds of volts of electricity to snap him out of his coma. Tom wondered if he would have ever agreed to such a treatment if it had been proposed. *Probably,* he conceded, *I was desperate enough to try anything.* Ultimately, though, it had been Shawn's newfound healing power that had finally roused Kyle from the coma.

Maybe Abendson needed to introduce Shawn to Gorinsky.

"Let me give it a try." He stepped forward and turned the wheelchair around to face him. Gorinsky did not protest being moved; he just kept on

staring blankly forward. His hands gripped the
armrests of his wheelchair. Tom spotted more scarring on Gorinsky's left hand. He knelt down to
make eye contact with the man, but the patient's
unfocused green eyes stared right through Tom as
though he was invisible. Stubble carpeted his jowls.
His jaw hung open slackly. A tiny tendril of drool
hung from the corner of his mouth. If he didn't
know better, he would have suspected Clayton of
lobotomizing the veteran as well as zapping him
full of current.

"Mister Gorinsky?" Tom said. "I'm with NTAC.
We'd like to ask you some questions. Is that all
right with you?"

Gorinsky gave no indication that he heard Tom.
Another bout of déjà vu struck Tom as he recalled
the hours he'd spent talking to his son's inert form.
Gorinsky didn't have feeding tubes hooked up to
him, as Kyle had, but Tom felt the same sense of
futility when it came to communicating with the
unresponsive returnee. He grimaced ruefully. *At
least I'm used to talking to people who can't talk back.*

"What do you think?" Diana asked. "Is it him?"

He scrutinized the silent inmate's face. Gorinsky
looked somewhat flabbier and more overweight
than the beefy leatherneck at the Market, no doubt

a result of his sedentary existence at the hospital, but the face was almost dead-on. Tom didn't remember the scar tissue on the man's throat, which extended all the way up to his chin, but it was possible that he had overlooked the burn marks during the earthquake and subsequent foot chase. He recalled the same face glancing back at him during that frantic pursuit through the lower levels of the Market. The fugitive's pissed-off expression had been very different from the vacant visage before him, but the basic features looked identical. Extracting a piece of paper from the pocket of his jacket, he held up a printout of the screen capture from the security footage. He looked back and forth between the black-and-white photo and Gorinsky. Marco had used his computer magic to enhance the image as much as possible.

"It's him," Tom said finally. He rose to his feet and looked at Diana. "I'm certain of it. This is the guy who got away from me yesterday."

"That's quite impossible," Clayton insisted. "Mister Gorinsky never left this room, let alone the hospital yesterday. My staff can attest to that."

"We'll need to take statements anyway," Diana stated, "from any nurses or orderlies who were on duty yesterday afternoon."

Clayton didn't put up a fuss. "Of course. I'll inform the staff to give you their full cooperation." He steered Gorinsky's wheelchair back toward the window. "Still, I'm certain there must be some mistake here. As you can see, Mister Gorinsky is in no condition to go gallivanting about the city."

Glancing around the room, Tom noticed various personal touches. A vase of fresh daffodils rested on the windowsill. An open box of "Applets & Cotlets" rested on the bedstand, next to the current issues of *Newsweek* and *Sports Illustrated*. A stuffed bulldog wearing a U.S. Marine uniform sat on top of a wooden chest of drawers.

"Does he get many visitors?" Tom asked. Somebody appeared to be taking an interest in the institutionalized patient.

"Just his brother," Clayton answered. "Phil Gorinsky. He visits fairly regularly, although not as often as he did in the beginning." He shrugged philosophically. "I find that even the most devoted friends and family start to curtail their visits if there are no real signs of progress. I suppose I can't blame them."

Tell me about it, Tom thought. His ex-wife, Linda, had sat at Kyle's bedside day and night for the first year or so, but eventually she couldn't

bring herself to haunt their son's hospital room
every day as Tom had. He had understood why
she'd given up hope, but it had still become a
source of friction between them. Ultimately, their
marriage had not survived their ordeal. He wondered what kept Gorinsky's brother coming back.
Faith? Optimism? A sense of obligation?

"Tom, look at this." Diana lifted the stuffed
bulldog from the dresser to expose a framed photo
propped up behind the toy. The black-and-white
photo, obviously taken in happier times, showed
a smiling Bill Gorinsky, proudly decked out in his
Marine uniform, posing with his arm around the
shoulders of another man who could have been his
mirror image. Aside from a navy uniform, the second man was a dead ringer for Gorinsky. "He has a
twin brother," Diana realized along with Tom. "An
identical twin."

Wait a second, Tom thought. *Was it the twin at
the market yesterday?*

He turned toward Clayton. "We're going to
need an address for the brother."

If Gorinsky was listening to the conversation,
there was no way to know.

SEVEN

Philip Gorinsky resided in Puyallup, northwest of Mount Rainier. The looming glaciers fed the silty green river flowing through the surrounding valley, irrigating blooming fields of daffodils on the outskirts of the city. Farmlands gradually gave way to more residential neighborhoods. As they pulled up to the curb outside Bill Gorinsky's brother's address, Diana spotted a VOLCANO EVACUATION ROUTE sign posted along the street. The blue and white metal sign, which flaunted a pictogram of a spewing volcano, was an unwelcome reminder of all that might be at stake every moment that Cooper DeMeers remained at large. She couldn't help glancing up at the mountain, which looked twice as imposing as it did from Seattle. If and when Rainier did blow its top, Puyallup would be one of the first communities to be flattened by a speeding lahar.

I just hope we're not wasting time investigating Gorinsky, Diana thought. But they had yet to determine conclusively the identity and intentions of the aggressive stranger who had accosted DeMeers at the Market the other day. Nor did they know the connection between the two men. *Maybe identifying Crew Cut can lead us to De-Meers?*

They approached Phil's home, a modest A-frame house fronted by a well-tended lawn and gardens. An American flag was proudly displayed from the porch roof. A ribbon-shaped sticker on the mailbox urged them to support the troops. A ceramic gnome peeked out from behind a rhododendron bush. A metal sign informed them that the premises were guarded by Olympic Security. The scene gave Diana a wholesome small-town vibe. She rang the doorbell.

"Coming!" a voice called from inside the house. When the door swung open a few moments later, to reveal the face and form of Gorinsky's twin brother, it was obvious at a glance that it had not been Philip Gorinsky whom Tom had pursued at the Market.

Whereas the twins had once been mirror images of each other, time and the arcane machinations of the future had played a cruel prank on the siblings. Phil was now nearly *sixty years older* than his institutionalized brother. Instead of the burly, red-headed sailor in the photo, a frail, silver-haired old man stood before them, supporting his weight with the help of a cane. Deep wrinkles creased his face, behind a pair of thick reading glasses. A hearing aid occupied one ear. Although it was a warm spring day, he wore an orange button-down sweater and slacks. A miniature flag pin gleamed upon his lapel. Age spots dotted his skin, which looked as dry and fragile as ancient parchment.

Diana wasn't too surprised by Phil's geriatric appearance. Despite their initial excitement at learning that Gorinsky had a twin, she and Tom had realized quickly enough that Phil would have aged normally the whole time his brother was missing. It was one thing to grasp that concept intellectually, however, and another to find yourself face-to-face with the bizarre reality. *It's like Einstein's "twin paradox" brought to life*, she thought. Born on the same day in 1922, one brother was now twenty-seven years old, while the other was in his eighties. *Talk about a time warp.*

"Hello?" the elderly gentleman asked, keeping the chain on the door. He peered at his unexpected visitors. "What's this about?" A feisty streak emerged as he eyed them suspiciously. "If you're selling something, I'm not interested."

Diana flashed her badge. "NTAC, Mister Gorinsky." She and Tom introduced themselves. "We'd like to talk to you about your brother."

"Is there something wrong?" Phil asked anxiously. "Is he all right?" He was visibly concerned about his sibling's well-being. "I was at the hospital just the other day and he seemed fine . . . well, as fine as he ever is."

"As far as we know, his condition is unchanged," she assured him. "But we'd still like to speak with you, Mister Gorinsky." She placed her palm against the door to hold it open. "Might we come in?"

"What? Oh, of course." He undid the chain and stepped inside to let them enter, looking mildly embarrassed that he hadn't invited them in before. "Forgive my manners. And please call me Phil. I haven't been 'Mister Gorinsky' since I retired from teaching back in eighty-six."

The living room was as neat and tidy as the

front yard. Copies of *Reader's Digest* and the AARP magazine rested on a polished wooden coffee table, next to a large-print edition of a Tom Clancy novel. The couch, wallpaper, and other furnishings were old-fashioned, but clean and in good condition. The carpet looked freshly vacuumed. The dust-free furniture and knickknacks smelled of Lemon Pledge. The cozy setting reminded Diana of her grandmother's old house. After the grungy squalor of DeMeers's basement dwelling, Phil's orderly domicile came as a pleasant relief.

Tom glanced around. "Do you live here alone, Mister Gorin—Phil?"

"I do indeed," the octogenarian replied. "Ever since my darling Eleanor passed away some time ago. I have a nurse who checks in on me twice a week, plus there are some nice ladies from my church who drop by now and then just to make sure I'm still breathing." A medic alert bracelet circled his wrist. "Bill moved in with me briefly, after he got back, but I'm afraid that . . . well, it didn't work out."

"So we understand," Tom said gently. "You have our sympathies."

"Thank you." Phil gestured toward the couch. "Please make yourself comfortable." He started to hobble toward the kitchen. "Can I interest you in some fresh lemonade?"

"No, thank you," Diana declined politely. She appreciated his cooperation and hospitality. They didn't get a lot of either nowadays. The agents sat down on the couch, while Phil cautiously lowered himself into a rocking chair in front of the unlit fireplace. A duplicate copy of that photo in Gorinsky's hospital room sat atop the mantle, alongside several other framed portraits of friends and family. The two young servicemen grinned at her from behind glass; little did they know what the future had in store for them. Looking closely at the old man in the chair, Diana thought she could still see the family resemblance. "Were you and your brother close?"

"We *are* close," Phil insisted, "even with all his troubles. People talk about the special bond between twins, but it wasn't just an old wives' tale in our case. We've always had a connection. When Bill was nearly killed by that Nazi bombing run during the war, I knew right away that something terrible had happened to him, even though I was stationed thousands of miles away in the Pacific at the time."

Diana remembered the burn marks scarring

Gorinsky's flesh, but took Phil's anecdote with a grain of salt. As far as she knew, there was no hard evidence supporting the idea that identical twins possessed a psychic bond. Then again, a few years ago she would have said the same thing about time travel, telekinesis, and any number of other unlikely phenomena . . .

"So you sensed that he had been injured somehow?"

"That's right." Phil shuddered at the memory. "But I also knew that he was still alive, just like I did after he disappeared in forty-seven, two years after V-J Day. The whole time Bill was missing, I always knew in my heart that he was still alive . . . somewhere."

*More like some*when, Diana thought.

"That must have been rough," Tom said, speaking from experience. Diana knew that he had hired private investigators to search for Shawn after his nephew disappeared.

Phil's voice turned bitter. "It was just so goddamn unfair, excuse the language." His knuckles tightened around the grip of his cane. "Bill had already come through so much. He'd survived the war, endured two years of rehab in a VA hospital, and was finally getting back on his feet again. He had his health back, he was starting college on the GI Bill, he was engaged to get married . . . he had his whole life ahead of him."

And then the future snatched him away, Diana realized. No wonder Gorinsky was so obsessed with getting back to his own time. He'd missed out on the best years of his life. "I guess that's why he's had so much trouble coping with his 4400 experience."

Phil nodded grimly. "Can you blame him? After the war, we were promised the American Dream, but Bill got cheated out of his share." His face took on a distinctly guilty expression. He hesitated before speaking again. "And I'm afraid there's more. Bill's fiancée, the girl he was supposed to marry . . . well, that was my Eleanor." He glanced up at a wedding photo on the mantle. Diana spotted the bride in several other portraits, aging gracefully over the course of a lifetime. "I hope you won't judge us too harshly. We both waited years for some word of what had happened to Bill, while growing closer all the while. Eventually, we turned to each other for comfort."

What's to judge? Diana thought sympathetically. It was an unusual turn of events, but not inconceivable under the circumstances. *I can see it happening.*

"We had a good life," Phil continued, a bit defensively. "I don't regret a thing. But it still came as quite a shock to Bill when he finally returned." Rising from his chair, he gazed mournfully at his late wife's portrait. "Eleanor was already gone by then, of course, taken by breast cancer a few years earlier. Perhaps that was for the best, at least for her sake."

Diana wondered if Phil ever blamed himself for his brother's mental collapse. The tragic story reminded her of poor Orson Bailey, one of the first 4400s she and Tom had investigated. A devoted husband, Bailey had returned just in time to watch his beloved wife die of Alzheimer's. Not for the first time, Diana had to ask herself what sort of grand design could possibly justify all the pain and heartache that had resulted from displacing 4400 people in time. Like Orson Bailey, Gorinsky's life and sanity had become collateral damage in the future's byzantine campaign to change the present.

"I'm sure he understands," she assured Phil, hoping it was true. "On some level, at least." Privately, though, she wondered if Gorinsky had truly forgiven his brother for marrying Eleanor in his absence. *Would April ever forgive me,* she thought hypothetically, *if I stole a fiancé from her?*

Not that anything like that was ever likely to happen.

Tom tactfully changed the subject. "Has your brother ever demonstrated any unusual ability?"

There was nothing in Gorinsky's file about an ability, but the returnees' unique talents often surfaced without warning. Maybe his file was out of date?

"That really happens?" Phil looked slightly taken aback. "I've heard stories, of course, but I thought maybe it was just ballyhoo to sell newspapers, like Bigfoot and flying saucers. It's hard enough to accept all that screwy time travel business they keep talking about, even though I can see with my own eyes that Bill didn't age a day while he was away." He shook his head in disbelief. Tired eyes implored the two agents. "Tell me how that makes any kind of sense. What kind of world are we living in where this sort of thing can actually happen?"

I wish I knew, Diana thought.

"Bilocation," Marco said.

The Theory Room at NTAC was the basement lair of Marco and his fellow brainiacs, where they applied their collective gray matter to the various mysteries presented by the 4400. The décor was as messy and unconventional as their minds. A movie poster for *The Monster That Devoured Cleveland* adorned one wall, next to a large dry-erase board covered with abstruse calculations and equations. Legal pads and computer disks were strewn about an assortment of cluttered desks and workstations. A "Jordan Collier" action figure perched atop a humming computer monitor. Christmas lights were strung up along the ceiling. Photos of crop circles and bug-eyed extraterrestrials were pinned to bulletin boards. Cardboard boxes, packed with old computer printouts, were stacked in the corners. The air reeked of microwave popcorn.

"Come again?" Tom asked, standing awkwardly by the door. He always felt out of his element in the nerds' domain, but had come to appreciate their frequent insights into NTAC's weirder cases. When you were dealing with situations as off the wall as the ones they encountered every day, it definitely paid to have some wild imaginations on your side. The two agents had descended to the Theory Room in hopes that Marco and his pals could explain how Bill Gorinsky could be at the Park Place Market two days ago while he was confined within Abendson at the same time.

"Bilocation," Marco repeated. Standing like a professor at the front of the room, he scrawled the word onto a blank board with a grease marker. "It's the ability to appear in two places simultaneously, just like your suspect apparently did."

Tom gave him an incredulous look. "There's actually a word for that?"

"Yep," Marco confirmed. "According to some sources, the phenomena has been around for centuries. Various saints, mystics, monks, and yogi are supposed to have been able to bilocate at will." He started to count them off on his fingers. "Saint Anthony of Padua, Saint Ambrose of Milan, Saint Severus of Ravenna, Saint Alphonsus Maria de'Liguori, Padre Pio of Italy, Pope Cyril VI. . . ."

"And Aleister Crowley," one of Marco's colleagues piped up. Tom knew the guy's name was Brady, but that was about the extent of his knowledge. Marco tended to act as spokesman for the think tank. "Don't forget him."

"Oh yeah," Marco added. "Him, too."

"So what are we talking about here?" Diana asked. "Some sort of astral projection?" She sat at a cluttered round table facing Marco. A lava lamp cast shifting red shadows over her face. "Gorinsky, if that's who it really was, certainly seemed solid enough at the Market the other day. He grabbed on to DeMeers at one point."

Marco didn't seem troubled by this detail. "That fits perfectly. In your classic bilocation scenario, the ectoplasmic double appears totally corporeal, and is able to interact normally with the physical world—until it evaporates back into the ether."

Tom nodded. "That would explain how he got away from me at that jade jewelry shop. I guess Gorinsky just stopped . . . bilocating . . . once he was out of sight."

"*If* it was Gorinsky," Diana reiterated. "We don't know that for sure."

"It was him," Tom said confidently. He had no more doubts on that score. Marco's explanation made sense . . . in a freaky 4400 kind of way. A thought occurred to him. "Gorinsky's been getting electroshock treatments at Abendson. Do you think that maybe it was the shock treatment that awakened his ability?"

"Actually, they don't call it shock treatment anymore," Brady corrected him. "The preferred term is 'electroconvulsive therapy.'"

Tom couldn't care less.

"You know," Diana recalled, "when Gorinsky grabbed on to DeMeers, Cooper acted like he'd received a minor electrical shock. Perhaps there is an electromagnetic component to his ability?"

"It's possible," Marco conceded. "The ECT could have stimulated the production of promicin in his brain." The newly discovered neurotransmitter had already been linked to the myriad abilities displayed by the 4400. "It's hard to say. We still don't know enough about what activates the returnees' latent abilities. Or how exactly ECT works, for that matter."

"In any event," Diana pointed out, "there's another mystery that still needs solving. What does Gorinsky want with Cooper DeMeers?"

Good question, Tom thought. A *Star Trek* calendar on the wall reminded him that DeMeers had eluded them for nearly forty-eight hours now. A nagging sense of urgency gnawed away at his patience. Although he couldn't say why, all his instincts told him that it was vitally important that they find DeMeers before Gorinsky did. Beckoning to Diana, he headed for the door.

"Let's take another look at that address book."

EIGHT

SONDRA JONNSON (disappeared December 9, 1993) worked as a tour guide for Seattle's Underground City. They found her down in Pioneer Square, hyping the tour to passing sightseers while handing out promotional brochures. Old-time streetlamps and an ornate wrought-iron pergola gave this historic stretch of downtown a nicely antique feel. A vintage streetcar trundled down First Avenue, past blocks of imposing Roman Revival architecture. An authentic Tlingit totem pole stood guard over the small brick plaza at the center of the square. A few yards away, a public drinking fountain was topped by a bronze bust of Chief Seattle himself. A sleeping wino added a bit more character to the neighborhood. Art galleries, clubs, bars, restaurants, and sidewalk cafés packed the surrounding red-brick buildings. After the Great Fire of 1889 burned the city to the ground, Seattle's founders had taken care to rebuild the downtown in stone.

Diana prayed it wouldn't be necessary to rebuild the city from scratch again.

"Trust me," Sondra told a family of tourists as they approached. She was a tall, strapping woman whose blond hair, blue eyes, and fair complexion betrayed her Scandinavian roots. A baseball cap shielded her eyes from the sun. A souvenir T-shirt advertised the Underground Tour. Hiking shorts exposed long, athletic legs. Flashing a blindingly white smile, she pressed some brochures into their hands. "You haven't really seen Seattle until you've seen what's underneath it. That's where the *real* history is buried."

Diana and Tom waited for the tourists to depart before approaching Sondra. "Excuse me, Ms. Jonnson?"

"Yes?" The woman turned her thousand-watt smile on the agents. She held out a brochure. "Are you interested in the tour?"

"Not right now," Diana said, producing her

badge. "NTAC. We'd like to talk to you for a few minutes if that's convenient."

Sondra's smile dimmed. A wary expression came over her Nordic features as she glanced at her wristwatch. She started to edge away from them. "Actually, I've got a tour starting in about twenty minutes . . ."

"This won't take long," Tom insisted. He moved to block her escape.

Sondra gave in. "All right." She nodded at a park bench underneath the totem pole. An iron fence enclosed a small garden behind the pole. "Over there." Diana sat down beside Sondra on the bench, while Tom remained standing. "What's this all about?"

Diana got right to the point. "How well do you know Cooper DeMeers?"

Sondra was one of the few 4400s listed in DeMeers's address book. They had also obtained phone records showing that DeMeers had called the tour guide on his cell phone right after he had escaped from them at the Market.

"Cooper?" Sondra feigned nonchalance . . . badly. "He's just a casual friend. We met in quarantine right after we got back from wherever." Homeland Security had briefly confined the 4400 after their return, before civil rights lawyers forced their release. "He works just up the street at the Market, so we get together for lunch sometimes. That's all."

Diana didn't believe her. Besides the damning phone records, she found it telling that Sondra had not yet asked them what they wanted with De-Meers. Perhaps she already knew that NTAC was looking for him?

"When was the last time you spoke with him?" Diana asked.

"I'm not sure," Sondra hedged. She fiddled clumsily with the brochures in her lap. "A couple of weeks maybe."

"That's funny," Tom said, looming over her. "We've got evidence indicating that he called you right after the earthquake Wednesday."

Sondra swallowed hard. "Oh yeah, right." Her azure eyes darted from side to side, as though looking for a convenient escape route. "I remember now. He was just checking to see if I was okay."

"Pretty thoughtful for a casual acquaintance," Diana observed. "Are you sure that's all you discussed?" Her voice held a warning tone. "Think carefully now."

To Diana's surprise, Sondra extracted a small

metal rasp from her hip pocket and started filing away at her teeth. She caught the two agents staring at her and blushed. "Sorry about that. Nervous habit. Ever since I got back, my teeth won't stop growing."

Tom and Diana exchanged startled looks. "Seriously?" Tom asked.

"You bet!" Sondra volunteered, a little too eager to change the subject. "It's pretty cool, really." She opened her mouth to show off rows of flawless white enamel. "All my old cavities filled back in, and I even grew back the tooth I lost during a skateboard accident in college. Ever since I became one of the 4400, I haven't had a single cavity. I don't even need to brush or floss anymore." She applied the rasp to an incisor. "The only drawback is that I have to keep filing the teeth down to avoid looking like Jaws."

Fascinated, Diana leaned in for a better look. The scientist in her briefly overcame the detective as she contemplated the woman's unusual ability. *Dental regeneration,* she thought, impressed by the potential implications for the human genome. *Just wait until Dr. Burkhoff hears about this . . .*

"I've been tempted to knock out another tooth," Sondra babbled on, obviously grateful to be talking

about anything other than her relationship with
Cooper DeMeers, "just to see how fast it would
grow back. But that strikes me as a bit extreme,
you know."

Dr. Burkhoff wouldn't think so.

Eying the rasp in Sondra's hand, Diana remembered the metal file she had found in DeMeers's
medicine cabinet, next to his toothbrush. *Sounds
to me*, she thought, *like they're more than just casual
acquaintances.*

So what else was she lying about?

"That's not in your file," Tom accused, deliberately putting her on the defensive.

All the blood drained from Sondra's face. "Is
that important?" she said anxiously. "I wasn't trying
to hide anything, I promise. It just seemed like no
big deal!"

"That's for us to decide." Diana kept the pressure on. "Does the name 'D. B. Cooper' mean
anything to you?"

"The hijacker guy?" Sondra blinked in surprise;
she looked genuinely baffled by the question.
"From the seventies?"

Diana guessed that DeMeers had never shared
his past exploits with the woman. Sondra probably
just thought that she was protecting her lover from

NTAC's nefarious clutches. "What about William Gorinsky?"

Sondra shook her head. "C'mon, folks," she pleaded. "Level with me here. Am I in some sort of trouble or not?"

"Not if you're telling us the truth." Diana felt a twinge of sympathy for the distraught guide. According to her file, Sondra had been a model citizen since returning to the present. There were no red flags or links to the Nova Group in her folder. Unlike Gorinsky and so many others, she seemed to have picked up the strands of her old life without a hitch. "You getting by okay, since you got out of quarantine?"

"What, are you my social worker now?" Sondra bristled momentarily, before regaining her composure. "Honestly, I've got nothing to complain about. From what I hear, I only missed out on the O.J. trial, Tonya and Nancy, and Monica Lewinsky. No great loss." She shrugged her shoulders. "I even got my old job back. And I can still use the exact same spiel I recited before I was abducted by the big Ball O' Light." She handed Diana a brochure. The flyer promised a captivating peek at Seattle's rowdy frontier days. "That's the nice thing about history. It doesn't change."

Diana managed a tight smile. *I know some people in the future who might disagree with that.*

Just down the street, at the Elliott Bay Book Company, a woman pretended to browse the self-help shelves while covertly observing the agents' encounter with Sondra Jonnson. Her spy-eyes picked up every nuance of the tense interrogation. *Good thing we never recruited her into Nova,* the woman thought. *That wuss caves too easily under pressure.*

She hit the speed dial on her cell phone. "Me again," she informed her cell leader. "Our friends at NTAC seem to have a lead on Cooper."

"Keep watching them," he replied. "Maybe they'll lead us straight to our seismic fugitive. I'll notify our operative to be ready to intervene."

"You got it." She ended the call as, two blocks north, the NTAC agents let Jonnson go about her business. Their clandestine observer was momentarily torn as to what to do; should she start watching Jonnson instead of the agents? Unfortunately, not even her remarkable eyes could look in two directions at once. *Better stick to the plan,* she decided. *We wouldn't want NTAC to get to Cooper while I'm looking elsewhere.*

Guessing that she had a long evening coming up, she headed for the café downstairs. Spying was thirsty work and she could use another chai. *Thank God for caffeine,* she thought, as she kept her eyes on Agents Baldwin and Skouris.

NINE

"I DON'T KNOW about you, but my butt is killing me."

Diana and Agent Garrity were parked across the street from Sondra Jonnson's apartment, a one-bedroom walk-up in Pioneer Square, above Doc Maynard's old saloon. They had been on stakeout for over five hours now, ever since DeMeers's suspected girlfriend had gotten off work. Garrity squirmed uncomfortably in the driver's seat of a nondescript brown Subaru. "You think maybe we're wasting our time?"

Jed Garrity was providing backup for Diana, while Tom carried out his end of tonight's surveillance operation. The dark-haired, thirtyish investigator was a good agent, she knew, despite his consistently pessimistic outlook. Garrity could always be counted on to expect the worst in any given situation. These days, alas, he was seldom proved wrong.

"I hope not," she replied, sitting shotgun beside him. She remained convinced that Sondra was hiding something, possibly the elusive Cooper DeMeers. Peering upward, she saw that the lights were still on in Sondra's apartment. Was she having trouble sleeping? *Tom and I left her pretty shook up this afternoon,* Diana thought. *Maybe we rattled her enough that she'll make a mistake?* Besides staking out her apartment, NTAC had also put a tap on Sondra's phone.

Pioneer Square's thriving nightlife was well under way around them. Music and laughter poured out the doorways of the neighborhood's many bars and nightclubs. Smokers congregated on the crowded sidewalks. Panhandlers hit up yuppies and college kids for loose change and the occasional cigarette. The neon sign of the local mission offered the vagrants an alternative to the streets. Scores of vehicles crowded First Avenue; parking was at a premium. A cloudless sky and mild temperatures invited plenty of pedestrian traffic.

Diana glanced at her watch. It was eleven-thirty; in theory, Alana had put Maia to bed hours ago. Diana's back ached from sitting in the car all night; she finished off a cup of cold coffee before deciding to check in with Tom. She pressed her cell phone to her ear.

He picked up on the first ring. "Hello?"

"Just touching base," she explained. "Sondra still hasn't budged from her apartment. What's new on your end?"

"Nothing much," he reported from Abendson. "Gorinsky's dead to the world."

It had taken a bit of arm-twisting, and the threat of a court order, to get Doctor Clayton to allow Tom to camp out in Gorinsky's room tonight, but the hospital director had eventually capitulated. The plan was for Tom to keep watch over Gorinsky's sleeping form while Diana and Garrity continued the hunt for DeMeers. If anyone tried to interfere with their investigation again, they wanted to know exactly what the confined mental patient was up to. Diana imagined Tom sitting diligently at Gorinsky's bedside, bored out of his mind. Talk about above and beyond; she knew how much he hated hospitals.

"I wish I slept this sound," Tom added. "The

guy hasn't stirred for hours. To be honest, I'm not entirely sure what I should be watching for. Do we think Gorinsky's 'astral double' is going to rise up out of his body like a ghost?"

"Beats me," she confessed. "This is my first case of alleged biloca—" Garrity nudged her with his elbow. She looked up to see Sondra Jonnson emerge from the building, clutching a paper bag of groceries. A jolt of adrenaline shot through Diana's system. "Hold on, something's happening!"

Pausing in front of the saloon, Sondra looked around cautiously to see if she was being watched. Diana slumped down in her seat, while Garrity made a show of checking his haircut in the rearview mirror. Sondra didn't give the Subaru a second look before taking off briskly down the sidewalk. A pack of clubbing Goth kids asked her for directions to Capitol Hill, but she was in too much of a rush to respond.

What's the big hurry? Diana wondered. *Anxious to get where you're going?*

Keeping Tom on the line, she and Garrity slipped out of the car and started after Sondra. The rowdy Friday night festivities made it easy to follow her unobserved. A stylish fedora helped to conceal Diana's features. Sondra kept nervously glancing back over her shoulders, but failed to spot the plainclothes agents amid the bustling crowd. Her furtive behavior struck Diana as a good sign. The jittery tour guide couldn't have looked more guilty if she'd tried.

"Looks like we're on to something," she whispered to Tom. "How's Sleeping Beauty?"

The last time they'd tried to apprehend De-Meers, some version of Gorinsky had gotten in the way. Diana didn't want any competition this time around.

"Out like a light," he reported. "You're good to go."

Up ahead, Sondra darted into a nearby alley. Diana hurried forward to peek around the corner. The ambient glow of one of the vintage streetlights provided just enough illumination for Diana to see Sondra descend a short flight of concrete steps to a basement door built into the side of the building on the left. A faded ghost ad for a turn-of-the-century headache tonic was painted on the sooty brick wall. More recent graffiti was scrawled atop the ancient ad. Garbage overflowed the top of a rusty metal Dumpster. Seattle's frequent rains had failed to wash the smell of urine away from the alley. Garrity made a face as he caught up with

Diana, who held a finger up in front of her lips.
Silence was the order of the moment.

Sondra held on to her groceries with one arm
while she fumbled with a set of keys. The basement door swung open and she disappeared into
the lower reaches of the building. The watching
agents gave her a ten-second head start before
following after her. In her haste, Sondra had left
the door unlocked. *Thank heaven for small favors,*
Diana thought. Her lock-picking skills were a
bit rusty. Beyond the door, a wooden staircase led
straight down into the Underground City.

After the Great Fire razed downtown Seattle
in 1889, city planners decided to take advantage
of the opportunity to rebuild Pioneer Square from
the ground up. Originally built upon tidal mud-
flats, frontier Seattle had suffered serious drainage
problems since day one, with toilets tending to
back up whenever the tide came in. A plan was
devised to raise the streets as much as thirty feet
higher; unfortunately, impatient landowners and
merchants went ahead and rebuilt their buildings
before the regrading plan went into effect. As a
result, when the streets were finally elevated, the
sidewalks and storefronts ended up one or two
stories below street level. For a time, pedestrians

had to use ladders to cross the streets, but eventually the sidewalks were covered over, turning the ground floors of the buildings into basements. The buried store entrances and sidewalks had languished for decades before being reinvented as a tourist attraction in the sixties. Diana had taken Maia on the tour a few summers ago.

The beam of her flashlight revealed a maze of musty passageways and interconnected basements. Debris lined walls of crumbling brick and plaster. Former doorways and windows were now blocked by packed earth and concrete. Rubble was strewn across the uneven floors. Built over sawdust landfill, the floors were cracked and sagging in places. Wooden walkways had been set up over the rougher terrain. Here and there, ornamental stonework and elegant columns confirmed that the dusty cellars had once served as the ground floors of fine mercantile establishments. An antique cash register rested upon the floor, next to the splintered remains of an old-fashioned rollback desk. An abandoned sign leaned against the wall, advertising the "South End Steam Baths." Rats scurried from the agents' approach. Cobwebs were draped like curtains in front of brick archways.

Diana guessed that Sondra knew this subterranean labyrinth like the back of her hand. *Of course*, she thought. *Where else would she hide De-Meers?*

She heard footsteps echoing ahead. The agents kept their flashlights aimed low to avoid betraying their presence. *Too bad we didn't bring night-vision goggles*, Diana reflected. They crept quietly along the wooden walkways. Light from above filtered down through cloudy glass cubes embedded in the sidewalks overhead. Moss hung from the ancient skylights. Legend had it that the district's once-abundant prostitutes had formerly paraded above the glass cubes with their prices written on the soles of their shoes, tempting the men below back when the underground corridors had still been in regular use. Diana wasn't sure she entirely believed that story, which she'd heard on the tour, but it certainly made for a colorful anecdote. She ducked her head beneath a rotting wooden water main.

"You know," Garrity whispered, "I'm not certain we've fully thought this through." He glanced nervously at the ceiling. "Do we really want to be underground with a guy who can allegedly trigger earthquakes with his mind?"

Good point, Diana thought. Being buried alive would definitely ruin her day, but it was too late to turn back now. She reminded herself that, according to Maia, she couldn't die just yet. *I still have to confront D. B. Cooper atop Mount Rainier.* Unless, of course, the future was tampering with the timeline again . . . It was like Marco said before: trying to reconcile predestination and time travel was enough to make your head spin.

"Cooper?" Sondra called out somewhere ahead. "Don't freak out. It's just me."

Just keep thinking that, Diana mused. She and Garrity exchanged a meaningful look. He drew his sidearm from its holster. *Sounds like we're on the right track.*

Sondra's voice came from beyond a rope stretched across an arched doorway. NO ADMITTANCE, warned a sign hanging from the rope. Diana recalled that only a small portion of the Underground was actually open to the public. She nodded to herself; it made sense that Sondra would store her fugitive lover in one of the areas off-limits to tourists. Torn cobwebs confirmed that someone had passed through the archway recently.

Lowering her voice, she tersely brought Tom up to speed. "We're closing in on DeMeers. Any activity with Gorinsky?"

"*Nada,*" he reported. "He's out cold, at least as

far as I can tell." He sounded frustrated at being so far from the action. "Good luck with DeMeers . . . and be careful."

"Will do," she promised. Stepping off the timber walkways, she and Garrity carefully made their way across the bumpy floor. Sticky strands of webbing clung to her face and hair. The murky darkness gave the buried catacombs a sepulchral quality; she couldn't help remembering a movie she'd seen on the late show once, about an immortal strangler lurking in the forgotten ruins beneath Seattle. She wondered if Cooper DeMeers was more or less dangerous than that fictional monster. *Guess we're about to find out.*

The glare of an electric light spilled around a corner ahead. As she and Garrity switched off their own flashlights and headed toward the light, Diana overheard snatches of conversation between Sondra and someone who had to be DeMeers.

"NTAC? They tracked you down already?" The alarmed male voice might have belonged to De-Meers. Diana couldn't be sure. "They didn't follow you here, did they?"

"No, I was careful," Sondra insisted. "Coop . . . what's this D. B. Cooper business all about? Is there something you're not telling me?"

Diana held her breath, anxious to hear De-Meers's answer. Would the runaway fishmonger fess up to his skyjacking past? The D. B. Cooper case remained the only unsolved hijacking in U.S. history. Never mind the 4400 connection for a moment; it would be quite a coup for NTAC if they finally bagged the legendary outlaw.

"Er, what do you mean?" he stalled, obviously in no hurry to answer the question. "You know NTAC. They'll use any excuse to lock us away."

Sondra wasn't buying it. "Be straight with me, Coop. Are you D. B. Cooper? And who the hell is William Gorinsky?" Her voice took on an hysterical edge. "I deserve to know exactly what you've got me mixed up in!"

"Please, baby. Calm down," he said soothingly. Diana caught a whiff of cigarette smoke. "You're right, you ought to know everything." He took a deep breath. "The truth is—"

Leaning forward, Garrity stumbled over a corroded metal pipe, which clattered loudly in the darkness. "What's that?" DeMeers exclaimed, cutting off his confession. "Who's there?"

Damn, Diana thought. *Talk about lousy timing!* Garrity shot her a sheepish look. She shrugged and drew her own gun. Their cover blown, she charged around the corner, holding the semiautomatic pistol in front of her. "NTAC! Nobody move!"

A single naked lightbulb, hanging from the ceiling rafters, exposed a ruined chamber that looked as if it might have once been used as an underground speakeasy during Prohibition. The rickety remains of a bar counter were propped up against the opposite wall, beneath a large cracked mirror in a filigreed frame. A shattered crystal chandelier and several empty wooden kegs had been shoved carelessly into a corner. Fresh groceries were spread out atop a moldering billiards table. Diana spotted a carton of Raleigh filter tips among the supplies. The torn green felt reeked of mildew and mouse droppings. A rumpled sleeping bag stretched atop an inflatable mattress, beside a small stack of newspapers and magazines. An elevated toilet seat, some three feet above the floor, hinted at the plumbing challenges that had led to the Underground's creation in the first place. *Looks like DeMeers has made himself at home,* Diana noted, *no doubt with Sondra's able assistance.*

The startled couple were backed up against the bar, their hands held over their heads. Diana was relieved not to see any weapons in their hands; the only thing DeMeers was holding was a lighted cigarette. The smoke tickled her nose.

"Don't shoot!" Sondra cried out frantically. "We surrender!"

DeMeers glared at her. He had traded his orange rubber overalls for a sweater and jeans. His bushy whiskers needed a shave. Two days' worth of stubble dotted his shaved scalp. The gold tooth gave him a vaguely piratical appearance. "I thought you said nobody followed you!"

"I didn't see them, I swear!" Tears streamed down her face. She gnashed her teeth.

"Quiet, both of you!" Diana barked. She heard Garrity bringing up the rear. Despite his mishap, it seemed that they had the situation under control. Neither DeMeers nor his girlfriend looked like they were planning to put up a fight. She kept them fixed in her gun sights nonetheless. "We've got him, Tom," she informed her partner via cell phone. "We're bringing them in now. Why don't you meet us back at HQ?"

Garrity stepped forward with two pairs of handcuffs. "Cooper DeMeers, Sondra Jonnson. You're under arrest for obstruction of justice." It was still a bit early to charge DeMeers with hijacking or premeditated earthquake-generating; all they really had on him right now was his failure to cooperate with their investigation. "You're both coming with us."

The suspects' eyes widened in shock. Their jaws dropped. Diana wasn't quite sure why they were so stunned by this turn of events; they already knew NTAC was after DeMeers. Then Diana realized that the two returnees weren't staring at her or Garrity. They were looking beyond them at something—or someone—else.

"You!" DeMeers gasped. "From the Market!"

"Watch out!" Sondra shouted.

Praying that she wasn't falling for the oldest trick in the book, Diana glanced back over her shoulder—to see Bill Gorinsky standing in the entrance to the old speakeasy. The beefy veteran filled up the doorway, his fists clenched at his sides. He was dressed just as he had been at the Market two days ago. Semper Fi was emblazoned on his tight green T-shirt. The camouflage trousers were army surplus. Psychic projection or not, he certainly looked solid enough. A trace of ozone tickled her nostrils. She wondered again if the double was electromagnetic in nature.

Garrity spun around in surprise. The handcuffs

jangled in his grip. "Holy crap!" he blurted. "Is that the mental hospital guy?"

"Tom!" Diana said urgently into the phone. "Gorinsky, he's here!"

"What? Are you sure?" She heard him jump to his feet. "I'm staring right at him!"

"So am I." Looking more closely, she saw that the figure in the doorway was definitely the same man they had encountered at Abendson, albeit with a few subtle differences. He was in better condition than the flabby, out-of-shape mental patient, nor did she see any of the wartime scarring the real Gorinsky was afflicted with. His youthful face was fresh and clean-shaven. Perhaps the man's astral double represented some sort of idealized version of himself? She'd have to run that hypothesis by Marco if and when she ever got out of here. "I guess bilocation isn't just a theory anymore."

She hesitated, unsure where she should be pointing her gun. "William Gorinsky," she addressed the newcomer, "you're intruding upon a federal investigation. Step away from the door and surrender to our custody." She still didn't understand Gorinsky's role in this affair, but she was prepared to drag his ectoplasmic butt all the way back to NTAC if that's what it took to get some answers. "Don't give us any trouble."

He pointed at DeMeers. "I just want him. The rest of you should stay out of my way."

Was it just her imagination or was there an odd, tinny quality to Gorinsky's voice, like an old juke-box recording? "Sorry," she told him. "That's not going to happen."

"Your choice," he said ominously. "Don't say I didn't warn you."

"I don't understand!" DeMeers protested. "What's happening? Who is this guy?"

He sounded genuinely confused. *Join the club,* Diana thought. His puzzled outbursts threatened to distract her from Gorinsky. There were suddenly too many variables to keep track of. *We're outnumbered here.*

Garrity came to her rescue. "You keep an eye on these two," he suggested, indicating DeMeers and Sondra. "I'll deal with Gorinsky."

With his gun in one hand and the cuffs in the other, he approached Gorinsky. "All right, put your hands out," he instructed the unarmed intruder. If he was apprehensive about confronting some sort of freakish apparition, he didn't show it. "Let's take this nice and easy . . ."

Gorinsky abruptly grabbed Garrity's arm. Electricity crackled and Garrity stiffened as though jolted by a powerful shock. The ozone smell got stronger. The stocky ex-Marine delivered a savage karate chop to Garrity's neck, dropping the stunned agent to the floor. Garrity's gun slipped from his fingers. Gorinsky kicked the weapon into a corner, away from Diana and the others. He stepped over Garrity's twitching body.

"Garrity!" Diana cried out in alarm.

Gorinsky advanced toward DeMeers. "You're coming with me," he repeated.

"Not so fast!" Diana stepped between Gorinsky and his target. Turning her back on DeMeers and Sondra, she aimed her automatic at Gorinsky's broad chest. "Don't make me shoot!"

Gorinsky sneered. "Take your best shot."

He came at her and Diana discharged her weapon. The gunshot echoed deafeningly inside the claustrophobic confines of the underground chamber. The acrid smell of cordite added to the pungent atmosphere. Sondra shrieked in panic.

Bits of brick and plaster went flying as the bullet passed through Gorinsky and slammed into the wall behind him. He hesitated, glancing down at his chest, then grinned at the conspicuous absence of any visible wound. "How about that?" he chuckled.

Diana couldn't believe her eyes. Gorinsky's T-shirt wasn't even singed. *I know I hit him. There's no way I missed at this range.* More evidence for the astral double theory: despite appearances, the figure before her was not composed of flesh and blood. *So how am I supposed to stop him?*

"Diana!" Tom shouted into her ear. In the tumult, she had almost forgotten that she still had him on the line. "What's going on there?"

"It's Gorinsky. He took out Garrity." She emptied her clip into Gorinsky, yelling over the blare of gunfire. The muzzle flashed repeatedly in the murk. "The bullets aren't stopping him!"

Gorinsky lunged at her, knocking the gun from her hand with a swipe of his arm. It clattered to the floor several feet away. She gasped and stepped backward, but his big hands closed about her throat. An electric tingle spread from her neck to her toes. Ozone filled her lungs. Her cell phone sparked and slipped from her fingers as she struggled to defend herself. Numb fingers lacked the strength to tear Gorinsky's hands away from her neck. "Tom!" she croaked hoarsely. "Help . . . !"

* * *

Tom suddenly wished *he* could be at two places at once.

Stuck in Gorinsky's hospital room, miles away from the action, he could only listen helplessly as his fellow agents came under attack . . . from the very same individual lying in front of him.

William Gorinsky lay flat on his back beneath the covers, barely moving. The overhead lights were dimmed, with only a solitary lamp on an end table giving Tom enough light to read by during his nocturnal vigil. An open magazine lay forgotten upon a chair as he paced anxiously around the room, his cell phone glued to his ear. He heard Diana's own phone crash onto the floor. Her anguished voice could barely be heard. "Tom . . . help!"

"Diana!" he shouted into the phone. "Garrity!"

No one answered.

His fists clenched in frustration. He had to do something, but what? Tom peered intently at Gorinsky's face. The patient's eyes flickered as though dreaming. A slight sneer curled his lips. The man's body was here, but his spirit was somewhere else. In the Underground City, it seemed, threatening Diana.

His mind racing, Tom remembered how Gorinsky's double had vanished into thin air at the Market. Maybe if he roused Gorinsky here, the double would disappear again? It was worth a shot; anything was better than doing nothing while his partner was in danger. He thrust his phone into his pocket.

"Gorinsky!" He grabbed the sleeping man by the shoulders and shook him roughly. Gorinsky's body flopped limply in his grasp, like an empty shell. His pajama top slipped, exposing more of the ugly burns on his left shoulder. "Wake up!" Gorinsky's eyelids fluttered, but refused to open. "Wake up, damnit!"

Desperate, Tom kicked over a bedside table. A vase of flowers and a cheap clock-radio crashed to the floor, but the clamor failed to wake Gorinsky from his trance. Clutching the patient's collar, Tom slapped him hard across the face. The blow knocked Gorinsky's head to one side, but had little effect. Gorinsky's eyes opened, but the lifeless green orbs stared blankly into space. There was still nobody at home. Tom shouted into the man's face. "Gorinsky! Get back here, you sleepwalking son of a bitch!"

The commotion attracted the hospital's night staff. "Hey, what's going on?" an orderly exclaimed

indignantly as he charged into the room. A horri-
fied-looking nurse was right behind him. "Leave
that patient alone!"

Tom realized just how bad this looked, but there
was no time to explain, even if he could. Instead he
yanked his sidearm from its holster and waved it
in the orderly's face. "Back off!" he ordered. "Don't
get any closer!"

The orderly threw up his hands and backed
away. The nurse turned and ran for help. Tom
heard her shouting in the corridor outside. He
guessed she'd be calling in the hospital's security
guards any minute now, not to mention the Seattle
Police Department. One way or another, he was
going to have a lot of explaining to do. This wasn't
exactly by the book.

But that didn't matter now. All he cared about
was stopping Gorinsky's rampaging doppelganger.
Keeping one eye on the door, he glanced around
the room. His frantic gaze fell onto the fallen
clock-radio. Lying amid the broken shards of the
vase, the radio was still plugged into a wall socket.
A desperate idea occurred to him.

*Electroshock, eh? Diana says nobody really knows
how it works . . .*

Releasing his hold on Gorinsky's collar, he let

the man's sagging head and shoulders drop back onto the bed. Tom snatched a pitcher of water off the top of the dresser and splashed the contents in Gorinsky's face. The cold spray did not revive the patient, but Tom hadn't really expected it to. He had another option in mind. Taking hold of the radio and its cord, he yanked the cord from the back of the appliance, exposing torn copper wires. Tom smiled grimly. His fingers wrapped around the severed cord's rubber insulation. He stuck a rolled-up magazine between the patient's jaws.

Time for your shock treatment, Mister Gorinsky . . .

Before anyone could arrive to stop him, he applied the naked wires to Gorinsky's damp forehead. Electricity sparked and the patient's entire body spasmed. Gaping eyes bulged from their sockets. His teeth bit down hard on the latest issue of *National Geographic*. An inarticulate moan escaped his clenched jaws. Tom jerked the cord back, breaking the connection, but Gorinsky kept on convulsing. For an instant, Tom thought he saw the shimmering blue outline of *another* Gorinsky superimposed on top of the writhing body in the bed, then the glowing aura faded, leaving actinic violet spots in Tom's vision. Gorinsky's blood-streaked eyes, alive and aware, met his for just a second. "No . . ." the patient murmured, spitting out the magazine. His lips were cracked and bleeding. A tear leaked down his cheek. "Not fair . . ."

He collapsed lifelessly into the bed. His chest stopped heaving. Glassy eyes stared into oblivion.

Jesus Christ, Tom thought. He yanked the plug from the wall socket. *I didn't mean to kill him!* He placed his fingers against Gorinsky's throat, searching in vain for a pulse. The smell of burnt hair rose from the corpse's scalp. He heard heavy footsteps running toward the room. *I just wanted to save . . .*

"Diana!"

He reached for his phone . . .

The older he got, the harder Phil Gorinsky found it to fall asleep at night. That hardly seemed fair, but what could you do? It was just something that came with old age, along with aching joints and regrets. Some nights, like tonight, he just sat up reading until he finally drifted off to sleep in his rocking chair. A wool comforter protected his legs from the late-night chill. A hardcover library book was propped up on his lap. The oversized print accommodated his failing vision.

He tried to concentrate on the plot, something

about a terrorist plot to blow up the Statue of Liberty, but his thoughts kept wandering off. That visit from those two NTAC agents had troubled him more than he liked to admit. Why was the government looking into Bill's case after all this time? Although polite, the agents had been deliberately vague about the nature of their investigation. *Why did they ask me about whether Bill had acquired some sort of supernatural ability?* Bill's doctors had never mentioned anything of the sort. *As if my poor brother doesn't already have enough problems . . . !*

He looked up at the photo on the mantel, the same one those agents had seemed so interested in. Eleanor had taken that photo, right before Uncle Sam shipped them both overseas. That seemed like a lifetime ago, which he guessed it had been. Except for Bill, that is; it had only been a few years for him. *Small wonder he's so messed up in the head.* Phil gazed at the old snapshot with melancholy nostalgia. They'd both looked so young and hopeful back then. Bill was still young, of course, but was there any hope left for him? A twinge of guilt reminded Phil that he hadn't visited his brother for a couple of days now. *I'll have to catch a ride to the hospital tomorrow.*

Giving up on his novel, he laid the book facedown on his lap. He leaned back in the rocking chair, resting his head against a cushion. Closing his eyes, he started to doze off . . . until a sudden start jolted him awake.

Bill!

His eyes snapped open and his worn-out heart was pounding like a jackhammer. He lurched unsteadily to his feet. The comforter and library book tumbled to the floor. A dizzy spell came over him, and he reached out for the mantel, accidentally knocking over the framed photo, which crashed onto the hearth. Phil knew at once that something terrible had happened to his brother; this was just like that time in '45, only worse somehow.

Bill was dead . . . or was he?

A tingling sensation rushed over his skin. Every hair on his body stood on end. He shut his eyes, only to see brilliant sparks flashing against the inside of his eyelids. His fingers and toes went numb. Lightning crackled in his ears. He tasted blood in his mouth and realized that he had bitten his own tongue. His heart thundered in his chest.

What's wrong with me? Am I having a stroke?

Letting go of the mantel, he groped for the medic-alert bracelet on his wrist. His trembling fingers pressed the emergency button, just as another wave of dizziness washed over him. A storm raged inside his skull. All at once, he could barely remember his own name. *Phil? Bill . . . ?*

The old man collapsed onto the carpet, only a few feet away from the splintered glass frame of the photo. His frail body convulsed upon the floor.

Choking hands cut off Diana's breath. Gorinsky's determined face was only inches away from her own. She couldn't feel his breath, but the ozone smell was overpowering. Her aching lungs screamed for oxygen. Static crackled in her ears. The room began to spin as she felt herself blacking out. Darkness encroached on her vision.

I'm sorry, Maia. I didn't want to leave you an orphan again . . .

A blinding electrical flash dispelled the darkness. Gorinsky's hands stopped squeezing her throat. Gasping for breath, Diana staggered backward. As her vision cleared, she realized that the murderous apparition was nowhere to be seen. Gorinsky had vanished into the ether, just as he had before.

But why? She checked hurriedly to make sure

DeMeers was still present. To her relief, the suspected hijacker and his girlfriend were still backed up against the wall. Their flabbergasted faces held bewildered expressions. "What happened?" Sondra asked, gone white as a ghost. "Where'd he go?"

I wish I knew, Diana thought. The unstoppable 4400 had left without his prize. "Stay right where you are!" she ordered the couple while she retrieved her gun from the floor. The last thing she needed right now was for DeMeers or Sondra to give her any trouble. "You're still under arrest."

A groan came from Garrity's prone form. He stirred upon the floor. Wincing, he hauled himself up into a sitting position. "What happened?" he asked, sounding dazed and disoriented. "Where am I?" Diana guessed that Gorinsky's electroconvulsive zap had scrambled Garrity's short-term memory. "Skouris?"

She started to explain, then heard another voice calling her name. "Diana?" Tom called to her from the fallen cell phone. "What's happening? Answer me, Diana!"

"Hang on!" she called out to him as she scrambled for the phone. There were scorch marks on its casing, but at least it was still working. "I'm here, Tom." She glanced at Garrity, who was slowly rising to his feet. He looked as if he was starting to remember where he was. "We're both okay. Gorinsky just vanished." She sniffed the air; even the distinctive ozone smell was gone. "I don't know why."

"I think I can answer that," Tom said glumly. He rapidly briefed her on the events at Abendson. Diana found herself torn between gratitude for her partner's quick thinking and shock that Gorinsky was dead. Tom sounded pretty shook up, too.

"Oh my God," she whispered. "Are you okay?"

"I'll manage," Tom said. She heard strident voices in the background. "But I'm going to be tied up here for a while, straightening out this mess. Don't worry about me, though. You and Garrity just concentrate on bringing in DeMeers."

"Count on it," she told him. "And, Tom . . . thanks." She had no doubt that her partner had just saved her life for the umpteenth time. *But who's counting?* Ending the call, she returned the phone to her pocket. She looked over at Garrity. "You up to this?"

He nodded, despite looking a little under the weather. "Man, we don't get paid enough for this craziness." He recovered his own pistol from the dirt. Shaking his head to clear the last of the fuzz from his brain, he approached DeMeers and Sondra once more. "Now then, where were we?"

"That's it?" DeMeers protested. "You're still not going to tell us what's going on?" His composure crumbled as his temper hit its limit. He threw his cigarette onto the floor and stomped it out beneath his foot. His face flushed behind his beard. Veins pulsed at his temples. "This is insane. Why can't you people just leave us alone!"

The broken chandelier started rattling in the corner. A trickle of dust began falling from the ceiling. A faint vibration rattled the forgotten speakeasy.

Another earthquake? Diana stared accusingly at DeMeers. No way was this another coincidence . . .

"Stop it," she ordered, brandishing her gun. "Right now."

"Stop what?" He waved his empty hands over his head. "I'm not doing anything!"

His panicked expression suggested that he was telling the truth. Diana guessed that he had no conscious control over his tectokinesis, at least not yet. Many of the returnees had needed time to master their new abilities. As the floor quivered beneath her, it was unclear whether DeMeers's time had run out. The concrete floor cracked and buckled.

"I knew it," Garrity said dourly. "I just knew this was going to happen."

"Cooper! What are they talking about?" Sondra demanded. Tottering unsteadily upon her feet, she grabbed on to his arm for support. She stared at her lover as though she had never seen him before. "Are you doing this?"

"I don't know!" He clutched his head. Veins throbbed across his skull. "I don't understand!"

The tremors increased in intensity. The cracked mirror crashed down onto the floor, shattering into dozens of pieces. A wooden keg toppled over. Decades' worth of dust rained down from overhead, obscuring Diana's vision. She covered her mouth with her hand to keep from choking on the flying sediment. Fighting to keep her balance, she braced herself against the rocking billiards table. Groceries bounced atop the moldy green felt; a six-pack inched toward the edge. The more agitated De-Meers became, the more the seismic paroxysms threatened to bring down the Underground on their heads.

"DeMeers . . . Cooper," Diana called out to him. "You have to calm down!" She laid her sidearm down on top of the table. "Look, I'm putting down my weapon. Nobody here wants to hurt you." Following her lead, Garrity lowered his gun as well. "We just need to understand this ability of yours." That wasn't entirely true—there was still the matter of that hijacking thirty-five years ago—but that was the least of Diana's concerns at the moment. "You need to calm down and let us help you . . . for all our sakes!" She considered reloading her gun with tranquilizer darts, but it seemed to be too late for that. *It might just upset him more.*

Sondra seemed to get the message. "Please, honey, listen to her." A rafter cracked loudly above them and she let out a frightened yelp. "You gotta stop this. Just close your eyes and think happy thoughts."

"I . . . I'll try," DeMeers promised, closing his eyes as instructed. Diana held her breath as she watched the man assume a more meditative de-meanor. He inhaled deeply, only to end up coughing on the airborne debris. The walls trembled as he struggled to bring his breathing under control. His purple face started to pale back to pink. He unclenched his fists. The swollen veins shrunk in size until they were only faint blue streaks beneath his scalp.

"That's it!" Sondra encouraged him. "You can do it!"

At first nothing happened, but then the tremors gradually subsided. Diana let out a sigh of relief as the floor stopped shaking. Clouds of dust settled onto the ground. The chandelier fell silent. Maybe they weren't going to end up entombed after all.

"That's more like it." She cautiously let go of the billiards table. "I think we're okay now."

DeMeers hesitantly opened his eyes. He looked as surprised as anyone else to find the potential cave-in averted. "I did it," he murmured in disbelief. "It really is me."

So it appears, Diana thought. Being careful not to alarm him, she holstered her gun. Garrity started to come forward with the handcuffs again, but Diana discreetly signaled him to back off. "Thank you for your cooperation, Mister De-Meers. If you and Ms. Jonnson could come with us now, we'd like to take you back to NTAC for observation." She wiped the dust from her face. "You must realize by now that your new ability has to be managed somehow. It's not going to just go away on its own."

"I guess not," he muttered. All the fight had gone out of him. He squeezed Sondra's hand. "Sorry, babe. Bet you didn't know I was a one-man disaster area."

She gave him a comforting smile. "It will be okay, Coop. We'll get through this."

Diana admired the other woman's optimism and loyalty to her boyfriend. She wished she could be so confident that everything was going to turn out well in the end, but Maia's unfulfilled prophecy still cast a pall over the future. *Just take things one day at a time,* she advised herself. *That's all we can do right now.* The sooner she got DeMeers into an NTAC holding cell, properly dosed and tranquilized, the better.

She gestured toward the exit. "After you."

TEN

THE INTERROGATION ROOMS at NTAC were not meant to be cozy. Soundproof ceramic tiles covered the walls, cutting the chamber off from the rest of the world. A rectangular blue-steel table occupied the center of the room. Matching metal chairs were strictly functional. A one-way mirror allowed outside observers to view the proceedings without being seen. The temperature was deliberately kept a few degrees warmer than necessary, the better to sweat answers out of uncooperative suspects. The bare gray walls offered no distractions.

Cooper DeMeers sat at the table opposite Tom and Diana. Although dosed with the inhibitor and a

mild sedative, he still looked distinctly apprehensive as the two agents sat down across from him.
Perspiration gleamed upon his bare scalp. A bright
orange jumpsuit had replaced the dusty clothes he
had been wearing when he was brought in. At Diana's request, he was not shackled. A tranquilizer
pistol rested against Tom's hip just in case the med
techs hadn't gotten DeMeers's dosage right. Seattle
didn't need another earthquake.

Diana introduced Tom to the suspect. "Are they
treating you all right, Cooper?"

"Well enough," he replied. "How is Sondra?"

"She's fine," Diana assured him. As far as they
could tell, her only crime had been helping De-
Meers hide from NTAC. "She's been released on
her own recognizance."

"That's good," DeMeers said, visibly relieved by
the news. "She's a great lady. She doesn't deserve to
get hassled on my account."

Tom decided to get straight to the point. He
hauled up a box he had carried into the interrogation room and poured its contents onto the
table in front of DeMeers. Scads of D. B. Cooper memorabilia, extracted from DeMeers's foot
locker, spilled across the tabletop. The scrapbooks,
paperbacks, videos, and other items made an

impressive pile. The evidence had already been checked out by the lab boys. DeMeers's prints were all over them.

"Quite a collection," Tom observed. "Souvenirs of your historic jump? You like to take them out sometimes and bask in your notoriety? Must really stroke the old ego to know that people are still talking about you after all these years."

DeMeers had initially blanched at the sight of his belongings, but he quickly recovered. "You think I'm D. B. Cooper?" He scoffed at the very idea. "Is that what this is all about?"

"Come on, Cooper," Diana urged. "Level with us." She ticked off the points of similarity. "You disappeared about the same time as D. B. Cooper. You match the physical profile. You have skydiving experience. You're both bourbon drinkers. You even smoke the same brand of cigarettes."

"So?" he challenged them. "Is that all you've got?" He leaned back in his chair, appearing a bit more relaxed. "Look, you saw where I worked. I sling fish for a living." He laughed bitterly. "You think I'd do that if I had two hundred grand stashed away somewhere?"

Not if you lost it somehow, Tom thought. Back in 1980, nine years after the hijacking, about six thousand dollars of the ransom money had washed up on the shore of the Columbia River on the border of southern Washington. Found by a picnicking family, the soggy twenties had been identified by their serial numbers. Subsequent searches had failed to turn up the rest of the $200,000, but Tom wondered if perhaps all of Cooper's ill-gotten gains had ended up in the river somehow. Maybe the bulk of the money had been washed out to sea?

"Then what's with the collection?" Tom waved the original FBI wanted poster in DeMeers's face. The prisoner's stubborn denials frustrated Tom. This wasn't just about solving a decades-old mystery; it was crucial that they determine whether DeMeers was indeed the man Maia had seen in her vision. "Why the fascination with D. B. Cooper?"

"It's just a hobby," he insisted. "Some people obsess over Jack the Ripper or the JFK assassination. Others search for Bigfoot or the Loch Ness Monster." DeMeers shrugged. "I collect D. B. Cooper paraphernalia. It's no big deal."

Tom didn't believe him. "It's got to be hard keeping this secret all these years. Even from your girlfriend. Don't you ever just want to tell somebody who you really are, take credit for what you did?"

"Nice try," DeMeers snickered. "But even if I

was D. B. Cooper, which I'm not, why risk going to prison for something that happened thirty-plus years ago? Bad enough that I got carried off by a glowing ball of light for three decades. You think I'd want to trade my freedom for a brief taste of fame?" He rolled his eyes at the sheer absurdity of the idea. "Besides, it's the *mystery* of D. B. Cooper that keeps people talking. If he ever came forward, there would be one last flurry of headlines, then he'd disappear into obscurity forever. He'd end up just a forgotten footnote in the history of crime."

"Sounds like you've given this some thought," Diana accused him. She looked over his file. "I see you were actually working at Sea-Tac Airport as a bartender back in 1971. What was the matter? Did you get tired of serving drinks to people who were actually going somewhere, flying off to interesting and exciting locations while you were stuck behind a bar washing glasses?" DeMeers scowled; Tom wondered if Diana was hitting a nerve. "I can see where that would get pretty old after a while. It must have been tempting to get on a plane yourself, maybe go for one big score that would change your life for good?"

"Spare me the amateur psych profiles." DeMeers shifted his weight, showing signs of impatience.

"Look, are we done with this D. B. Cooper crap yet? I thought you were going to help me control my ability."

"What do you think the shots are for?" Tom chose not to mention Maia's prophecy just yet. Instead he swept the souvenirs aside and produced the inflammatory manifesto they had found in DeMeers's apartment. The flyer was sealed inside a transparent evidence bag. "What's your connection to the Nova Group?"

"Nova?" This time DeMeers seemed genuinely startled by the accusation. "I don't have anything to do with that bunch." He nodded at the flyer. "I just picked that up in a coffee shop on the Ave 'cause it looked interesting, you know. I'm a 4400; naturally it caught my attention. That doesn't mean I'm some kind of terrorist."

No, just a former skyjacker, Tom thought. Still, DeMeers's explanation made sense. Unlike a few minutes ago, Tom didn't get a sense that the prisoner was lying to them. "So you don't support the Nova Group's agenda? Then why did you run from us at the Market the other day?"

"I just freaked out, okay!" DeMeers raised his voice, and Tom tensed automatically. His fingers drifted toward the grip of his tranquilizer, but no tremors shook the interrogation room. Apparently the inhibitor was doing its job. "First that creepy Marine showed up looking for me, then you folks charged onto the scene." His eyes lit up as a theory formed in his mind. "That Marine, the disappearing guy who attacked us in the Underground . . . is he part of the Nova Group? Is that what's got you all wound up?" His voice faltered as he tried and failed to put all the pieces together. "But what's that got to do with me?"

"We were hoping you could tell us that," Diana admitted. "Had you ever met him before?"

DeMeers shook his head.

"He's a 4400," Tom pointed out. "You would have been in quarantine together."

"Along with over four thousand other people!" He fidgeted restlessly in his seat; Tom figured he was probably craving a nicotine fix. "You think we all know each other? We were crammed in like cattle there."

That was a slight exaggeration, but Tom conceded the point. Even after two and a half years of dealing with the 4400 on a daily basis, he still didn't know all their names and faces by heart. It was certainly possible that DeMeers and Gorinsky had never met before.

"Who the hell is that guy anyway?" DeMeers glanced uneasily around the room, as though half expecting his ectoplasmic stalker to materialize at any moment. "Are you sure I'm safe here?"

"For the record," Diana informed him, "his name was William Gorinsky."

DeMeers didn't miss her use of the past tense. "Was?"

"He's dead," Tom said tersely. "You don't need to worry about him anymore."

DeMeers didn't ask how Gorinsky died. Maybe he didn't want to know.

"Does the name mean anything to you?" Diana asked.

"Not that I can think of." He paused to search his memory, then shook his head again. "So what happens now? How long are you people planning to hold me?"

Good question, Tom thought. Inhibitor or not, he didn't feel comfortable releasing DeMeers as long as Maia's prophecy remained unfulfilled. But right now they couldn't even be a hundred percent sure that they had the right guy. He flirted with the idea of confronting DeMeers head-on with the content of Maia's vision, in hopes of getting him to crack, but that was probably something he ought to run by Diana first. Better to broach the subject more obliquely.

"That depends," he told DeMeers. "How often do you visit Mount Rainier?"

The question caught the other man completely by surprise. "What the hell? What you want to know that for?"

Before Tom could continue this line of inquiry, there was a knock at the door. Tom and Diana looked over to see Nina standing in the doorway. "Sorry to interrupt," their boss said with a somber expression on her face. "But we have a situation."

Now what? Tom wondered.

DeMeers was taken back to his cell, and Tom and Diana joined Nina in her office, where two visitors awaited them. One of them was a short man of Middle Eastern descent wearing a tailored Armani suit. He had an equally expensive haircut and neatly manicured nails. Tom put his age in the late forties, early fifties. Strands of silver infiltrated his black goatee. A young Asian woman accompanied him.

"Agent Baldwin, Agent Skouris," Nina explained, "meet Mister Rahmen Aziz, an attorney representing The 4400 Center, and his assistant,

Simone Tanaka. They're here on behalf of Cooper DeMeers."

Tom didn't like the sound of that. The 4400 Center had been set up by the late Jordan Collier, a business tycoon who had returned to the present along with the rest of the 4400, to represent the returnees and advance their mission, at least as Collier conceived that mission to be. Following Collier's shocking assassination, Tom's nephew, Collier's personal protégé, had inherited the reins of the Center. Tom generally trusted Shawn to do the right thing, as he had by helping them hunt down the Nova Group, but NTAC and the Center seldom saw eye to eye, especially these days.

He eyed Aziz warily. "I don't believe we've met."

"That's correct, Agent Baldwin, but I've been employed by the Center for some time now." He had a deep, mellifluous voice well-suited to coaxing juries. "My responsibilities have expanded recently, due to the unfortunate death of Matthew Ross." The lawyer shook his head sadly. "Quite an unexpected tragedy. It took us all very much by surprise."

"Yeah. Us, too." Someday soon, Tom knew, he would have to deal with the Isabelle Tyler situation. According to his contacts in the future, she was a lot more dangerous than even Diana knew. But Maia's apocalyptic prophecy took priority right now. "How can we help you, Mister Aziz?"

The attorney nodded at his assistant, who handed him a sheath of documents. "We have reason to believe that DeMeers is being held against his will and without legal representation." He presented the documents to Nina. "We're requesting that he be turned over to The 4400 Center for his own safety. As you know, Homeland Security has often dealt harshly with the 4400, in violation of their constitutional rights."

Tom wondered how Aziz had found out about this situation so fast. DeMeers had been in custody for less than twenty-four hours. Did Sondra Jonnson go straight to The 4400 Center after she was released?

"The Inhibitor Scandal was an aberration," Nina insisted. "Those responsible are facing federal charges."

"So you say," Aziz replied, "but you'll forgive me if I fear that the government's antipathy toward the 4400 does not begin and end with Dennis Ryland. These are perilous times we live in. *Habeas corpus* is not what it used to be. I don't want Cooper DeMeers to disappear into NTAC's holding cells indefinitely, or, even worse, be shipped off to some secret prison beyond our reach."

"Mister DeMeers surrendered voluntarily," Diana pointed out.

"I'm not convinced he was given much choice in the matter." Aziz seemed like the kind of lawyer who was very comfortable addressing judges and juries. "I would like to speak with DeMeers immediately to see just how 'voluntary' his cooperation is."

Would DeMeers walk out if given the opportunity? Tom didn't want to take that chance, not if he was still capable of setting off a volcano with his mind. *I'd just as soon keep Seattle in one piece.*

Nina was obviously on the same page. "DeMeers is the subject of an ongoing investigation. We have probable cause to believe that he poses a serious threat to national security."

"All the more reason we must have a full accounting of the charges against him," Aziz stated. " 'National security' is all too often used as a rationale to deny an individual his rights under the law." He puffed out his chest. "If you're not prepared to grant us access to DeMeers at this time, we will have no choice but to seek a court order demanding his release."

Nina stuck to her guns. "Cooper DeMeers isn't going anywhere until we determine that it is safe to release him."

"We'll see what the courts have to say about that." Aziz turned toward the door and beckoned for Simone to follow him. "A pleasure meeting you, agents. No doubt we'll be in touch again."

"Yeah. No doubt." Tom watched them leave with a sinking feeling in his stomach. This was a complication they didn't need. "What do you think?" he asked Nina once their unwelcome visitors were out of earshot. "Do they have a chance at getting DeMeers away from us?"

"Possibly." She looked tired; Tom knew she had been up all night smoothing over the mess he had made at Abendson. If not for her efforts, he'd probably be cooling his heels in a jail cell right now. As it was, he doubted that he'd be welcomed back to Abendson anytime soon. They seemed to frown on people electrocuting their patients. "In the past, the courts have granted us broad powers in dealing with the 4400, but trying to hold a man on the basis of a psychic vision might be pushing it. Can we conclusively link him to that skyjacking back in seventy-one?"

"Not yet," Diana admitted. "Our case against him on that front is still pretty circumstantial."

Nina sighed wearily. "Well, keep on it. Aziz will have a harder time prying him away from us if we can prove that Cooper DeMeers and D. B. Cooper are one and the same."

"We'll do our best," Diana promised. She turned toward Tom. "Back to the drawing board?"

"Just give me a few minutes first," he said as they headed back to their own office. He extracted his cell phone from his pocket. "I need to make a call."

"Oh, hi, Uncle Tommy. What's up?"

One of the advantages of being related to Shawn was that Tom had a direct line to his nephew, allowing him to bypass The 4400 Center's various levels of bureaucracy. For privacy's sake, Tom had stepped into Garrity's empty cubicle to make the call. Jed was taking the day off on doctor's orders after being zapped by Gorinsky's hostile double. Diana had stubbornly shrugged off her own brush with death.

"You got a minute?" Tom asked. "I think we need to talk about this DeMeers situation."

"DeMeers?"

"A 4400 we brought in for questioning last

night," Tom explained. "We just had a visit from one of your lawyers, a Rahmen Aziz."

"Oh right," Shawn said. "That guy you picked up in the Underground City. My people briefed me on that this morning. Sorry to space out on you like that." His tone was apologetic. "I've got a lot on my mind right now."

Tom thought his nephew sounded kind of distracted. *Wonder if he's got his hands full with Isabelle.* Between running the Center and dating a homicidal superwoman from the future, Shawn had to be feeling the strain. *That's way too much responsibility for a kid his age to have to cope with.*

"So it wasn't your idea to send Aziz over here to spring DeMeers?"

"If I remember right," Shawn replied, "Rahmen brought the matter to me on his own initiative. But he made a good case for the Center getting involved. Jordan created this place to look out for the best interests of the 4400. This sounds exactly like what he would've wanted us to do in this case."

"Then Collier would have been wrong," Tom insisted, "because I've got to tell you, Shawn, that this is a seriously bad idea." He wished he could tell Shawn about Mount Rainier, but NTAC was still keeping a tight lid on that scenario. "You have no idea what this DeMeers character might be capable of."

"No offense, Uncle Tommy, but I can't just take your word for it." Tom could tell he had Shawn's full attention now. "NTAC's come down on us too hard too often. Heck, we'd probably still be in quarantine if the courts hadn't forced you guys to release us." Like the rest of the returnees, Shawn had not appreciated being placed in captivity right after his return. "Not to mention the time you rounded us all up during the inhibitor epidemic. I don't want to bust your chops, but if you think this guy is so dangerous, you're going to have to prove it. That doesn't seem unreasonable to me."

Tom played his trump card. "Listen to me, Shawn. Maia Skouris saw DeMeers cause a major disaster, sometime in the near future." In actuality, the truth was somewhat more complicated than that, but Tom didn't want to muddy the waters any more than he had to. "You know about Maia. You've got to realize that we have to take her visions very seriously."

"I don't know." The Maia angle seemed to give Shawn pause. "I'll tell you what, I'll talk the matter over with Richard." Tom recalled that Richard Tyler, Isabelle's father, had recently taken over as

co-director of The 4400 Center, sharing power
with Shawn. "But I'm reluctant to undercut my
own people, especially when they seem to be doing
their jobs. I appreciate your concerns regarding Maia, but, in the long run, we can't hold our
policies hostage to her visions. That strikes me as a
very dangerous precedent."

"I see," Tom said, disappointed. "Well, thanks
for listening to me." He sensed that this was as
much as he was going to get out of Shawn for the
time being. "One last question: was it Sondra Jonnson who got the Center involved in this case?"

"Who?" Shawn asked. "I don't think so. I don't
recognize the name."

Then where had Aziz gotten his information
from? "Are you sure about that, Shawn? Can you
look into that for—?"

A woman's voice, somewhere in the background,
interrupted him. "Come on, Shawn!" she said impatiently. Tom recognized Isabelle's imperious
tone. "I'm getting bored."

"Gotta run, Uncle Tommy." Shawn sounded
harried and more than a little anxious. Tom
guessed that Isabelle wasn't a girl you kept waiting,
not if you wanted to stay in one piece. "Talk to you
soon."

Tom heard a click at the other end of the line. A dial tone informed him his call was over. *Damn,* he thought. *That didn't go the way I wanted it to.* He considered trying to contact Richard Tyler, but thought better of it. Tyler was a decent man, but he was possibly even more suspicious of NTAC than Shawn was. *I can't see him overruling Aziz.*

Frustrated, he went looking for Diana. Maybe she had a clue as to what they should do next, because right now it felt like everyone and his brother was conspiring to keep them from saving Seattle. Where were their "friends" in the future now that they needed them?

Still, at least we don't have to worry about Gorinsky anymore . . .

ELEVEN

"BUT, SHAWN, you promised we'd go flying kites in Gas Works Park today. It's supposed to be an ideal romantic outing." Isabelle thrust a glossy periodical in Shawn's face. "*Seattle* magazine says so!"

At moments like this, it was easy to remember that, despite her twenty-something appearance, Isabelle was still in her terrible twos. "I'm sorry," Shawn replied as he strolled down the carpeted hallway toward Richard Tyler's office at The 4400 Center. Isabelle tagged along beside him. "I just need to talk to your dad about something."

"But it's Saturday," she whined. "Why do you have to work today anyway?"

The last thing Shawn wanted to do was involve Isabelle in this latest crisis. The gruesome death of Jamie Skysinger, only three days ago, was still fresh in his mind. "That's why I get the big bucks," he said breezily, hoping to fend off further inquiries. As they approached the open door of Richard's corner office, he saw that Isabelle's father was also putting in extra hours this weekend. Richard was huddled behind his desk, poring over reports. *I figured he'd be here,* Shawn thought. Running the Center was a lot of work, as he knew from personal experience. Shawn had originally resisted sharing his authority with Richard, but he had to admit that there were advantages to not having to manage the whole enterprise on his own. *This job is too big for just one person.*

"Excuse me, Richard." He rapped lightly on the open door as he entered the office. Isabelle attempted to follow him in, and looked positively flabbergasted when he gently closed the door in her face. "Sorry. Private business."

He half expected her to blast down the door with her mind or something, but, to his relief and surprise, she stayed outside in the hall. *Guess I lucked out this time.*

"Shawn?" Richard Tyler looked up from the

paperwork on his desk. Isabelle's father was a tall, lean black man in his early thirties who had once served as an Air Force pilot during the Korean War. He had a tense, worried expression. "What is it? Is something wrong?" He glanced apprehensively at the door. "Is this about Isabelle?"

Richard initially disapproved of Shawn's relationship with his newly adult daughter, but recently he seemed more worried about Isabelle herself. Although protective of his child, he was also well aware of her volatile nature—and lethal potential. If anything, he had come to accept Shawn as a stabilizing influence on Isabelle. Not that anybody could really control her . . .

"No," Shawn replied. For once, Isabelle wasn't the problem. "Do you remember the DeMeers situation?"

Richard had been present for Aziz's original briefing. "I remember. The returnee NTAC picked up last night."

Shawn updated him on his call from his uncle. Over Isabelle's protests, he had also taken the time to review the case in more detail. "There's more. According to Aziz, NTAC really believes this guy can trigger earthquakes and volcanoes, just like the one Maia Skouris saw in her vision."

"Are we sure about that?" Richard gazed out his office's expansive picture window at the white-capped mountain hovering over the horizon. "Where's Aziz getting his inside information from?"

Shawn flipped quickly through a folder of papers. "I'm not sure. Aziz's report just mentions 'confidential sources.'" It was too bad that Aziz wasn't on hand to answer Richard's questions himself, but Shawn was reluctant to spoil what was left of the lawyer's weekend. He'd confer with Aziz again on Monday. In the meantime, he was less concerned with how their lawyer found out about DeMeers's alleged ability than with the potentially catastrophic implications. "So how do we want to handle this? I don't like the idea of NTAC snatching our people off the streets, but I'm not eager to see Seattle wiped out by a volcano, either."

"I know what you mean," Richard admitted. "But I still think DeMeers is better off in our hands." He rescued a fax from the papers on his desk. "Did you know that your uncle electrocuted a mentally ill 4400 at Abendson last night, about the same time that his partner was taking DeMeers into custody?"

"What?" Shawn snatched the document from

Richard's hand and hastily scanned the report. He flinched involuntarily at the sight of the hospital's letterhead; he still had nightmarish memories of his own recent confinement at Abendson. The fax offered a terse but chilling account of the tragic events in Ward 59. "I must have missed this."

"NTAC's claiming the death was accidental," Richard said. "Baldwin was just trying to stop this Gorinsky from using his ability against Diana Skouris. But I believe this incident demonstrates the extreme lengths NTAC will go to if they think a 4400 poses a threat. I know Baldwin is your uncle but looking out for DeMeers's personal well-being is simply not going to be his top priority, not if he's convinced that DeMeers is dangerous." He reclaimed the damning fax from Shawn. "Hell, he and Skouris wanted to take *you* into custody during your recent mental . . . lapse. Believe me, it took a lot of arguing on my part to convince them to let us commit you to Abendson instead. If you were anybody else, you might still be in an NTAC holding cell."

To be fair, Shawn thought, *I did almost kill Maia while I was insane.* He couldn't really blame Diana for wanting to put him away after that. It dawned on him that he still hadn't had a chance to apologize to Diana and Maia for what happened. *I need to do something about that soon.*

"If it's up to me," Richard continued, "I'd rather have our own people looking after DeMeers, helping him learn to control his ability, than let the government lock him away forever, drugged out of his mind."

"Okay," Shawn agreed. What Richard was saying made sense. *DeMeers is one of us; we should take responsibility for him.* "Let's have Aziz keep working the legal angles. In the meantime, we should try to learn more about DeMeers, find out what kind of person he is." Shawn knew only too well that there were some very bad apples among his fellow returnees; the Nova Group had proved that beyond the shadow of a doubt. "You ever met him?"

Richard shook his head. "Not that I remember."

"Me neither." Besides Nova, Shawn recalled, there had also been that serial killer guy who had used his ability to brainwash other people into committing new murders for him. Shawn had no problems with NTAC locking that slimeball up and throwing away the key. "I don't want to find out we're protecting another Oliver Knox or Daniel Armand."

"Understood," Richard said. "I'll get right on it."

Isabelle knocked impatiently at the door. "Shawn? Are you going to be much longer?"

"I'll be right with you." He winced at her voice. "One more thing," he told Richard: "I think we should keep Isabelle out of the loop on this one. We don't want her to . . . overreact."

Isabelle had gone on a killing spree the last couple of times that Shawn had been threatened. He didn't want to know how she'd respond if she thought the entire city was in danger. She might decide to go after DeMeers herself—and heaven help NTAC or anyone else who got in her way.

"That sounds like a good idea to me," her father said.

Isabelle paced restlessly in the hall. *What's taking Shawn so long?* she fumed. *And why is he excluding me like this?*

The glossy magazine in her hand, which promised "The Ten Most Romantic Outings in the Emerald City," seemed to mock her foiled plans for the afternoon. So far she had resisted the temptation to rip the magazine to shreds, but if this delay dragged on much longer she wasn't going to be responsible for her actions. She glared irritably at the closed door cutting her off from both her boyfriend and her father. Ugly abstract art hung on the hallway walls.

This is all Tom Baldwin's fault, she thought bitterly. It was the call from Shawn's uncle that had derailed their Saturday outing. She didn't know what "Uncle Tommy" had bugged Shawn about, but obviously it had been enough to lure Shawn away from her side. *Is he trying to break us up on purpose?* She had never told Shawn about the time that, under orders from the future, Tom Baldwin had come close to killing her. He hadn't been able to go through with it in the end, but she knew Tom still considered her some kind of dangerous monster. *Bad enough he tries to execute me. Now he's interfering with my love life?*

She was about to get Tom on the phone and give him a piece of her mind when the office door *finally* swung open and Shawn and her dad joined her in the hall. "Hello, honey," her father said, giving her a hug. "Sorry to keep you waiting."

"That's okay," she lied. "I didn't mind." She looked hopefully at Shawn. "Are we ready to go? We can still get some good kite-flying in."

He made *that* face, the one that he was making

more and more often lately: a sort of pained grimace that suggested that he would rather endure a root canal than spend another minute in her presence. "I'm so sorry, Isabelle, but something has come up. Maybe you can go to the park without me?"

She couldn't believe her ears. "That sort of defeats the point." She was looking forward to them spending some quality time together, especially after their disastrous date at the Space Needle. Was that what this was all about? Did Shawn blame her for that terrorist's death? *It's not fair,* she thought indignantly. *Doesn't he realize that I saved his life . . . again?* "What's so important that you can't take the afternoon off?"

"Nothing you need to worry about," her father insisted. "Just budgets and such."

"Maybe I can help," she volunteered. "I'm good with numbers."

In fact, that was an extreme understatement. She had mastered advanced calculus in less than a day and probably knew more about higher mathematics than most of the professors at the state university. *Still, no need to brag about it,* she thought, impressed by her own modesty. *That would just be rude.*

"Actually," Shawn said, "it's more about politics than numbers. Got to keep all the different departments happy, you know." He tried to guide her toward the elevator. "Thanks anyway, though."

Don't treat me like a child, she pouted. But she held her tongue, determined to prove to Shawn that she wasn't the crazy, out-of-control person he thought she was. "I just want to help out my two favorite guys."

"That's really sweet, honey," her father humored her. "Hey, I might have a project for you. I've been meaning to have someone look over our medical database to see if any of our people are showing any long-term side effects as a result of inhibitor poisoning. If you like, I can set you up at a monitor down in the infirmary."

Sounds like busywork to me, Isabelle thought. She knew a wild goose chase when she heard one. They were hiding something from her, but she could see right through them. It took all her patience and self-control to keep from demanding that they tell her the truth right here and now. Instead she went along with this transparent charade. "Sure. Let me at that database. I'll zip through it in no time."

Both men looked visibly relieved that she wasn't

throwing a fit. Like she was some kind of spoiled kid.

Fine, she thought spitefully, *I can keep secrets, too.* Like the fact that she had been covertly meeting with Dennis Ryland. Intent on keeping up with current events, she had discovered Ryland's new position at the Haspel Corporation before it had even made the back pages of the news. Instead of serving time in a federal prison, the mastermind behind the inhibitor scandal had been rewarded with a cushy job in the private sector, where he was continuing his campaign to neutralize the 4400 by any means possible. This had all been done very quietly; she doubted that even Tom Baldwin or his partner had heard about Ryland's new position yet. But it was all there in the fine print; you just had to be able to read between the lines.

Isabelle knew she had enemies, at NTAC, among the 4400, even in the future. That being the case, securing some powerful allies had struck her as a good idea. If her destiny really was to exterminate the 4400, as the late Matthew Ross had insisted, then that put her and Dennis Ryland on the same side. And if she chose to defend the returnees instead, then infiltrating Haspelcorp could have its advantages as well. Shawn and her father would take her a lot more seriously, she figured, if she managed to get to the bottom of Ryland's schemes against the 4400.

Isabelle liked having a foot in both camps. *Everyone keeps telling me I have a destiny,* she thought, *but I prefer to have options.*

She chucked the useless magazine into a waste bin.

TWELVE

William Gorinsky was buried with full military honors in a hillside cemetery overlooking Puyallup. Clouds and drizzle provided an appropriately gloomy atmosphere. Umbrellas blossomed above the heads of the funeral party. An honor guard composed of two servicemen fired shots into a bleak gray sky. An American flag draped the casket. Buglers being in short supply, a portable CD player delivered a recorded rendition of "Taps."

Standing apart from the other mourners, Tom listened silently to the farewell salute. A dark overcoat protected him from the rain. Alana stood beside him, sharing his umbrella. She wore a stylish but conservative black suit. "Are you all right?" she whispered to him softly.

"Yeah, more or less." He tugged at the band of silk constricting his throat; weddings and funerals were about the only times he broke down and wore a tie. "Thanks for coming with me today."

"Of course, Thomas." She gave his hand a comforting squeeze. "I know this has to be difficult for you."

That's for sure, he thought. Nevertheless, he felt obliged to pay his respects. Diana had offered to accompany him as well, but he had insisted that she spend Sunday with her daughter instead. *I was responsible for Gorinsky's death, not her.*

Oddly enough, the coroner's report had ruled out electrocution as the cause of death. According to the autopsy, the shock from the power cord had not inflicted enough damage to kill Gorinsky, nor had he suffered any sort of heart attack. In the absence of any other theories, speculation centered around the electromagnetic nature of Gorinsky's ability. Had Tom short-circuited him somehow by jolting him out of his bilocated state? Perhaps Gorinsky's physical form hadn't been able to survive the shock of being forcibly disconnected from his astral double? In the end, it didn't really matter.

One way or another, Tom realized, *he died at my hands.*

Gorinsky's funeral was sparsely attended. Thanks to his fifty-seven-year absence from history, the scarred veteran had outlived most of his contemporaries. Phil Gorinsky watched the proceedings from a wheelchair. A nurse stood by, shielding the old man with a black umbrella, while a uniformed Marine presented Phil with the flag from his brother's casket. "Taps" continued to play as the coffin was slowly lowered into the earth.

Tom realized he couldn't put off speaking to Phil any longer. Letting go of Alana's hand, he approached the retired schoolteacher. A cold rain pelted his head and shoulders. "Excuse me, Mister Gorinsky?"

He was shocked by the change in the senior citizen's appearance. Philip Gorinsky seemed dramatically weaker and more debilitated than he had been just three days earlier. His wrinkled skin was bleached of color. Hollow cheeks and sunken eyes gave him a cadaverous aspect. Despite a heavy coat and blanket, his palsied fingers shook as they held the folded flag in his lap. His brother's death had obviously taken quite a toll on him.

Phil looked up at Tom. "Agent Baldwin."

Tom was impressed that the old man remembered his name. "Forgive me for intruding, but I wanted to express my sincere condolences on your loss. I really wish things could have turned out differently."

He braced himself for a venomous outburst. Tom still wasn't sure what he could have done differently to save Diana and the others, but Phil was entitled to feel angry about his brother's death. If venting at Tom made the surviving twin feel better, the agent was willing to take a little verbal abuse. It was the least he could do for the man.

For a second, he thought he saw a flash of resentment in the elderly veteran's rheumy eyes, then Phil surprised him by saying, "It's all right, Agent Baldwin. You were just doing your duty, I understand that." He watched his twin's casket disappear into the ground. "My brother was . . . disturbed . . . and he wasn't getting any better. Maybe he's finally at peace now."

"I hope so," Tom said, grateful for the man's forgiveness. He eyed Bill's withered frame with concern. "How are you holding up, sir?"

"At my age, holding up is harder than it sounds." He shrugged his bony shoulders. "I suspect I'll be joining Phil and Eleanor soon." His voice wheezed from his lungs. "But not just yet. I like to think I still have a few more innings in me."

Tom started to compliment Phil on his attitude, but the man's nurse interrupted. "Excuse me, I really need to get Mister Gorinsky out of the rain."

"Right." Tom stepped aside to let the nurse wheel Phil toward a waiting ambulette. "Take care of yourself, Phil."

Alana rejoined him as he watched the ambulette pull away. She brought him under the cover of their umbrella. "How'd it go?"

"Better than I expected, actually." They clung together, sharing the warmth of their bodies. "It still seems a damn shame, though. Bill Gorinsky could have enjoyed a long, full life like his brother. He never asked for what happened to him."

"I know," Alana said gravely. She had been abducted only five years before. "None of us did."

THIRTEEN

A WEEKEND IN a holding cell hadn't made Cooper DeMeers any more forthcoming.

"How many times do I have to tell you?" he griped. "I'm *not* D. B. Cooper!"

Seated across from him in the interrogation room, Diana kept a close eye on the veins beneath the prisoner's stubbly scalp. NTAC's headquarters was a lot sturdier than either the Market or the Underground City, having been constructed in full compliance with Seattle's building codes, but she didn't feel like testing its limits this afternoon. *Two earthquakes in one week is quite enough for me, thank you very much.*

Tom kept up the pressure. "Why do I feel like you're still not leveling with us, Cooper?"

"What does it even matter anyway, after all these years?" DeMeers blurted in exasperation. "Don't you folks have better things to do? I thought there was a war on terror going on."

In fact, the 9/11 terror attacks had been one of the reasons that Diana had transferred from the CDC to Homeland Security. Here in Seattle, however, the return of the 4400 had trumped the threat of mere human terrorism, at least as far as NTAC was concerned. As far as they knew, al-Qaeda wasn't capable of igniting Mount Rainier with a thought.

Tom looked to Diana for her input. She knew exactly what he was thinking. They weren't getting anywhere and time was running out. Rahmen Aziz could show up with a court order freeing DeMeers at any moment. Clearly, a change in strategy was required. She nodded thoughtfully at Tom. It was time to put all their cards on the table.

"Here's the thing, Cooper." Tom put deliberate emphasis on their suspect's first name. "We happen to know a little girl who can see the future. She tells us that 'D. B. Cooper' is going to cause Mount Rainier to erupt sometime in the near future." His voice took on a sarcastic edge. "You don't know any returnee who might have the ability to do that, do you? Maybe a fortyish white male who disappeared around 1971?"

"Thousands of people could be killed in a disaster like that," Diana stressed. "Whole cities could be wiped out."

DeMeers looked genuinely stunned and horrified by the picture they were painting. He practically had to lift his jaw off the table. "But . . . but I would never do anything like that! I wouldn't dream of it." His initial shock morphed into indignation. "What sort of monster do you think I am?"

"D. B. Cooper threatened to blow up a jet full of innocent passengers," Tom reminded him.

"But nobody really got hurt!" DeMeers exclaimed. "He let all the passengers off at Sea-Tac. There wasn't even really a bomb . . . or so some people think, that is."

Any doubts Diana still had about D. B. Cooper's true identity were rapidly evaporating. "I'd like to think that," she told him. "And nobody's saying you're a monster. You're just another 4400 who can't entirely control his ability yet." As a peace offering, she offered him a pack of Raleigh cigarettes and a matchbook. "If you'll just be honest with us, we can try to fix things so that nothing terrible happens because of you."

She didn't mention that Maia's visions had *never* been proved wrong. Now was not the time for another philosophical debate on free will versus predestination. Besides, Maia didn't always see the whole picture, just bits and pieces of the future. Just a few weeks ago, for instance, she'd seen herself being kidnaped again, but not that Tom would eventually manage to talk the future into returning her to the present. *I have to believe that we haven't seen the full story here, either.*

"I don't know," he said hesitantly. Accepting the cigarettes, he gratefully lit up and took a couple of long draws on the cigarette to steady his nerves. "I'd like to help you, but . . ."

His voice trailed off into silence. Diana guessed that he was still afraid of being prosecuted for that long-ago hijacking. She wished she had the authority to offer DeMeers some sort of clemency in exchange for his full cooperation, but neither she nor Tom was empowered to make any deals of that nature. *Maybe we should ask Nina to talk to the FBI about that, before Aziz whisks DeMeers away from us.*

"But what?" Tom pressed him. He shoved an ashtray across the table. "Aren't you concerned by what we just told you? Don't you care that you could be responsible for the biggest disaster in U.S. history?"

"Maybe that little girl is wrong!" DeMeers said desperately, reaching for straws. "How do I know that you're not just making this up to trick me?"

His faced reddened. A plump vein beat out a silent warning upon his forehead. He was so visibly upset that Diana feared that they might have pushed him too hard. To her dismay, the ashtray started vibrating like crazy. She felt a faint rumble beneath her chair. The table rattled. Diana grabbed on to it for support.

Damn it, she thought. *Looks like we went too easy on the inhibitor . . .*

Tom jumped to his feet. He reached for the tranquilizer pistol at his waist, but she signaled him to hold off for a moment. Maybe she could still talk DeMeers down, like she had in the Underground.

"Cooper!" She kept her voice low, for fear of agitating him further. "Just calm down. Everything's going to be okay. There's no need to panic. We'll work this out somehow." His frantic eyes locked on to hers. She prayed she was getting through to him. "That's right. You can do this. Just think of Sondra. You know she wouldn't want you to lose control again . . ."

DeMeers closed his eyes. He took deep, calming breaths. Diana tried to do the same as she waited anxiously to see whether the crisis had been averted again. Tense moments stretched on endlessly until the ashtray stopped vibrating and the rumble faded away. Diana collapsed against the back of her seat. Beneath her sweater, she was drenched in sweat. Her pulse was racing. She swallowed hard.

That was a close one!

One eye at a time, DeMeers checked to see if the interrogation room was still intact. "Is it over?" he asked tentatively. "Did I stop it in time?"

"Seems like it," Tom said. His hand came away from his holster and he signaled the med tech standing by behind the shiny one-way mirror. A young Filipino woman in mint green scrubs entered the room carrying a hypodermic. Her ashen complexion suggested that she had experienced the quake as well. "I think we're done for the time being."

She could hear the frustration in his voice. It was going to be difficult to apply the third degree to a suspect who triggered earth tremors whenever he got riled up. *We're going to need a whole new approach here,* she realized, *assuming we get another shot at him.*

As if on cue, Nina appeared in the doorway. "Tom, Diana. If I can have a word with you?"

Diana experienced a flash of déjà vu as they convened outside the interrogation room. Through the transparent side of the one-way mirror, she saw the med tech nervously administer an inhibitor/tranquilizer mix to DeMeers. She hoped the other woman wasn't trembling too hard to find the vein.

"Let me guess," Tom said. "Aziz is here to spring DeMeers."

Nina shook her head. "Just the opposite. The NSA is taking him off our hands. They're ordering that he be shipped to a remote, seismically inert location and kept carefully medicated." She didn't look terribly pleased by this development. "I'm guessing they'll never let him set foot anywhere near the continental United States again."

"Isn't that a bit extreme?" Diana protested. She had just promised DeMeers that everything was going to work out for him, that NTAC would work with him to resolve this dilemma. "Aside from the hijacking, which we can't prove, he hasn't actually threatened anyone on purpose."

"Washington thinks the magnitude of the risk justifies these measures. To be honest, I'm not sure they're entirely wrong." She spotted Diana glaring at her in disbelief. "Don't give me that look. It's your daughter's visions that have got Washington convinced that the entire Pacific Northwest is at stake."

"We're still not one hundred percent certain that we've got the right guy," Tom pointed out. "Just give us a little more time with him. We're making progress. I'm pretty sure that he was about to open up when all the shaking started. He just needs some time to process what we told him."

"Sorry," Nina said. "It's out of my hands. These orders come from the highest level. The transfer will take place within twenty-four hours. In the meantime, the NSA wants him bottled up tight."

Diana watched helplessly as a pair of armed guards escorted DeMeers from the interrogation room. He slumped between them, obviously doped to the gills. There was no way they were going to get any more out of him in that state.

"So much for that," Tom said, reaching the same conclusion. Nina headed back to her office, leaving the two agents alone. They stared through the glass into the empty room beyond. "Is that it? Case closed?"

Diana wasn't so sure. "Not according to Maia."

She wondered if she still had a trip to Mount Rainier in her future.

"Nine A.M. sharp? That works for me. Just make sure there are no delays. I want Cooper DeMeers in our custody before I finish my first cup of coffee."

Dennis Ryland hung up the phone. He smirked in satisfaction, imagining the frustrated look on Tom Baldwin's face as his prime suspect was taken away from him. Ryland didn't consider himself a petty man, but he had to admit that there was a certain pleasure to be had in getting back at his backstabbing former friend and protégé. If not for Baldwin and his partner, Ryland's role in the inhibitor program might never have been discovered, and the 4400 would have no longer posed a threat to the nation's security. *I should have reassigned both of them*, he castigated himself, *once they started developing emotional ties to the returnees.* But who could have guessed that a level-headed scientist like Skouris would end up actually *adopting* one of the menaces?

I certainly didn't see that one coming.

Still, he couldn't complain. Leaning back against the genuine leather upholstery of his executive chair, he contemplated his sumptuous corner office. With its imported Italian furniture and tasteful objets d'art, it was considerably grander and more comfortable than his old digs back at Homeland Security. The private sector had its advantages, chief among them less governmental interference and oversight. Ironically, he was in a better position to take strong, decisive action against the 4400 now than he had been in as a mere federal employee. With the NSA contracting its investigation of the Nova Group out to Haspelcorp, he was right where he needed to be.

The six-figure salary was just a bonus.

It's a shame I can't be there tomorrow, he mused, *just to see the look on Tom's and Diana's faces when they say good-bye to Cooper DeMeers for good.* He couldn't wait to get the alleged earth-shaker into the hands of Haspelcorp's eager scientists. General Randa was already intrigued by the possible military applications of DeMeers's ability . . .

"Let me guess. Iced *vente* chai soy, right?"

"Right on the money," she confirmed. By now,

the friendly baristas here knew her order by heart.
She was a regular at this particular Starbucks, with
good reason. The cozy coffee shop offered a perfect view of NTAC's inner sanctums, provided you
were equipped with the right sort of spy-eyes. As
she paid for her drink, she kept one eye on the ongoing developments at their enemy's headquarters.
Things had just taken an unexpected turn.

"You ever going to try something different?" the
boy behind the counter asked.

Was he flirting with her? If so, he was going to
be disappointed. She had more important matters
to occupy her mind. "Sure. Come September, I'll
want a *hot* chai."

Assuming this Starbucks, along with the rest of
Seattle, was still around next fall . . .

"Thanks." Sipping her afternoon dose of caffeine, she headed for her favorite table, where she
flipped open a copy of *The Volcano*, a local arts
and entertainment newsletter. The paper was just
a prop, protective coloration to help her blend in
with her surroundings, but it was hard not to see
the paper's masthead as an omen of sorts. The
spewing mountain reminded her of just how much
was at stake where Cooper DeMeers was concerned.

Her cell phone swiftly connected her with her cell leader. "Listen up. We've got trouble." She quickly outlined the NSA's intention to spirit DeMeers away to an undisclosed location beyond their reach. "The transfer is tomorrow morning."

"That doesn't give us much time," her leader acknowledged. "We're going to have to move quickly."

FOURTEEN

F‌REE FALL WAS a bitch.

Ten thousand feet above the snowbound wilderness, Cooper plunged through the freezing night sky. His stomach seemed to lunge up his throat as he accelerated downward at a breath-stealing clip. A heavy overcoat, gloves, and sunglasses provided scant protection against the frigid wind. For a second, he regretted leaving his tie back in the cabin of the plane, not that the thin strip of fabric would have made much of a difference; it felt like ten below, not counting the windchill factor. He lost his brown loafers almost immediately, leaving nothing but a pair of thick wool socks on his feet. The briefcase containing the so-called bomb was torn from his grasp. He wondered if anyone would ever find it.

He couldn't believe how cold it was, even more so than he had anticipated. *I should have waited until spring,* he thought, even though that really hadn't been an option. The divorce had practically cleaned him out; between his mounting debts and alimony payments, he would have been bankrupt long before warm weather returned to the Northwest, especially given the lousy state of the economy. Massive layoffs at Boeing had sent the whole region into a tailspin. *Besides, if I'd stalled any longer, I'd have lost my nerve for sure . . .*

Two parachutes were strapped to his torso, one to his back and another to his chest, just in case of an emergency. He felt confident that the Feds had not sabotaged any of the four chutes he had demanded; they wouldn't have taken the chance that he might have forced one or more of the hostages to jump with him. That was the idea at least. He had thought this all out ahead of time, and so far everything had gone according to plan. A fabric bag, loaded down with over twenty pounds of cash, was tied to his waist by sturdy nylon cords; he had cannibalized one of the extra chutes for the fabric and cords. The weight of the bag tugged on his hips as it dangled below him. The chutes were slightly different than the T-7's he had used back in Korea, but the basics didn't seem to have changed too much.

What goes up, must come down . . . in one piece, preferably.

All sense of falling vanished as he reached terminal velocity, roughly 120 miles per hour. He struggled to maintain a stable arch position, his belly to the earth, but the ferocious winter winds pummeled him relentlessly, making it all but impossible to control his descent. His sunglasses went flying, and he squinted into the fierce gale. This was nothing like that jump he had made over Sukchon during the war. Only a daredevil or a maniac would attempt to land a parachute during a winter storm, the night before Thanksgiving, no less. So what did that make him?

Desperate, that's what.

A sudden jolt yanked him upward as the automatic activation device on his chute went off. No matter how much you were prepared for it, the chute's deployment always came as a shock. Pins and needles stabbed his frozen fingers as they tugged on the risers. The parachute billowed above him, or so he assumed; it was so dark that he could barely see the outline of the canopy. On the brighter side, any air force planes tailing the 727 wouldn't be able to spot the parachute, either. The jet's relatively slow speed would also challenge any other aircraft's attempt to shadow the 727. Most military aircraft would zip right past it.

Or so he'd figured when he cooked up this scheme.

Looking down, he saw storm clouds directly below him. Dense mist enveloped him as he dropped into the mass of heavy, black clouds. Snow pelted his face. Ice and sleet glazed his defenseless body, soaking through his meager overcoat, business suit, and thermal underwear. The turbulence was unbelievable. Raging winds buffeted him from all directions, so that he was tossed about like a leaf in a hurricane. A violent updraft jerked him dozens of feet higher, then dropped him just as abruptly. Any attempt to maintain a proper diving posture was a lost cause. Vertigo and nausea assailed him; he clenched his chattering teeth to keep from vomiting into the wind. Sleet splashed against his face like a tidal wave; he felt as if he were drowning beneath an arctic sea. Lightning flashed within the storm clouds, way too close for comfort. Blinding bursts of bright red electrical fire forced him to squeeze his eyes shut. The wind howled in his ears, punctuated by deafening booms of thunder. He clasped his hands over his ears, but the din was still loud enough to torture his eardrums, which felt like they were on the verge of bursting. Terrifying possibilities raced through his brain. What if the wind tangled the canopy or tore loose the straps across his torso? What if a stray burst of lightning set his parachute aflame?

This is crazy, he thought. *I'm a goner for sure.*

He had always known that the odds were against him on this stunt. But what other choice had he had except to roll the dice on one all-or-nothing gamble? A shrink would no doubt claim that Cooper had some kind of lunatic death wish, and, to be honest, that probably wasn't too far from the mark. His life had being going downhill for months now, ever since he'd lost his job at Boeing in the big bust, but not for much longer. One way or another, all his troubles would be over soon . . .

Blame Hollywood, he thought. After all, he had gotten the idea from that movie last year. Ever since he'd seen *Airport,* which had showed him how easy it was to smuggle a bomb aboard a commercial jetliner, the plan for tonight's risky caper had been forming in his mind. At first it had been just a wild idea, something to fantasize about during all those long, tedious hours tending bar at the airport, but as time went by, and his life and finances continued to go down the toilet, the notion had grown into an obsession, until finally it had been all he could think about: one bold act that could change his life for good. *Better to go out in a blaze of glory than let poverty and failure eat you away by inches.*

At least that's what he'd thought before. Who knew glory could be so cold?

The brutal turbulence abated slightly as he fell out of the clouds into the snowy sky above the drop zone. Forcing his eyes open, he peered downward, trying in vain to penetrate the murky wilderness below. No house or street lights gleamed in the dark, confirming that he was more or less where he was supposed to be. In theory, there should be nothing beneath him except miles of rugged forest and a few scattered farms. He had planned to aim for an open field or clearing, but clearly he had underestimated the severity of the weather. Even now, powerful winds carried him horizontally over the forest at breakneck speed. There was no way to control his descent. Any minute he expected to be impaled upon a treetop.

Unlike in Korea, there were no spongy rice paddies waiting for him below.

And no medals, either.

Dangling beneath him, the money bag hit the trees first, giving him a split second of warning before he came down right after it. He twisted in the harness just in time to slip between two towering pines. Branches and needles scratched his face and hands. A wrenching halt gave him whiplash as the canopy fouled in the branches overhead. Dislodged snow tumbled onto his bare head. Swinging like a pendulum, he smacked face first into a solid tree trunk. The impact set his head ringing. Tasting blood, he spit out a broken tooth.

It was a rough landing, but it could have been worse.

A lot worse.

His numb fingers fumbled with the clasps of his harness. He half slid, half fell to earth, where a deep snowbank broke his fall. Exhausted, he lay on his back beneath the trees, staring up at the tangled canopy many feet above him. For a few perilous moments, he was tempted to just lie there and not get up. He'd always heard that freezing to death was a relatively painless way to go, like drifting off to sleep. His eyelids sagged as he settled into the snow . . .

Then he remembered the money. Had he managed to hang on to the cash during his fall? Suddenly anxious to find out, he lurched to his feet and groped for the bag. A sigh of relief misted before his lips as he found the ransom money half buried in the snow a few feet away. Despite his tumultuous descent, the bag had not come open. All ten thousand of the unmarked twenties were still inside. Enough money to start a whole new life somewhere a hell of a lot warmer than here. Costa Rica maybe, or Tahiti.

How about that? he marveled. *I did it!*

Euphoria momentarily overcame both the weather and his injuries. He pressed a handful of snow against his aching jaw, letting the cold numb the pain from his missing tooth. A rush of adrenaline fueled his depleted muscles as he looked about for a safe place to stow his loot. These woods were going to be crawling with cops and reporters come morning, and he couldn't risk getting caught with the ransom on his person, even if he still retained enough strength to lug the twenty-one-pound bag of cash back to civilization, which was doubtful. He would have to come back for it later, after things had cooled down some. It was going to be a long, agonizing wait, but at least he wouldn't be tempted to spend the money too freely or too quickly. In fact, he shouldn't even quit his job right away, or people might get suspicious. He had deliberately flown out of Portland just to reduce the odds of being recognized at the airport. The smartest course would be just to go about his life as though nothing had changed while figuring out the best way to launder $200,000 in cash. Then quietly relocate to the Caribbean . . .

But first he had to get out of these damned woods before he froze to death.

Slicing apart the spare parachute with a pocket knife, he wrapped the waterproof fabric around his stockinged feet. The improvised footware wasn't ideal, but hopefully it would save his toes from frostbite. Hefting the bulging money bag, he hiked through the snow until he judged that he had put enough distance between himself and the abandoned canopy. The frozen earth was too hard to bury anything in, so he trudged toward a large fallen log instead. His gloved hands dug out a large quantity of snow from inside the log, then stuffed the bag deep into its hollow interior. He carved his initials—his *real* initials—into the bark. The possibility of any searchers spotting the crude "CDM" did not concern him; within minutes, the falling snow would cover the telltale inscription.

But could he find the log again later? Fishing a miniature compass from his pocket, he hurriedly got his bearings. A snowcapped mountain rose above the forest to the northeast. *That would be Mount St. Helens,* he surmised, recognizing the southwest face of the mountain from his research. Not a bad landmark to remember. He'd have a better sense of his location, of course, once he located the nearest road or residence. For now, the looming mountain would have to do. *It's not like it's going anywhere in the near future.*

The heavy physical activity helped him fend off the bitter November chill, but he knew he had to find shelter soon. Two hundred grand wasn't going to do him any good if he died of exposure before morning. According to his watch, it was a little after eight-thirty. Dawn was nearly twelve hours away. He rummaged through his pockets to confirm that he still had his cigarette lighter. If worse came to worse, he'd start a fire to thaw out. The cops weren't going to scour the forest by night, right? Chances were, they'd wait until the sun rose, and the storm passed, before launching any major search operation.

The merciless cold seeped straight through his sodden garments into the very marrow of his bones. His teeth chattered no matter how tightly he clenched his jaws. His face felt raw. His chapped lips were cracked and bleeding. Rasping breaths fogged the air. He couldn't feel his toes or fingertips.

On second thought, maybe he needed to light that fire right away.

A blinding white glare caught him by surprise. *What the—?* Shielding his eyes with his hand, he gazed up into the light, expecting to see a FBI helicopter hovering above him. *It's impossible,* he thought in despair. *How did they find me so fast?* He threw up his hands before some trigger-happy cop could fill him full of lead. "Don't shoot! I surrender!"

But there was no helicopter, only a glowing ball of cold white light descending through the tree branches like Glinda's bubble in *The Wizard of Oz.* The glare was so intense, he had to avert his eyes. For an instant he thought that the incandescent sphere was going to crash right into him, but then it paused in midair several yards above his head. Luminous coils reached down from the globe, wrapping themselves around his torso and lifting him off his feet. A tingling sensation rushed over his entire body, instantly banishing the chill of night. Every fiber of his being felt like it had been shot full of novocaine; he couldn't move a muscle. Hairs rose up all over his skin. A freakish wind lifted his soggy brown hair. Unable to resist, he was drawn inexorably toward the mysterious ball of light. A high-pitched hum filled his ears, swelling in volume until it sounded like the roar of an invisible ocean. Defying gravity, his feet dangled above the snow-covered ground.

Wait! he thought frantically. *What's happening?* He tried to cry out, but his paralyzed vocal cords refused to cooperate as he ascended against his will. For a heartbeat, he wondered if he was hallucinating. Or had he actually died during his jump and this was Heaven come to claim him? It was all too surreal to be believed. *This wasn't part of the plan!*

The last thing he saw, before he vanished into the light, was Mount St. Helens standing guard over his buried fortune . . .

Cooper DeMeers awoke with a start. Glancing around in confusion, it took him a second to recognize his surroundings: a bleak detention cell in a subbasement beneath NTAC's Seattle

offices. The austere gray walls were devoid of
decoration. A stainless-steel commode rested
across the chamber from his cot. The overhead
lamp had been switched off for the evening, but
light from the corridor outside penetrated his cell
via a horizontal slit cut at eye level into the heavy
steel door locking him in. The air had a sterile,
antiseptic smell. Muffled sobs and snores came
from the adjacent cells. Guards paced in the hall.

That's right, he recalled, *I'm a prisoner.*

He flopped back down onto his cot, his restless body awash in sweat. He peeked at his wrist
to check the time, only to remember that the Feds
had confiscated his watch. Judging from the silence
outside, he guessed that it was well after midnight.
Long hours stretched before him. He didn't know
what was more discouraging: his present captivity or
the fact that he had just endured *that* dream again.

So what else is new? Clad in his convict-orange
jumpsuit, he brooded darkly in his cell. Bad enough
that he had to relive that hellish jump every damn
night, but what else did he have to show for it,
except for the infuriating knowledge that his big
score had been snatched away from him by fate
and, if you could believe it, some time-traveling do-
gooders from tomorrow? Thanks to his involuntary

detour to the future, his stolen fortune had probably sat untouched for years—until Mount St. Helens erupted nine years later, burying the drop zone in ash and altering the landscape beyond recognition. That freak disaster was almost more galling than his original abduction. For the first few days after he had gotten back, he had actually entertained the notion that the $200,000 might still be waiting for him up in the woods—until he found out about the cataclysmic events of May 18, 1980. *It's not fair*, he thought for possibly the five zillionth time. *How was I supposed to know that the damn mountain was going to blow up while I was away?*

Granted, it was possible that years of floods, fires, and avalanches had already dispersed his hidden stash of twenties far and wide. Since washing up on the shores of the twenty-first century, he had wasted hours poring over topographical maps of the region trying to figure out how exactly $5,880 of the ransom money had ended up on the banks of the Columbia River, where that lucky eight-year-old had found it. According to the Internet, the FBI had eventually paid young Brian Ingram a reward of nearly three thousand dollars, which the kid had reportedly spent on a motorcycle and VCR. *Stupid brat made out better than I did*, Cooper thought bitterly. *All I got was a missing tooth—and thirty-five years in limbo.*

Unable to get back to sleep, he sat on the edge of the cot, cradling his head in his hands. He felt groggy, hungover, probably because of all the tranquilizers they had been pumping into him. Not that he blamed NTAC; his unwanted new ability scared him as much as anyone else, maybe even more so. *Why give me such a horrific ability?* he wondered. *What possible good can that do anyone?*

He heard more footsteps outside, growing louder as they neared his door. A guard going about his rounds, presumably. Cooper wondered if maybe the guard could get him an aspirin. He felt a headache coming on.

"Excuse me," he called out. He got off the cot and walked barefoot over to the door. "I don't want to cause any problems, but can you—"

The footsteps halted right outside the door. "Cooper DeMeers?"

The tinny voice sounded familiar, but Cooper couldn't place it right away. "Yeah, that's me." Placing his face against the cold steel door, he peered out through the eye slit.

William Gorinsky stared back at him.

A frightened yelp escaped Cooper's lips. His

heart skipped a beat. *They told me he was dead!*

Yet there was no mistaking the beefy figure standing outside the cell. It was undeniably the same guy who had come after him at the Market and in the Underground, the menacing stranger who had disappeared right before Cooper's eyes three nights ago. But how had he gotten past all of NTAC's security—and why was he here in the first place?

You're supposed to be dead!

"What are you?" Cooper whispered, his mouth as dry as a desert. "What do you want from me?" He backed away fearfully from the door. "Why won't you leave me alone?"

Gorinsky didn't bother to explain. "Stand back," he said unnecessarily. There was a loud electrical zap and the cell door slid open. Nothing but empty air now separated Cooper from the other man, the one who should have been six feet under by now. The acrid smell of burnt circuitry filled the cell.

"K-keep away from me!" Cooper stammered. His back was pressed up against the far wall of the cell. He screamed for someone to save him from the intruder. "Guards! Somebody! Help!"

Gorinsky scowled impatiently. "C'mon, hurry up!" He beckoned to Cooper. "I'm breaking you out, you moron!"

"You there!" A guard's voice intruded on the scene. "Step away from the cell and put your hands where I can see them!"

Gorinsky ignored the command. "Don't you know what they're planning?" he snarled at Cooper. "They're going to lock you up for life, numbskull! This is your only chance!"

Could that be true? Cooper didn't know what to think. Meanwhile, the commotion had awoken his fellow prisoners. The other inmates shouted for attention, demanding to know what was going on. How many people did NTAC have confined down here, Cooper wondered, and just how long had some of them been held prisoner? Over the last couple of years, he'd heard plenty of horror stories about innocent returnees who had been "disappeared" by the government and never heard from again, but he'd always been unsure how seriously to take such rumors. *Just a bunch of crazy conspiracy theories, or a preview of coming attractions . . . ?*

"This is your last warning!" the guard shouted at Gorinsky. "I'm authorized to use deadly force. Stand down or else!"

"Knock yourself out," Gorinsky taunted the guard.

Gunshots blared in the corridor. Flinching from the noise, Cooper expected Gorinsky to keel over,

spouting blood from gaping chest wounds, but the
intruder just muttered an obscenity and marched
away from the door, straight into the barrage of
gunfire. Bullets ricocheted off the doors and walls
outside the cell, striking sparks against the impervious metal, while the guard's voice grew increasingly panicky. "Oh, crap! You're one of *them*!" He
emptied his semiautomatic pistol without inflict-
ing any discernible damage to Gorinsky. "Drop,
damnit! What does it to take to put you down?"

An alarm went off belatedly. Blaring sirens
tortured Cooper's ears, adding to the cacophony
inside the violated cell block. He was surprised the
cell block hadn't gone into lockdown mode yet.
Maybe the guards were still trying to figure out
what was going on? He hesitated, uncertain how to
proceed. Mustering his courage, he peered around
the open doorway just in time to see Gorinsky
seize the hapless guard, who started twitching as
though zapped by a taser. Cooper instantly recalled
the minor electrical shock he had received the first
time Gorinsky had grabbed him at the Market, as
well as the way his mysterious stalker had attacked
those two NTAC agents in the Underground. *No
way,* Cooper thought. He wasn't sure exactly what
kind of ability Gorinsky had, but he knew he didn't

want to ever be on the receiving end of it. *You're not getting me that way!*

Gorinsky let go of the guard, who collapsed limply onto the floor. "What are you waiting for?" he hollered at Cooper, looking back over his shoulder. More guards came charging down the stairs at the end of the corridor. Metal grilles began to descend from the ceiling, between him and freedom. *"Run!"*

Cooper didn't need any further prompting. Unsure whom exactly he was trying to get away from, the guards or Gorinsky, he made tracks away from both of them. Other inmates shouted at him as he ran past their cells, begging for information or release, but Cooper couldn't afford to listen to their pleas. Like a baseball player diving for home, he slid beneath the descending grille only moments before it connected to the floor. He jumped to his feet and kept on running. Encountering a staircase beyond the cell block, he took the steps two at a time, his bare feet slapping against the cool concrete. Sheer terror and adrenaline exorcised his earlier grogginess. His heart was pounding a mile a minute. He prayed to God that he still had enough inhibitor in his system to keep his goddamn ability from bringing the entire building down on his head. He hadn't felt this scared since the last time he'd jumped out of a 727 . . .

A startled-looking guard suddenly appeared on the stairs before him. "Hold on!" the man shouted, reaching for his sidearm, but Cooper barreled right into him, knocking the guard flat on his back. On instinct, he snatched the pistol from the stunned guard's holster and hopped clumsily over his sprawled victim on his way up the steps. There was no turning back now, he knew. He had to get away or be locked up for life. Bursting from the stairwell, he found himself in the lobby of the building. NTAC's official seal was emblazoned on the polished marble floor. Metal detectors guarded the empty reception desk. He looked around frantically for the nearest exit.

To his surprise, he spotted a young Japanese woman standing right outside the front entrance. She called to him through a pair of wide glass doors. A sleek copper-colored Jaguar was parked at the curb behind her.

Who? Cooper wondered in confusion. As far as he knew, he had never seen the girl before. *Is she with Gorinsky?*

He couldn't hear what she was saying, but her intent was clear. He ran up to the door and tried to pull it open. It rattled in its frame, but refused to budge. *Locked*, he realized. *Figures*. Stymied, he looked helplessly at the woman, who pointed emphatically at the gun in his hand. *Oh right*, he thought sheepishly as she stepped away from the door. *I forgot*.

Wincing in anticipation, he took aim at the lock and fired. A loud report momentarily drowned out the shrieking alarms. He rammed the door open with his shoulder and dashed out onto the sidewalk outside. The nearly deserted streets and sidewalks confirmed that it was way past most people's bedtime. Streetlamps illuminated the landscaped grounds outside NTAC headquarters. Greasy puddles informed him that it had rained earlier. A clock tower revealed that it was nearly three in the morning.

"Hurry!" The woman grabbed him by the arm, practically dragging him toward the waiting sports car. She shoved him into the passenger seat, then scurried around to jump behind the wheel. "Buckle up!"

"Wait!" he pleaded. Things were happening too fast for him to keep up. "Who are you? What's this about?"

"No time for that." She threw the car into gear and accelerated away from the curb. Behind them, a night-owl bus honked and slammed on its brakes. The Jaguar rapidly left it behind, speeding north through the late night traffic. Tinted windows guarded their privacy. "You can thank us later."

Us? It occurred to Cooper that the nameless woman, if she was in cahoots with Gorinsky, didn't seem too concerned about leaving her partner behind to face the music. Then again, he recalled, Gorinsky could disappear into thin air. He might have already pulled another vanishing act by now.

Blocks sped by as he examined the woman behind the wheel. At least twenty years younger than him, she had the look of a sexy grad student. Her lustrous black hair had a pixie cut, but it was her striking brown eyes that really got your attention. Her dark bronze irises had a thin golden halo around them, giving her eyes an almost preternatural quality. *Trick contact lenses,* he wondered, *or a natural gift?* She was dressed for stealth, in a black sweater and slacks. Her tense expression grew more relaxed the further they got from NTAC. It looked like they might have made a clean getaway. A Starbucks coffee cup rested in the Jaguar's cup holder. The woman helped herself to a sip as she deftly navigated the city streets.

"Please," Cooper begged. "You gotta help me out here. Where are you taking me?"

"Someplace safe," she promised.

FIFTEEN

DIANA AND MARCO were working late, although she wasn't entirely sure why. Their laptops sat open atop her kitchen table, alongside a stack of blue folders from the office. Refrigerator magnets pinned Maia's artwork and school bulletins to the fridge. Buttery yellow walls gave the kitchen a warmer feel than Diana's work space downtown. Leftover slices of pineapple pizza—Maia's favorite—rested on top of the kitchen island nearby. Diana nibbled on a slice as she sorted through the papers on the table.

"Here." Marco handed her a steaming cup of hot tea, fresh from the microwave. "You look like you can use this."

"Thanks." She appreciated him staying up to work with her on this; she suspected that digging through evidence probably wasn't what he'd had in mind when he'd come over tonight. *Talk about a nice guy,* she thought. *I really don't deserve him.* "What time is it anyway?" She glanced at the clock over the stove. "Oh, God."

It was almost three-thirty in the morning. Maia had been asleep for hours, and Diana knew that she and Marco ought to be in bed, too. This being Monday, tomorrow was a workday. Her alarm clock was going to go off way too soon.

"I'm okay," he insisted. "I'm used to pulling all-nighters."

"No. This is ridiculous," she scolded herself. There was no point in working this case anymore, let alone losing sleep over it. Gorinsky was dead, and, as of a few hours from now, Cooper DeMeers was no longer her problem or her responsibility, thanks to the heavy-handed intervention of the NSA. "Why can't I let this go?"

"Well there's always Maia's unfulfilled proph-ecy," he reminded her.

This is true, she thought. It was difficult to achieve closure when, at the back of her mind, she was still dreading her inevitable encounter with "D. B. Cooper" atop an unruly mountain. But even putting that aside, there were still plenty of unresolved questions nagging at her brain, most of them involving William Gorinsky. How had the mentally disturbed veteran found out about DeMeers in the first place, and how had he managed to keep one step ahead of NTAC the whole time? And why had he been after DeMeers anyway?

Diana focused on that first question. Where had Gorinsky received his information from? She didn't want to think that there was a leak at NTAC, which meant looking somewhere else . . . like maybe Abendson Psychiatric Hospital.

Pages and pages of medical records from Ward 59 were spread out across the table. A court order had allowed them to obtain the files over Doctor Clayton's vehement protests. She hated to violate the patients' privacy like this, but if there was anything she had learned at the CDC, it was that sometimes public safety trumped privacy concerns . . . and that the best way to combat an infection was to trace it to its source. In this case, Ward 59. Marco sat down across from her as they continued to comb through lists of the hospital's staff and patients, looking for some connection to Cooper

DeMeers and/or the Nova Group. *If we can find something by morning,* she thought, *that might give us leverage we need to keep Cooper out of the NSA's clutches.*

The fact that Cooper's ability had definite military possibilities was not lost on her. She didn't want another Gary Navarro on her conscience.

"You know," Marco said, yawning, "a nice long rest in a padded cell is starting to sound better and better."

She knew how he felt. The long columns of names were already swimming before her eyes. The fact that the staff at Abendson seemed to have an unusually high turnover rate didn't make her and Marco's task any easier. No doubt the large concentration of 4400 patients contributed to the hospital's personnel problems; much of the public remained frightened of the returnees and their abilities, and the Nova Group's recent campaign of terror hadn't helped matters any. Diana wondered how many of Abendson's employees had quit over the Tess Doerner incident alone.

She yawned and rubbed her weary eyes. Maybe it was time to call it a night after all. She was about to suggest as much when a solitary name caught her eye, standing out from the others:

SIMONE TANAKA

Where do I know that from? The name definitely
rang a bell, but, in her sleep-deprived state, it took
her a moment to place it.

Rahmen Aziz's assistant.

"I think I've got something!" Excitement dispelled the fog from her brain. Using her laptop,
she quickly called up Simone's profile from their
4400 database. The mug shot in the file matched
the young woman she had met in Nina's office two
days earlier. "Listen to this. Simone Tanaka used to
be confined to Ward 59, along with Gorinsky, but
she was released six months ago."

Marco saw where she was going with this.
"Wanna bet they've stayed in touch?" He conjured
up Simone's file on his own computer. "Does she
have any known abilities?"

"Not that we have on record." She scanned the
woman's medical records. "But according to this,
she complained that she could see through people
and things, even when her eyes were closed. The
doctors thought she was hallucinating."

"Maybe not," Marco speculated. "Where the
4400 are concerned, it's hard to tell crazy from
coherent." He helped himself to the last slice of
pizza. "X-ray vision . . . wow! That's seriously retro.

Remember those goggles they used to sell in the back of comic books?"

"No." Diana was too busy trying to work out the full implications of her discovery to share Marco's nostalgia trip. *We've been assuming that it was Sondra Jonnson who enlisted Aziz on DeMeers's behalf, but what if Sondra had nothing to do with it? What if Simone informed Aziz—and Gorinsky? Just how much has she seen with those eyes of hers?*

"But I don't get it," Marco admitted. "Even if Simone and Gorinsky were in touch, why would she sic him on Cooper?"

"I wish I knew." She stared at the phone on the wall. Was it worth waking Tom to get his input or could this wait until morning?

The phone rang unexpectedly, startling her. *Did I do that?* she wondered momentarily, before remembering that she wasn't actually one of the 4400. She glanced anxiously at the clock on the stove. Phone calls at four in the morning were never good news. A horrible thought rushed through her brain. *Has something happened to April?* She had always feared that her sister would come to a bad end . . .

"You going to get that?" Marco asked.

His query jolted her into action. She snatched the phone from its cradle. "Hello?"

"Diana? It's me, Tom." Her partner's voice briefly reassured her; this wasn't about April. "I just heard from Nina. Cooper DeMeers has escaped from NTAC."

"What?" Diana felt a sinking feeling in the pit of her stomach. This wasn't over yet. "Are you serious?"

"Absolutely," Tom replied, "but that's not the weirdest part. According to witnesses, he was sprung by Gorinsky."

She blinked in surprise. "*William* Gorinsky?" She couldn't imagine that he was talking about the eighty-year-old brother in Puyallup. "But he's dead."

"Tell me about it," Tom said. "I attended his burial." Despite everything, he sounded slightly relieved that he apparently hadn't killed the man after all. "I guess his 'astral double' is still on the prowl."

"Is that even possible?" Diana was no expert on bilocation, but she found it hard to believe that Gorinsky's consciousness could survive the death of his physical body. Where was it getting its energy from? Time travel and telekinesis she could accept, albeit grudgingly, but she was still too much of a scientist to believe in ghosts.

"Who knows what's possible and impossible these days," Tom said. "Ask Marco the next time you see him."

Diana blushed, not quite sure whether she wanted to mention that Marco was sitting only a few feet away. It's not like it was a deep, dark secret that they were dating, but still . . . "I'll do that."

"In the meantime, the NSA is throwing a fit. Their agents are already fanning out in pursuit of DeMeers and they sound inclined to shoot first and ask questions later." She could tell from his tone that he was deadly serious. "If we want to keep Cooper alive, we need to find him first."

Diana remembered the lead she and Marco had just uncovered. "I think I know where to start looking."

Cooper had visited The 4400 Center before, although never quite under these same circumstances. Curiosity had drawn him to various open houses and fund-raisers sponsored by the Center, while his status as a returnee had entitled him to a guided tour conducted by one of the organization's many perky volunteers. To be honest, the place had given him a slightly cultish vibe, especially back when Jordan Collier was marketing himself as the second coming of L. Ron Hubbard or whomever. While he appreciated the Center's lobbying efforts, he had felt uncomfortable among the eager wannabes who flocked to the Center in hopes of achieving 4400 abilities of their own. He'd just wanted to get on with his life, not dispense cosmic wisdom to the masses. As if he'd actually had any such wisdom to impart.

Now the distinctive cylindrical building loomed before him like a sanctuary. Its silver exterior was clad in preweathered zinc panels, making it look like a futuristic fortress. A glass corona crowned the building. *Any port in a storm,* he thought, as he and his mysterious savior, who had finally volunteered that her name was Simone, ran toward the Center's tree-lined portico. They left a red Ford coupe at the curb, having traded cars in an all-night parking garage just in case someone saw the Jaguar peel away from NTAC. Cooper had changed out of his incriminating orange jumpsuit at the same time. Now wearing a flannel shirt and jeans provided by Simone, as well as a slightly snug pair of sneakers, he kept looking back over his shoulder in anticipation of flashing blue lights and sirens, but no police cars materialized. He felt hunted nonetheless.

If only he hadn't gone to see that damn *Airport* movie years ago . . . ! If he hadn't been in those frozen woods thirty-five years back, if he had never hijacked that plane, would that infernal ball of light still have found him? Would he still be a fugitive with an earthquake in his skull?

Only the future knew and it wasn't talking.

The windows were dark in the upper stories of the Center. Security lights in the front plaza left him feeling uncomfortably exposed. Despite his change of clothes, he couldn't wait to alter the rest of his appearance. *I'll shave my beard,* he thought, *and let my hair grow back.* The gold tooth would have to go as well. Maybe Simone knew a 4400 dentist he could trust?

She used a key card to open the front door. "You'll be safe here."

"Maybe." He stepped warily into the dimly lit lobby. No receptionist manned the front desk. They seemed to have the place to themselves. "Isn't this the first place they'll look for me?"

"This is just a temporary measure, until we can get you to a secure safe house." She locked the door behind them, which made him feel a little better. "In the meantime, NTAC isn't likely to stage a full raid on the Center unless they know for certain that we're holding you. There are too many 4400s here who are ready and willing to fight back."

That makes sense, he admitted. *The Feds wouldn't want to turn this place into the next Waco.* Not when they were still trying to live down the Inhibitor Scandal.

She escorted him upstairs to an office on the second floor, where they found a well-dressed Arab man waiting for them. "Rahmen Aziz," he introduced himself, shaking Cooper's hand. "Legal counsel for The 4400 Center. I've been trying to obtain your release from federal custody."

"Can you do that?" As a rule, Cooper didn't trust lawyers, but, boy, did he need one now. He could add a jailbreak and assaulting a guard to the list of charges against him. *Not that I had much choice, what with that spooky Gorinsky creep on the loose.*

Aziz shook his head. "Not anymore. I'm afraid the time for legal maneuvers is past. The NSA intends to bury you so deep that not even the Center and its resources will be able to liberate you." He let that sink in for a minute, before continuing. "You're a fugitive now, an outlaw . . . just like Nova Group."

Nova? Warning bells went off in Cooper's head. "Wait a second. I'm no terrorist."

"Terrorist. Freedom fighter." Aziz shrugged. "Today's labels don't matter. Nova Group is the defensive wing of the 4400, fighting back against a paranoid government that nearly exterminated us. I would think that your recent captivity would make you appreciate the vital necessity of an organization like Nova."

Spare me the sales pitch, Cooper thought. To be honest, he couldn't blame the Feds for wanting to keep their hands on a guy who could trigger earthquakes without even trying. "I'm not very political."

"You disappoint me, Mister DeMeers." Aziz gave him a withering once-over. His hands were clasped behind his back as he stood in front of an impressive mahogany desk. "One would not expect the legendary D. B. Cooper to be so hesitant to strike back at the authorities. Where's your rebellious spirit, famed in song and story?"

It wasn't about making a statement, Cooper protested silently. *I just needed the money.* "I'm not D. B. Coop—"

Aziz held up his hand. "Please, don't waste our time with perfunctory denials. As it happens, our benefactors in the far future blessed me with a singular ability: I can always tell whether someone is telling the truth or not by listening carefully to their heartbeat. A useful talent for an attorney, you must admit." He looked Cooper squarely in the eyes. "You *were* the notorious Dan Cooper." I know that and you know that. But that hardly matters now. I'm less concerned with what you did thirty-some years ago than with what you can do in the present. By all reports, you possess quite a remarkable ability of your own."

"You can have it," Cooper said bitterly. "I wish those bastards in the future had just left me alone."

"Tsk-tsk," Aziz clucked. "You see how the government and their stooges in the media have brainwashed you? The 4400 have been entrusted with the sacred responsibility of saving the world from an unimaginable future catastrophe. You must have faith that you have been endowed with your ability for a purpose."

"Easy for you to say." He bristled indignantly, despite his precarious situation. "You don't have to worry about setting off an earthquake or volcano every time you lose your cool. I'd be two hundred thousand dollars richer, and a whole lot happier, if those 'benefactors' you mentioned had stayed out of my life." Aziz and Simone were obviously fanatics; Cooper decided that he was in enough trouble without getting mixed up with this bunch. "Thanks for the jailbreak, but I'm out of here."

He headed for the door. The Canadian border was only about three hours away. The way he figured it, he had good odds of making it out of the country before NTAC or the NSA caught up with him. Once he got settled in Canada, under a whole new identity, he'd try to contact Sondra and see if she wanted to join him in exile. *On second thought,* he reconsidered, *maybe she'd be better off without me . . .*

Simone moved to block him, but he brushed her aside. "Forget about it. I'm not interested."

"You're making a serious mistake, Mister De-Meers," Aziz said. "I'm afraid we can't permit you to leave."

Cooper drew the semiautomatic pistol he had stolen from the guard at NTAC. "Try and stop me." A quaver in his voice betrayed his discomfort. Not counting the war, this was the first time in his life he had ever pulled a gun on anyone. He tried hard not to let it show. "I'm leaving now, and I don't want anyone following me."

"You're bluffing," Aziz accused him.

"Am I?" Gun in hand, he turned to face the lawyer. "You're the human lie detector. You tell me."

In fact, Cooper had no idea if he was bluffing or not. He was hoping Aziz couldn't tell, either. *Don't make me pull this trigger.*

The lawyer scowled, an encouragingly puzzled expression on his face. Cooper figured he'd made his point, until Aziz suddenly grinned in triumph. "Ah, excellent," he crowed, looking past Cooper at something beyond the escaped hijacker. "Just in the proverbial nick of time."

Cooper looked behind him to find William Gorinsky filling the doorway. Cooper started to swing the pistol around, but the other man was too fast for him. Gorinsky grabbed Cooper's shoulder, sending a numbing shock through the fugitive's arm. Cooper let out a startled cry as the gun slipped from his fingers. A second later, a backhanded blow sent him tumbling back into Aziz's office. He looked around frantically for the fallen gun, but Simone had already pounced on it. She gripped the weapon with both hands as she aimed it straight at his chest. "Don't move an inch," she warned him coolly. "Don't make a sound."

No trace of uncertainty glinted in her piercing gold-rimmed eyes. Cooper didn't need Aziz's special ability to know that she wasn't bluffing. He dropped to his knees and raised his hands over his head. *Christ,* he swore inwardly. *This just keeps get-ting worse and worse.*

"That's more like it." Aziz nodded at the new-comer. "Your timing is impeccable, Mister Gorinsky."

"No problem." Gorinsky entered the office and closed the door behind him. The click of the lock reminded Cooper of the prison he had just es-caped. "Now what?"

Aziz turned his attention back to Cooper. "I believe you've met Mister Gorinsky. A most valu-able operative. The lovely Simone recruited him some time ago." Gorinsky came up behind her and wrapped his arms around her waist. She nestled into him. Clearly, they were more than just comrades-in-arms. *Not bad for a dead guy,* Cooper conceded grudgingly. *Guess he's still solid enough to get lucky.*

"It was easy," she bragged. "After I got out of that miserable nuthouse, I knew Bill would mate-rialize up at Highland Beach eventually. He was obsessed with the place. I just staked the beach out until he showed up—or at least one of him did." She smirked at some sort of private joke. "Then I persuaded him to join Nova. An operative with a perfect alibi was just what we needed."

Hospital? One of him? Cooper had no idea what she was talking about; he felt like he'd missed the first part of a spy movie or something. "Please," he begged, "just let me go. I promise I won't tell anyone about you."

"It's not that simple, Mister DeMeers." Aziz stroked his goatee as he contemplated the kneeling captive. "There are bigger issues here than simply preserving the anonymity of a single Nova cell. The public already fears and distrusts the 4400. The last thing we need is for you to initiate a disaster that will turn the entire world against us."

Simone glared at Cooper down the barrel of the gun. "I still say we should dispose of him here and now. You know what the little girl predicted. We can't take the chance that her prophecy will come true."

"That would be a waste," Gorinsky argued. "This idiot can literally move mountains with his brain. We can use that kind of power."

"*If* we can control him." Aziz eyed Cooper skeptically, apparently of two minds on the subject. He sounded as if he was edging toward Simone's point of view. "So far, our friend here has been less than cooperative."

Cooper realized that he was only moments away from death. "Listen to me!" he pleaded. "I don't care what some crazy little girl said. I would never blow up Mount Rainier! Think about it, do I look like some kind of homicidal maniac? Why on Earth would I do something horrible like that?" His heart was pounding so hard that he was terrified that he was about to set off an earthquake at any moment, which would get him killed for sure. He prayed NTAC had injected enough inhibitor in his system to keep his ability out of commission for just a little while longer. "I promise, if you let me live, I'll never go within a hundred miles of Rainier or any other mountain. I'll move to the desert somewhere, away from any fault lines or volcanoes!"

"He's telling the truth," Aziz informed his compatriots. Hope flared in Cooper's heart as the dapper lawyer appeared to take the panicky offer under consideration. "Perhaps there's no need to make any rash decisions. Mister DeMeers isn't going anywhere unless we say so, and I admit that I'm reluctant to execute a fellow returnee if it's not strictly necessary. For all we know, the eruption the girl foresaw might still be weeks, months, or even years away. We have time to consider other options."

"Time?" Simone said incredulously. She wriggled free of Gorinsky's embrace. "Are you kidding me? NTAC has already rounded up every other Nova cell in town. They could be coming after us any minute now. This might be our only chance to stop this jerk from destroying Seattle!"

Aziz frowned. "Control yourself, Simone. Kindly lower your weapon."

"Like hell!" she snapped. "He has to die." She kept the pistol aimed at Cooper. Her black-clad body looked as tense as a coiled spring. "If you can't see that, then somebody has to get the job done."

Gorinsky stepped between Simone and Cooper. "Hold it!" he ordered. "Put that gun down!"

"Nice try," she said with a nearly audible smirk. "But you and I both know that I can shoot right through you without even leaving a scratch." Cooper braced himself for the end. He wondered if he would actually feel anything before the bullet tore through his heart. "So long, Mister D. B. Cooper. Nothing person—"

Before she could fire, however, Gorinsky swatted her arm to the side. The shot went wild, knocking an abstract painting from the wall. The framed artwork crashed loudly onto the carpet. "What the hell?" she protested. "Whose side are you on?"

"Not yours," he said brusquely. "Not anymore."

His fist clamped around her throat, choking her.

Electricity crackled and her svelte body stiffened. Gorinsky pried the pistol from her fingers before letting go of her neck. She dropped lifelessly onto the floor, facedown onto the carpet. Cooper couldn't tell if she was still breathing or not. Had the psycho killed his own girl?

"Simone!" Aziz stared in shock at Gorinsky. "What have you done?"

Gorinsky stepped away from the woman's fallen form. "Changed the agenda."

Taking advantage of the tumult, Cooper leapt to his feet and dashed for the door. *I have to get out of here,* he thought urgently. *These people are insane!*

"Uh-uh," Gorinsky grunted. Moving swiftly, he pressed the muzzle of the gun against the back of the fugitive's neck before Cooper could get to the door. The hijacker froze in place, almost too scared to breathe. "You're not going anywhere without me. I have big plans for you."

"Plans? What plans?" Aziz was at his wit's end, having completely lost control of the situation. The lawyer's polished exterior crumbled to pieces. "Have you lost your mind? What about our cause?"

Cooper caught on before Aziz. He knew a double cross when he saw one. Apparently, the lawyer's lie-detecting ability didn't work on *whatever*

Gorinsky was. Maybe because he didn't really have a heartbeat?

"Screw the cause!" Gorinsky barked. "Don't you get it? Simone was right: the Nova Group is history. It's every man for himself now." He spit disdainfully onto the carpet. "Besides, who cares about your stupid cause? I had my own reasons for joining this pinko outfit. But you were too blind to ever see that."

"What are you saying?" Aziz said, appalled. "You were a traitor all along?"

"More like a double agent," Gorinsky said. He prodded Cooper with the gun, nudging him toward the door. "We're getting out of here now."

Ever since Gorinsky had first appeared at the Market, Cooper recalled, the stalker had been trying to abscond with Cooper. Now it appeared that he was finally getting what he wanted, although Cooper was still in the dark regarding the other man's motives. *I don't get it*, he thought. *What does he want me for?*

Aziz ran between them and the door, blocking the exit with his body. "I can't let you do this. He's too dangerous!"

"That's what I'm counting on," Gorinsky said as, without hesitation, he swung the pistol away from Cooper's neck and shot Aziz in the gut. The blare of the gunshot, going off only inches away from Cooper's right ear, was deafening. He nearly jumped out of his sneakers.

Oh my God! Cooper reacted. *He shot the bastard!*

Clutching his chest, Aziz slid to the floor, leaving a gory streak on the door behind him. Dark venous blood seeped through his fingers and trickled from the corner of his mouth. An agonized expression contorted his face. He gazed up at Gorinsky in shock. "We . . . trusted you . . . Simone trusted you . . ."

"Tough luck," Gorinsky answered callously. His voice held nothing but scorn for his former leader. He nudged the fallen lawyer with his foot. "Maybe your pals in the future will come through for you . . . but, you know, I don't think they'll bother."

A bullet hole perforated the door. Cooper wondered if anyone had heard the gunshot. The offices directly outside were all empty this early in the morning, but he was aware that several returnees actually resided in the Center, mostly in private apartments on the third floor of the building. He had briefly checked out the accommodations himself before deciding that the Center wasn't for him. Maybe the gunshot had awoken somebody upstairs? He found himself hoping that someone was dialing the police at this very moment. Given a choice, he'd rather take his chances with the authorities than stick with Gorinsky. He had just seen firsthand exactly how dangerous his stalker was. *He just shot somebody in cold blood!*

Gorinsky kicked open the door and shoved Cooper from behind, forcing him to step over Aziz's writhing body. "Move it," Gorinsky ordered. "We're going for a drive."

The gunman forced him down the stairs to the lobby and out to the parking lot. Behind them, lights clicked on behind the windows of The 4400 Center as the residents woke to discover Gorinsky's gruesome handiwork. Cooper heard muffled screams and shouting.

"I don't understand," he blurted, completely lost. "Where are we going? What do you want?"

Gorinsky's clean-cut face darkened. "To get revenge on the future."

SIXTEEN

A MUFFLED BANG roused Shawn from an uneasy sleep. He lay awake in the dark, uncertain what he had heard. A gunshot? A firecracker? He squinted at the digital alarm clock by the bed and saw that it was past 4 A.M. *Did I really hear something,* he wondered, *or did I just dream it?* Grisly nightmares, of Isabelle calmly exterminating his friends and family, had troubled his slumber ever since he'd finally succeeded in drifting off to sleep. The blare of the gunshot fit right in with the violent scenarios surfacing from his unconscious mind. Convincing himself that he had dreamed the whole thing, he closed his eyes to catch a few more hours of sleep.

Then he heard another bang.

That's no dream, he realized with a start. *This is for real.*

Isabelle stirred beside him, her nude body partially draped over his. "Shawn?" she murmured groggily. "What is it?"

"Probably nothing," he lied, sliding out from under her. He grabbed a bathrobe off a chair and tied the belt around his waist. Whatever was happening, he didn't want Isabelle involved; she was too powerful and unpredictable. Her presence could only escalate the situation. "Just go back to sleep."

Fortunately, she wasn't fully awake yet. No doubt her own repose had been blissfully serene. "Shawn?" Blinking the sleep from her eyes, she woozily lifted her head from the pillow. "Wait for me . . ."

He pretended he didn't hear her.

Exiting his private suite, which had formerly belonged to the late Jordan Collier, he stepped out into the hall where he found Richard Tyler up and about. *Guess he's a light sleeper, too,* Shawn thought. "You hear that, too?"

Richard nodded grimly. "Two gunshots." He had seen combat in Korea and knew what he was talking about. "Coming from downstairs."

Shawn heard people stirring in the other apartments. Worried faces started peering out of doorways. Devon Moore, his personal assistant, looked to him anxiously. "What's going on?" she asked. "Are we in danger?" A chorus of competing voices echoed her fears. "Was that a gun?"

Shawn guessed that he probably wasn't the only one remembering Jordan Collier's assassination. A concealed sniper had shot Collier to death right outside this very building. The ghastly sight of the bullets tearing through his mentor's body was burned forever into Shawn's memory. *Who is shooting at us now?* he worried. *The Nova Group again? But I thought I was their primary target, along with Isabelle?*

"Everybody stay in their rooms until further notice," Richard ordered, taking charge. Shawn was impressed by his cool head in the crisis. "I'm sure our security personnel already have the situation in hand, but everyone should stay put just in case."

His words seemed to calm the other residents, who retreated back into their quarters. Shawn followed Richard down the stairs toward the executive offices on the second floor. He gulped as he realized that neither of them was armed. Would

Richard's telekinetic abilities be enough to defend them if they came under attack? Last he'd heard, Isabelle's father could only levitate a few small objects at a time.

To his relief, a team of uniformed security guards had already located the origin of the disturbance: Rahmen Aziz's office. Horrifying details hit Shawn one after another. The blood-smeared door. The bullet hole through the splintered wood. Aziz lying across the threshold of the office, bleeding to death . . .

"Oh my God!" Richard exclaimed beside him. "What happened here?"

Shawn didn't wait for an explanation. He knew what he had to do. Rushing to Aziz's side, he knelt down by the injured lawyer. A crimson puddle spread out from beneath Aziz, soaking into the carpet. "Give me room!" Shawn ordered the guards, who stepped back to let him work. He placed his palms against Aziz's bleeding torso. The hot stickiness of the blood made him gag, but he didn't withdraw his hands; two-plus years as a professional healer had given him a pretty strong stomach. Mustering his strength, he closed his eyes in concentration. His healing ability had failed to save Jordan Collier from his gunshot wounds, but maybe he could still save Aziz if he moved fast enough.

A phantom pain stabbed him in the abdomen. *Only one wound,* he sensed. *Good. That gives me a chance.* He let his own life force flow into the lawyer's body, amplifying Aziz's ordinary healing factors to the nth degree. Contrary to popular opinion, he didn't actually suck out people's injuries or ailments; he just infused them with the strength to heal themselves . . . at great cost to his own endurance. A grimace contorted his face, and his limbs trembled, as he poured his youthful vigor into the dying man. Mercifully, the bullet had already passed through Aziz's body so there was no need to expel it. Shawn only had to hold on while the damaged bones and tissues knitted themselves back together. He opened his eyes to keep a close watch on his patient. Blood stopped flowing from the shrinking hole in the lawyer's gut. The color began to return to Aziz's face. His ragged breathing grew stronger and steadier. *He's going to make it,* Shawn realized. *Thank God!*

Breathing heavily, Shawn lifted his hands and leaned back onto his ankles. He felt as though he had just run a marathon, but he couldn't complain;

he knew he had just saved the other man's life. Aziz reached out and squeezed Shawn's bloody hand. "Thank you," he whispered. "Forgive me for plotting against you. We were wrong to seek your death."

Huh?

Shawn took a moment to recover before turning his attention back to the ongoing crisis. Richard emerged from the violated office, shaking his head. Shawn recalled that, up until recently, the office had belonged to the late Matthew Ross. Now Aziz had nearly died there as well. *It's almost like there's a curse over the place.*

"We found another casualty," Richard reported. "Simone Tanaka. She's alive, but in no condition to talk right away." He glanced back at the office. "No trace of the shooter. Looks like he got away." He conferred briefly with the security guards. "No indications of forced entry, either. Could be an inside job."

One of us? Shawn looked accusingly at Aziz. "What happened here? What were you saying about a plot?" A theory popped into his brain. "Did Simone shoot you? Did you have some sort of falling-out?"

"No," the lawyer whispered weakly. Although

no longer at death's door, he was still pretty shaken up. "Not Simone. Gorinsky."

The guy Uncle Tommy electrocuted? Now Shawn was really confused. "I thought he was dead."

Before Aziz could explain, Shawn heard footsteps racing toward them. *Please don't be Isabelle,* he prayed, before looking up to see his uncle and Diana Skouris rushing onto the scene. "NTAC!" Tom said, holding up his badge. The guards hesitated, unsure whether to let the government agents through, but Shawn signaled that it was okay. The agents' eyes quickly took in the gruesome scene.

"Good Lord," Diana said. "What's happened here?"

Simone Tanaka's file had listed The 4400 Center as her permanent address. Tom had driven straight here, rendezvousing with Diana right out front. He had hoped to interrogate Simone regarding her connection to William Gorinsky; instead they found themselves arriving at a crime scene.

"Boy, am I glad to see you," Shawn greeted them. Fresh blood splattered his hands; staggering to his feet, he wiped them off on his bathrobe. Tom's gaze shifted from his nephew to Rahmen Aziz, whose shirt front was also soaked in blood. He guessed that Shawn had just performed one of his trademark healings. Had someone attacked Aziz?

Simone? Tom speculated. "Want to fill us in?"

Shawn quickly brought them up-to-date, while Richard Tyler confirmed the particulars. Tom and Diana exchanged a startled look when they heard that Simone Tanaka had also been victimized—by Gorinsky, reportedly. The supposedly dead veteran had beaten them to the punch again. *What's it going to take to stop him,* Tom thought. *He keeps turning up like a bad penny.*

"You folks got here pretty quickly," Shawn commented.

"We were already on the way," Tom explained. "To see Simone."

"She's still in pretty rough shape," Richard said, gesturing toward the office behind him. Shawn started to head toward the door, but Richard restrained him. "I don't think it's life-threatening, Shawn. You can take it easy for a minute."

"You sure?" Shawn asked. His gait was a little unsteady, as though healing Aziz had taken a lot out of him, but he looked ready to heal the other casualty without hesitation. Tom was impressed by his dedication to his calling. "Maybe I should check on her anyway."

"Shawn!" Isabelle suddenly appeared at the other end of the corridor, wearing a violet silk kimono. Her brown eyes widened in alarm as she spotted the crimson stains on his robe. Tom didn't miss the look of dismay on Shawn's face as his imperious girlfriend arrived on the scene. "You're hurt!"

As she rushed toward the crime scene, a pair of guards foolishly attempted to block her approach. "Back off!" she warned them as, with a wave of her hand, she flung both of them away from her with a casual display of telekinesis. The guards smacked against the walls on either side of the oncoming woman, but not too hard; neither was knocked unconscious. Tom figured they had gotten off lucky. By her standards, Isabelle had been positively re-strained.

What was it the future had called her again? *A terrible evil?* Tom wondered again if he had made a mistake not to kill her when he'd had the chance.

"I'm all right, Isabelle!" Shawn said wearily. "It's not my blood."

"Oh." Looking around, she swiftly put the pieces together. "What's going on?"

"Everything is under control, Isabelle," Richard informed his daughter. "This is none of your concern. Please return to our rooms."

Isabelle was taken aback by his suggestion. "But . . . what if you need me?"

"NTAC is here. Our security forces are doing their job. The criminal has fled the building." Richard addressed her firmly; Tom watched carefully to see how the precocious superwoman reacted. "The most helpful thing you can do right now is go back upstairs and let us handle this. I'll be with you shortly."

Isabelle still resisted the idea. "Shawn?" She looked to her reluctant boyfriend, as though hoping he would overrule her father.

No such luck.

"Just do what your dad says," Shawn told Isabelle, taking Richard's side. "We've got all the help we need right now."

This was *not* what Isabelle wanted to hear. Her expression soured. Expecting fireworks, Tom's hand drifted stealthily toward his handgun, just in case. *Too bad I left that damned hypo at home,* he thought; according to an emissary from the future, the syringe contained the only weapon that would stop Isabelle for good. She opened her mouth to protest her exclusion, but then, apparently thinking better of it, bit down on her lower lip. Much to Tom's surprise, she spun around and stalked off without another word. Everyone present let out a collective sigh of relief.

Guess we dodged that bullet, Tom thought. *For now.*

Diana looked grateful to get back to the business at hand. "So, where were we again?"

"Talk to Aziz," Shawn suggested. "He seems to know what's going on."

The lawyer had achieved a sitting position, his back up against a wall. Tom and Diana crouched down in front of him. "All right, Aziz. Talk. Who did this to you . . . and why?"

Aziz was a lot less self-assured than he'd been in Nina's office two days ago. Apparently being shot in the stomach had put the fear of God into him. "Gorinsky. He turned on us, attacked Simone, then me. I'm not sure why."

"Where is he now?" Tom asked.

"I don't know, I swear it." He kept fingering his bloody stomach, as though he still couldn't entirely believe that the bullet wound was gone. "He fled with DeMeers. Took him prisoner."

"Cooper?" Diana's ears perked up. "What does he want with Cooper?"

Aziz shook his head. "I wish I knew. He betrayed us all . . . said something about getting revenge on the future." His sweaty face went pale as an appalling thought struck home. "Dear God, what have I done? What if I've brought about the very disaster I sought to avert?" He clutched Diana's arm. "You! Your daughter is the one who foresaw this. You know what's at stake. You have to stop him!"

"Who do you mean?" Diana asked. "Cooper or Gorinsky?"

"I'm not sure," Aziz confessed. "But none of us are safe while Cooper is in the hands of that madman. You have to get him back." Guilt was written all over his face. His voice took on a defensive tone. "I swear, I never intended any of this. I was just trying to protect another 4400!"

Tom guessed that the lawyer wasn't telling them the full truth, but there would be time enough to pick apart his story later. Right now he tended to agree with Aziz: finding Cooper DeMeers was their first priority.

Which meant finding out why William Gorinsky was still walking the earth.

"Go home, Isabelle. Get out of our way, Isabelle."

The nerve of them . . . just who do they think I am?

Isabelle fumed silently as she changed out of the

kimono in the quarters she shared with her father. The suite wasn't quite as luxurious as Shawn's, but it certainly beat the rustic log cabin where she'd lived with her parents when she was just a toddler. Those days were long over, however, so why did her father still treat her like a child?

She stared at her reflection in the mirror over her dresser, seeing a full-grown woman with a distinctly pissed-off expression. She didn't know whom she was more angry at, her father for dismissing her like that, or Shawn for not standing up for her. What was the good of having a boyfriend—aside from the sex, that is—if you couldn't count on him to back you up?

Maybe Dennis Ryland at Haspelcorp was right all along and none of the 4400 could be trusted. Isabelle didn't want to think that was so, particularly where Shawn and her dad were concerned, but they seemed determined to drive her away, no matter how hard she tried to prove herself. The eyes in the mirror took on a coldly calculating glint.

That could be a serious mistake on their part.

The mirror shattered as she angrily blasted the glass into pieces.

SEVENTEEN

"BUT HOW CAN Gorinsky's doppelganger still be alive?" Diana asked. "In theory, his physical body, brain and all, is dead and rotting now." She made a mental note to see about having the veteran's body exhumed just to be certain he was really dead. "Where's he getting his energy from?"

"Good question." Marco's voice emanated from the speakerphone on Aziz's desk. Diana, Tom, Shawn, and Richard were all gathered around the desk, while the Center's security guards escorted Simone and Aziz, in handcuffs, down to the Center's infirmary. Marco himself was still back at Diana's apartment, babysitting Maia. "The only explanation I can come up with is that Gorinsky's double is somehow drawing on someone else's life force."

"He can do that?" Tom asked.

"Possibly," Marco said. "The literature of parapsychology is filled with accounts of psychic vampirism, where one individual leeches energy from another. There's been entire books written on the subject. And we've witnessed similar phenomena since the 4400 returned. Look at the way Isabelle Tyler's accelerated growth drained years from her mother's life. Lily Tyler aged fifty years the same night that Isabelle went from a toddler to an adult in one fell swoop."

Diana glanced uncomfortably at Richard; apparently Marco didn't realize that Lily's grieving husband was in the room with them. His wife had died of old age shortly after Isabelle's transformation. Richard winced slightly at Marco's glib reference to the tragedy, but otherwise maintained a stoic demeanor. Diana sympathized with his loss; Lily Tyler had been a beautiful and caring woman. *If only her daughter took after her more . . .*

"So who is Gorinsky sponging off?" Tom wondered aloud. "Is there any way to find out?"

Diana suddenly remembered the special bond that Philip Gorinsky claimed to have shared with

his twin brother. "What about Phil? He insisted
that there was a connection between them. Whom
else would his brother's disembodied spirit gravi-
tate to? Maybe Gorinsky latched on to his twin's
body and is draining Phil's life force, cerebral
energy, or whatever to sustain himself? Just like
Isabelle and her mother."

"That's it!" Tom said, his face growing more
animated. "I saw Phil at Gorinsky's funeral and
he looked like death warmed over. At the time, I
chalked it up to grief over his brother's death, but
I bet that Gorinsky was already feeding off him."
He looked disgusted at the thought of the old man
being exploited like that. "It's probably been going
on since Gorinsky flat lined at Abendson."

"Makes sense to me," Diana agreed. "At least as
much as any of this does." She leaned toward the
speakerphone. "Thanks, Marco. I think we can
take it from here."

"Okay," Marco said, sounding exhausted. She felt
sorry for waking him after already keeping him up
all night. "Good luck . . . hang on a second." Diana
heard Maia's voice in the background. "Maia's up.
She wants to talk to you. She says it's urgent."

Uh-oh, Diana thought. *This doesn't sound good.*
She waited apprehensively while Marco passed the

phone to her daughter. "Maia? What is it, honey? Is something wrong?"

"Mommy?" Maia sounded wide awake . . . and worried. "It's time."

Diana recognized the spooky certainty in her daughter's voice. It was the same tone Maia used whenever she delivered one of her oracular pronouncements. Even after two years, moments like this sent a shiver down Diana's spine. "Time for what?"

"It's time for you to go to the mountain."

Diana's heart sank. She knew what this meant: Rainier was about to wake up. *I guess we know where Gorinsky is taking Cooper,* she thought despairingly. *Right back to where this all began.*

"Mount Rainier?" Diana asked, even though she already knew the answer. Tom, Richard, and Shawn all looked equally chagrined by Maia's latest prophecy. Diana's brain swiftly worked out the logistics. The mountain was approximately three hours away by car. Gorinsky had a head start on them, but if they hurried they might still be able to catch up with him. *Maybe we can commandeer a helicopter?*

"Yes," Maia confirmed. "I just saw you there. Again."

Only for a moment did Diana consider defying the girl's prediction and staying away from

Rainier. Her course was clear. Fate and duty both compelled her to pursue Gorinsky and to try to stop Cooper from blowing up the whole mountain. "Where on Rainier, honey? It's a big place."

"There's a bridge—a high, scary one—over a river, with rocks and rapids way below. The bridge is swinging back and forth, like it's going to come apart any minute. You're on the bridge, Mommy, way up high over the rocks." Maia's eyes were wide with fear. "If you fall . . . !"

"I won't fall, honey," Diana promised. "But what kind of bridge. Like for cars?"

Maia shook her head. "No, it's for people. A rope bridge, like at the playground, but longer and higher. It wobbles when you walk on it."

A suspension bridge, Diana realized. Probably on one of the hiking trails up on the mountain. She tried to see if Maia could narrow the location down any further. "Does the bridge have a name? Did you see a sign anywhere?"

"No, Mommy. I'm sorry. Please, promise me you'll be careful. I don't like what that mountain shows me."

"Don't worry," she assured her daughter. She and Maia had already had several serious talks concerning her job; Maia knew her mother's work sometimes placed her in danger, but that Mommy always came home in the end. "Tom and I will both be very careful, just like we always are."

"But Tom's not going with you," Maia declared. "Alana is."

"What?" Tom blurted in surprise. As far as Diana knew, Alana was waiting for him back at the house they shared on Parkside Avenue. "Alana?"

Diana was equally startled. Alana Mareva was a teacher and gallery owner, not a field agent. She didn't even work for NTAC. "What do you mean, honey? Why Alana?"

"She has to go with you," Maia repeated with that same eerie certainty. "And that other woman. The one with the eyes."

Simone?

"We need to get ready to evacuate if we have to," Richard said to Shawn, while the visiting NTAC agents conferred among themselves. Shawn and Richard stood in front of a plate-glass window, staring out at the pristine white mantle of Rainier. "We don't have to tell them exactly what Maia predicted, but we need to be ready to clear out of here on a moment's notice, just in case NTAC can't stop Cooper from triggering an eruption."

"Good idea," Shawn agreed, but he couldn't help wondering how long they could keep Isabelle in the dark. She wasn't going to be happy when she found out how much they had concealed from her concerning the threat posed by Cooper DeMeers. "Let's get everybody up and packed. We've had earthquake drills before, so they should know what to do. Can you arrange to have some buses on hand?"

"I can do that," Richard said. "I'll also have our people quietly contact the returnees who live off-site."

They were talking thousands of people here; was it even possible to alert that many people without starting a panic? And what about the millions of ordinary people who weren't connected to the 4400? Shawn found it hard even to imagine the scope of the disaster that might be awaiting them. This could make the Great Fire of 1889 look like a summer barbecue.

I hope Uncle Tommy and Diana know what they're doing, Shawn thought. He glanced over at Tom and Diana, who appeared to be getting ready to make their departure. "Give me just a minute," he apologized to Richard before walking over to where the two agents were huddled. There was something he needed to say while he still had the chance. "Excuse me, Diana?"

She looked at him. "Yes?"

"Before you go, I just wanted to apologize to you . . . for hurting Maia last week . . . when I was ill." His memories of those horrible days were garbled and chaotic, but eyewitnesses had confirmed that he had nearly killed Diana's daughter in a deluded attempt to "heal" her. "You have to know that I would have never done anything to harm her if I'd been in my right mind."

Diana examined him thoughtfully, weighing his apology, before finally speaking. "I understand, Shawn. It wasn't your fault. Daniel Armand had messed with your mind." She reached out and took his hand. "I admit I was upset at the time, but I can't forget that you also saved Maia's life, when she was dying of inhibitor poisoning." She cracked a thin smile. "I think we're even."

"Thanks," Shawn said, grateful for her forgiveness. No matter what happened next, with Isabelle or the mountain, he was glad to get that off his chest. He turned back toward Richard, who was waiting to work out the evacuation plans. "Take care, Diana. And you, too, Uncle Tommy."

He wondered if he would ever see them again.

EIGHTEEN

Tom MADE GOOD time getting to Philip Gorinsky's house in Puyallup. This early in the morning the traffic had been light on I-5. A glance at his watch informed him that it was a little past five in the morning. In theory, Diana and Alana were en route to Rainier by now, along with Simone Tanaka.

Don't take any unnecessary chances, he urged them silently. He gazed south at the looming mountain. It didn't look like it was about to pull a St. Helens, but Tom knew that looks could be deceptive where the 4400 were concerned. If Rainier blew, there was little chance that the women would get away in time. *I don't want to lose you both.*

He hated staying behind like this, while his partner and his girlfriend—undoubtedly the two most important women in his life—flew into jeopardy atop a slumbering volcano. But what else was he supposed to do? Maia had been quite emphatic on the subject and they ignored her prophecies only at their own peril. Presumably, this was the way things were *supposed* to happen.

But that doesn't mean I have to like it.

Parking the Chevy at the curb, he approached Phil's humble domicile. Even in the early morning gloom, he could see that the old man's lawn and gardens showed signs of neglect. The grass needed mowing, while weeds had sprouted up in the formerly tidy flower beds. Tom found this an ominous sign; he had only met the man twice, but he already knew that it wasn't like Phil to let things go to seed like this. Diana's theory was looking even more on-target. Being haunted by the spirit of his dead brother had clearly taken a toll on Phil's housekeeping.

Given the hour, it came as no surprise that the house's windows were all dark. Tom felt bad about disturbing the old man so early in the morning, especially if their suspicions proved incorrect, but there was too much at stake to wait for the sun to come up. If William Gorinsky was using his surviving twin as some sort of human battery, they needed to know about it—especially with Diana and Alana heading for another confrontation with the murderous apparition. *He almost killed Diana last time.*

Ringing the doorbell produced no results, so he tried pounding loudly on the front door. "Mister Gorinsky? Phil?" He shouted loud enough for the old man to hear him, but received only silence in response. "It's Agent Baldwin from NTAC. I really need to speak to you."

Nothing.

He glanced fretfully at the neighboring houses, relieved not to see any lights coming on inside the homes. The last thing he needed right now was a well-meaning neighbor calling the cops. His NTAC credentials would keep him out of trouble, but he didn't look forward to having to explain why he was harassing an eighty-year-old veteran at five in the morning. *"You see, officer, we have reason to believe that he is supplying cerebral energy to his dead twin's ectoplasmic double. . . ."*

Looking around, he decided that the neglected lawn, as well as the continuing silence from inside the house, constituted probable cause that the old man was in need of immediate assistance. Taking a few steps back to get a running start, he smashed the door open with his shoulder. To his relief, no sirens blared. Apparently Phil had neglected to activate his house's security system before turning in.

More evidence that all was not as it should be.

"Phil? Don't be alarmed. It's me, Tom Baldwin."

He quickly located a light switch and turned on the lights. A rapid scan informed him that Phil had been too weak or impaired to look after the interior of the house as well. Dust coated the coffee table and fireplace mantel. The carpet needed vacuuming. A TV dinner, mostly untouched, was going bad on an end table. A wool comforter lay in a heap in front of the empty rocking chair. Tom guessed that nobody had looked in on Phil for a few days.

Ragged, stertorous breathing quickly led Tom to Phil himself, whom he found sprawled on the kitchen floor. Cold water gushed from a faucet over the sink. A shattered mug lay on the floor near his head. It looked as if Phil had been fixing himself a cup of tea when he'd suddenly been stricken. *No wonder the security system wasn't on yet.* Tom wondered if the octogenarian's collapse had coincided with Gorinsky's sudden appearance at NTAC or The 4400 Center.

Or maybe he had just had a stroke?

"Phil!" He knelt down beside the older man and hurriedly checked his pulse. He felt a weak but steady beat beneath his fingers. *Okay*, he thought. *At least he's still alive.* He gently rolled Phil onto his back and tried to rouse him. "Phil? Can you hear me?"

The unconscious senior citizen failed to respond. Tom was reminded of Gorinsky's inert state that night at Abendson, when his hostile doppelganger had attacked Diana and Garrity in the Underground. Phil's eyelids fluttered. His lips murmured inaudibly. His right hand was clenched shut, perhaps around the grip of a phantom semi-automatic?

What was Gorinsky doing right this very minute?

Reaching for his cell phone, Tom started to dial 911, then hesitated. Did he really want to involve some clueless paramedics in this? What if he needed to fatally break the connection between Phil and his twin's rampaging double? Tom didn't want to harm the old man, especially after what had happened with his brother, but suppose Diana and Alana came under attack by the seemingly unstoppable Gorinsky? Tom wrestled briefly with his conscience. What if he was wrong and Phil was just in a diabetic coma or something? Would he ever forgive himself if he didn't get the innocent retiree immediate medical attention?

Damnit, he thought. There was really no choice at all.

He dialed 911. "Hello, I'd like to request an ambulance."

He hoped he wasn't fatally compromising Diana's pursuit of Gorinsky.

After giving the dispatcher Phil's name and address, he pocketed his cell phone and pondered what to do next. Phil's lips started moving again so Tom leaned forward in hopes of making out what he was saying. The old man's voice was so faint that, even with his ear only inches away from Phil's face, Tom could barely hear him.

"Keep moving. . . ."

"Keep moving," Gorinsky ordered Cooper. "Faster."

The killer's gun had been aimed at Cooper's head for hours now, but Cooper had hardly grown used to the situation. If anything, he was getting more freaked out by the minute as the tranquilizers in his system gradually wore off. After fleeing The 4400 Center, and hot-wiring a random car from the Center's parking lot, Gorinsky had forced Cooper to drive south toward Mount Rainier. In order to avoid the ranger stations at the entrances to the park, they had left the car alongside a lonely mountain road a few miles short of the Nisqually gateway and set off on foot through the woods. Now Cooper found himself on a forced march toward the last place on Earth he wanted to set foot on: the snow-covered volcano up ahead.

Dawn painted the enormous glaciers a rosy shade of peach. Cooper stumbled through the uneven terrain of a dense old-growth forest. It was an overcast, foggy morning. Towering firs and hemlocks obscured his view. Faint sunlight filtered down through the heavy green canopy overhead. Moss and lichen clung to the trunks of the trees. A stream gurgled somewhere nearby, reminding Cooper just how thirsty he was. Birdsong greeted the sun. Woodpeckers tapped loudly against solid bark. Logs, fallen needles, and fungi littered the forest floor as they hiked uphill through the foliage. Cooper was already breathing hard. His legs were killing him. His flannel shirt wasn't enough to keep out the morning chill. He needed a jacket or something.

"Please," he pleaded. "I need a break."

"Tough." Gorinsky didn't sound winded at all. Was he just in better shape, or did dead men not need to breathe? "Your NTAC pals will be coming after you any time now. I'm not letting them steal you away from me again."

"They're not my friends!" Cooper protested. "I didn't want anything to do with any of you people! I just wanted to be left alone!"

"Keep your voice down!" Gorinsky barked. He peered about warily, although it seemed unlikely that they were being watched by anything other than wildlife. The barrel of his pistol jabbed Cooper between the shoulder blades. "And step on it. We haven't got all day."

For the one hundredth time, Cooper wished that he hadn't snatched the damn gun from that guard back at NTAC. Then again, Gorinsky could presumably just zap him instead. "For God's sake, can't you let me know what this is all about?" He kept his voice low to avoid provoking the trigger-happy gunman. "Maybe we're on the same side."

Frankly, he doubted that was the case, but he was willing to say anything to find out what

Gorinsky was really after—and where exactly he fit into the picture. *Is he after the $200,000? If so, he's in for a hell of a disappointment!*

"We ought to be," his captor said grudgingly. "From what I hear, those bastards in the future screwed you over, too. Just like they did to all of us." Venom dripped from his words; Cooper could practically hear the man's blood pressure rising as he finally gave voice to the simmering fury that seemed to be driving him. "I had a great future in front of me. The best years of my life. College, a career, a great girl . . . and they stole it all away, because of some complicated plan to change history. Well, I'll teach them to mess with my American Dream. I'll spoil their goddamn plan if it's the last thing I do!"

Cooper was confused. "But . . . I thought you belonged to the Nova Group? Don't you believe that the 4400 are destined to save the world?"

"Not if I can help it," Gorinsky snarled. "What do I care about what happens to some heartless SOBs thousands of years from now, after what they did to me? Screw them and their stupid master plan!" Spittle sprayed from his lips. "I was only with Nova because of Simone, and because I wanted to be where the action was, right in the

middle of things, so that I could sabotage the future's plans at a crucial moment. I was just waiting
for the right opportunity—and then you came
along."

"What do you mean?" Cooper asked. He was
afraid he knew, but needed to hear it anyway.
"What do you want from me?"

Gorinsky laughed joylessly. "What do you
think, numbskull?" He pointed at the northern
flank of Rainier, which was barely visible through
the teeming pines. "You're going to blow up that
mountain for me, just like the little girl predicted.
If we're lucky, we'll wipe out most of Seattle and
the 4400, too." He chortled loudly. "That should
sure throw a monkey wrench into the future's
plans!"

"You want to kill all those people, cause a major
disaster, just to get back at the people who abducted us?" Cooper couldn't believe what he was
hearing. "You're insane!"

"Says the man who jumped out of a jetliner with
a bomb in his suitcase," Gorinsky mocked him.
"You're no one to talk. The way I figure it, we're
both on borrowed time, so we might as well go out
with a bang." He prodded Cooper with the pistol
once more. "Now shut up and keep walking."

Cooper realized there was no point in trying to
reason with Gorinsky; the man was obviously out
of his mind—and willing to sacrifice both of them
to get his revenge on the future. Cooper's only
hope was to get away from the killer somehow. In
the meantime, he struggled to stay calm, for fear
of setting off another earthquake before he had
a chance to escape. He wasn't sure how long the
inhibitor in his bloodstream was supposed to last,
but it was bound to wear off eventually. *I need to get
out of here before that happens,* he thought. *If I can.*

Knowing that he was on a suicide mission didn't
make the arduous hike any easier. In time, they
stumbled onto a trail of sorts. Poorly maintained,
it appeared to be the proverbial road less traveled;
still, it beat trekking through the underbrush. The
path led steeply upward, so that they were fighting
gravity the whole way. Without a watch, Cooper
couldn't keep track of the time, but he figured that
they had been walking for at least a couple of hours
by the time they finally passed the tree line and left
the forest behind. Sloping subalpine meadows rose
before them. Acres of spring flowers blossomed in
the misty sunlight, despite the generous patches
of snow still frosting the hillside. Melting snow
gurgled down the mountain. Cooper looked about

anxiously for other hikers, but it was still early and the unmarked trail appeared to be far from the beaten path. He spotted a ranger cabin on the other side of the meadow. For a second, hope sparked inside him.

"Don't even think about it," Gorinsky growled in his ear.

Veering in direction, he forced Cooper to take the long way around the cabin. Within minutes they had lost sight of the rustic structure. Cooper's spirits sagged. So much for being rescued by a forest ranger. He was still stuck with a killer, with no help in sight.

They waded through an icy stream that stung Cooper's aching feet. The cold water soaked right through his ill-fitting sneakers. The higher they climbed, the more aware Cooper was that he was hardly dressed for a long hike up a mountain. Hugging himself to fight the cold, he longed for a heavy jacket or sweater. A chilly wind bit into his face and bones. He took a moment to scoop a couple of handfuls of water into his mouth. The ice-cold water tasted delicious and went a long way toward restoring what was left of his strength. At least he didn't feel like he was about to drop at any minute.

"That's enough," Gorinsky declared. The stalker himself seemed impervious to the cold, hunger, thirst, or fatigue, or maybe he was just too crazed to care. He gave Cooper an impatient shove that sent the weary fugitive stumbling across the slippery stones beneath his feet. "You better not be stalling on purpose."

"I'm not, I swear!" Cooper waded back onto dry land. Water streamed from his sneakers. "I'm just exhausted. I'm out of shape."

"Then save your breath for the climb," Gorinsky said, doing his best impression of a drill sergeant. The brawny leatherneck looked like one, too. "And stop dragging your feet. It will all be over soon."

That's what I'm afraid of, Cooper thought.

It only got colder as they continued to gain altitude. The flowering meadows gradually gave way to piled snow and rock. Boulders jutted from deep gullies carved out by forgotten avalanches. Banks of loose scree piled at the base of weathered granite cliffs. Switchbacks led them on a zigzag route up the colossal mountain. The snow was ankle-deep at times. The freezing wind left Cooper shivering. He hadn't felt this cold since that hellish November night thirty-five years ago, right before that big ball of light changed his life forever. They had ascended above the cloud cover by now, leaving the morning fog behind, but he could see his own breath misting before him. The increasingly steep grade had him panting in exertion. They passed a waterfall, cascading down a rocky cliff. The spray from the falls sprinkled his face, but did little to ease his suffering. He panted over the roar of the falling water.

"Please, I can't keep this up," he gasped. Part of him almost wanted to reach the end of the hike, even if that meant his own volcanic demise. "How much higher are we going?"

"As high as we can get." Gorinsky peered up at the rugged immensity of Rainier, which now practically blotted out the sky. No matter how long they hiked, the mountain's snow-topped crown still seemed to tower above them in the distance. "I don't know what sort of range your ability has, but I want to get you as close to the top as possible, just to be sure."

Cooper prayed that the killer wasn't crazy enough to think they could actually make it to the summit. They weren't remotely equipped to tackle any serious mountaineering, especially this early in the spring. Freak storms, blizzards, and avalanches killed off climbers all the time, and Cooper had never scaled a mountain in his life. *He's going to get us both killed,* he thought, *which might not be such a bad thing.* Given a choice, he'd rather be buried alive in an avalanche than set off a volcano that killed thousands.

"Huh," Gorinsky grunted as they rounded a turn. "Take a look at that."

Directly in their path, a narrow suspension bridge spanned a deep ravine. Creeping up to the edge of the precipice, Cooper saw foaming rapids at least one hundred feet below. The skinny bridge was only a few feet wide, barely enough for one hiker to squeeze through at a time, but looked over two hundred feet in length. A rusty sign was posted at the entrance to the bridge: ONE PERSON ON THE BRIDGE AT A TIME. DO NOT BOUNCE OR SHAKE BRIDGE.

"You first," Gorinsky ordered.

Cooper gulped and stepped out onto the bridge, which swayed alarmingly beneath his tread. He grabbed on to the guide ropes for dear life. His wet sneakers squished against the wooden floorboards as he hoped that the crude bridge was better maintained than the rest of the trail. A howling wind keened in his ears. He could hear the coursing river crash against heavy boulders far beneath him. *Don't look down,* he told himself, but the perverse temptation was impossible to resist. Peeking down between bouncing wooden slats, he experienced a sudden attack of dizziness and abruptly looked away. *Who would have guessed,* he thought sourly, *that the notorious D. B. Cooper was afraid of heights?*

Too bad he hadn't thought to ask for a parachute.

He briefly considered throwing himself off the bridge, ending his ordeal once and for all, but a stubborn urge to live won out over his better judgment. He wasn't ready to die just yet, no matter what Gorinsky had in mind. *Does that make me a hero or a coward?*

After what felt like forever, he reached the opposite end of the bridge and gratefully stepped onto solid rock once more. "All right," Gorinsky shouted at him from across the ravine. "Step away from the bridge and keep your back to me. You even think about messing with the bridge while I'm on it, and I'll empty this entire gun into your miserable hide. You got that?"

"I understand."

Cooper waited helplessly while the bridge rattled beneath his captor's boots. Gorinsky made it across the span faster than Cooper had, barely giving the hijacker time to wonder about whether he had just missed his best chance to give Gorinsky the slip.

But where was he supposed to go? Looking ahead, he saw that they had arrived at the end of the trail: a rocky saddle between two distant peaks. The site offered a spectacular view of the misty woodlands and vast glacial valleys below, as well as the immense upper reaches of the mountain soaring above them, but Cooper was in no position to appreciate the scenery. Any chance of escaping Gorinsky seemed to have dropped away like the forbidding cliffs before them. There was no place to run, nowhere to go but down.

He was trapped.

Gorinsky surveyed the mountainside and reached a similar conclusion. "Looks like this is as high as we get." He smirked in anticipation. "Hope you've still got one last good eruption in you, 'cause it's showtime."

He stepped back and nodded at Cooper.

"Bring on the fireworks."

NINETEEN

"WELL," DIANA ASKED, "have you spotted them yet?"

The mountain rescue helicopter swooped above the northwest face of Mount Rainier. Simone Tanaka, both her wrists and ankles shackled, sat up front with the pilot to permit her a better view of the endless white slopes below. Gazing out her own window in the rear of the copter, Diana understood why Maia had foreseen that Simone should accompany them in the pursuit of Cooper and Gorinsky. Literally hundreds of square miles of wilderness were spread out beneath them; even with an entire team of agents and rangers swarming the scene, there was no guarantee that they would be able to locate the two men in time. A pair of high-powered binoculars rested in Diana's lap, but Simone's enhanced vision was still their best shot at tracking the fugitives down. *Let's just hope those eyes of hers live up to the hype.*

"I'm looking, I'm looking!" the young woman snapped. The medics at The 4400 Center had cleared her for this expedition, but Simone's nerves seemed stretched to the breaking point. She raised her voice to be heard over the whir of the rotors. "Believe me, I want to find those two as much as anybody."

That's probably true, Diana conceded. She figured their proximity to the mountain guaranteed Simone's cooperation. None of them wanted to be this close to Rainier with Cooper still unaccounted for. "What about the bridge?" she pressed. "Maia mentioned a swinging bridge."

"You know how many freaking wooden bridges there are down there?" Sarcasm colored Simone's voice. "I don't suppose that spooky kid of yours told you anything more specific? The name of a trail or waterfall maybe?"

"Doesn't work that way," Diana said coldly. Insulting her daughter was not the way to get on her good side. She instructed the pilot to make another pass; coming from Seattle, the fugitives would probably have entered the parklands from the southwest. "Keeping looking," she ordered Simone. "The more help you give us, the lighter your sentence is likely to be."

The way Diana saw it, they already had the young woman linked to Gorinsky, the jailbreak, and possibly even espionage charges for spying on NTAC. A closer look at her file had revealed a history of radical politics dating back to the early 1970s, and, after last night's events, NTAC would be going over her more recent activities with a fine-tooth comb. Diana wouldn't be surprised to find out that Simone and Aziz were both involved with Nova Group to some degree. She was in big trouble.

Assuming we survive the next few hours.

"You think I don't know that?" Simone whined. She leaned forward in her seat, scanning the sprawling meadows, forests, and glaciers below. Handcuffs rattled around her slender wrists. "I'm doing the best I can!"

But would that be enough? The missing men had been on the loose for hours now. They'd had plenty of time to make it to Rainier if that was indeed what Gorinsky had in mind. State troopers

had reported finding an abandoned car right outside the park, but nobody had yet confirmed that
it was the same vehicle the fugitives had stolen
from the parking lot at The 4400 Center. What
if, at this very moment, the two men were headed
for Oregon or Canada instead? Maia's prophecy
was the only real "evidence" pointing them toward
Rainier. Diana couldn't help hoping that maybe,
just maybe, her daughter was wrong for once.

But she knew better than that.

"No luck yet?" Alana asked. Tom's girlfriend sat
beside Diana in the back. She had come along on
this mission without any argument. Diana appreciated her cooperation; tracking down dangerous
fugitives was hardly part of the schoolteacher's
job description. It said a lot about Alana that she'd
been willing to drop everything and join them on
this manhunt, despite the significant risks involved.
Both women were wearing snow gear hastily req-
uisitioned from Alana's closets. Fortunately, they
were about the same size; Alana's clothes were a
little baggy on Diana, but that had been the least of
her worries. Just as long as they kept her warm . . .

" 'Fraid not," Diana admitted. She settled back
into her seat in order to converse with Alana without shouting. The cockpit tilted vertiginously as

the copter banked sharply to the left. Diana instinctively grabbed her armrest.

Alana peered out her own window at the magnificent vista below. "I only wish I knew why I was here. Do you think it has something to do with my ability?"

The raven-haired, exotically beautiful teacher possessed the unique ability to create artificial realities that were practically indistinguishable from the real thing. Diana had personally experienced Alana's gift only a few weeks ago, when Maia had been kidnapped by a covert operative from the future. Alana had helped Diana cope with her daughter's disappearance by taking her into an imaginary reality, partially constructed from Diana's own memories, in which she and Maia were still together. That virtual realm had felt so convincing, so *real*, that Diana had almost let herself disappear into the illusion forever. Only the safe recovery of the real Maia had ultimately lured her out of the phantom existence Alana had conjured up for her.

"I assume so," she replied. "But don't know how."

"Perhaps we can figure it out," Alana suggested. "What do we know about these men, Gorinsky and DeMeers?"

Diana wondered how much Tom had already told her about the case. They had a solid relationship—she doubted that there were any secrets between them—but maybe Tom had been too busy to keep Alana up-to-date on his work. They had been chasing "D. B. Cooper" for nearly a week now and Diana was definitely feeling the strain. *To think this all started with a field trip to Mount Rainier . . . !*

"Here's what we know so far," she began, giving Alana a concise rundown on what they had already learned about both men. "Hard to say who's the most dangerous. Cooper's ability poses the greatest threat, but I don't get a sense that he actually wants to hurt anybody. Gorinsky, on the other hand, has already attacked several people. He's mentally unhinged, not to mention legally dead."

Alana nodded. "I can't help feeling sorry for him, though. There's something tragic about his story. Thomas spoke of this at Gorinsky's funeral, how the poor man never got to live a long, full life like his brother." A pensive look came over her face. "You know, Diana, recently I've been helping the children at the Center deal with the trauma of their abduction by using my ability to fill in the years they missed while they were away. It's a kind of therapy, that sometimes yields various positive results. Perhaps—"

Before she could complete her thought, Simone shouted excitedly. "There they are! I see them!" The cuffs on her wrists forced her to point with both hands. "Down there, to the right!"

Diana had to take her word for it. Even with binoculars, all she could see from this height were miles of trackless wilderness and glaciers. The pilot looked to her for guidance. "Take us down," she instructed him. Finding a safe place to land was going to be a challenge, but there was no way around it. "Get us as close as you can!"

Cooper made one last try to get Gorinsky to see reason.

"Listen to me!" he pleaded. "It's not late. We don't have to do this." The edge of the lofty ridge dropped off sharply behind him. Jagged spurs of granite jutted from the packed snow and ice like the fins on a dinosaur's back. Rainier itself was like a slumbering dragon, just waiting to wake up and spew fire from its gullet. "Think of all the people at risk. We're talking mass murder here!"

Gorinsky was unmoved. "Guess the future should have thought of that before they messed

with me. This is on them, not us. We're the goddamn victims here!" He waved the stolen gun at
Cooper. "What are you waiting for? Do it!"

"It doesn't work that way! I can't control it. I
don't know how." Cooper tried to stay calm, to
keep his pulse and breathing steady, but how was
he supposed to do that when a deranged gunman was thrusting a pistol in his face on top of a
sleeping volcano? Just try to keep cool under those
conditions! It was harder than jumping out of an
airplane.

Gorinsky scowled. "Your ability worked pretty
good before, when I came after you in the Market
and Underground." His free hand reached out
for Cooper. Static electricity crackled around his
beefy fingers. A whiff of ozone polluted the pure
mountain air. "Maybe you just need the right mo-
tivation."

"No! Keep away from me!" Panicking, Cooper
instinctively stepped backward, only to feel weathered stone give way beneath his foot. He toppled
over the edge, about to plummet to his death, but
Gorinsky grabbed his arm and yanked him back
onto the ridge. Cooper barely had time to wonder
whether he should be relieved or dismayed when
a painful electric shock jolted his system. His jaws

clamped together, barely missing his tongue, as he spasmed precariously atop the icy saddle. An agonized cry escaped his clenched teeth. Static crackled in his ears.

"How you like that, buddy?" Gorinsky gloated. His high-voltage fingers dug into Cooper's arm, refusing to let go. "That enough to get your juices flowing?"

The current halted abruptly, giving Cooper a moment to catch his breath. Shaking, he dropped to his knees in the snow. Gorinsky's fingers closed tightly on his shoulder.

"Don't worry," the killer said. "I'm not planning to fry you. I just want to make you hurt—like this!"

A fresh shock electrified Cooper's entire body. His heart beat erratically. Plump veins surfaced on the backs of his hands. Violent convulsions shook his debilitated frame . . . and the mountain began to tremble in sympathy. The ridge shuddered beneath his feet, almost throwing him off. A cascade of snow tumbled over the edge. A low rumble, immeasurably deep, rose from Rainier's volcanic interior.

The inhibitor! Cooper realized even through his torment. *It's not working anymore!*

"That's more like it!" Gorinsky whooped jubilantly, even as he teetered atop the shaking ridge. He sent another burst of electricity blasting through Cooper. "Keep it up!"

The tremors slowly increased in intensity. Avalanches roared down the sides of the nearby peaks, burying the trails below. Cataracts of ice water gushed down crumbling cliffs.

Oh my God! Cooper thought. *I can't stop it. It's really happening!*

"That's enough, Gorinsky!" A woman's voice cut through the deep bass rumble of the mountain. "Get your hands off him!"

Cooper looked in desperation toward the source of the voice.

Gun in hand, Agent Skouris stepped off the bridge.

"Diana? What's happening? Talk to me!"

Frustrated, Tom shook his cell phone, as though that would get rid of the static interfering with his call to Diana. Reception between here and Rainier was spotty at best. Diana had alerted him when Simone had first zeroed in on Gorinsky and Cooper, but since then he'd only picked up snatches of her voice between the static. In theory, she and Alana were closing in on the fugitives—and that was all he knew. *They could be confronting Gorinsky right now!*

"Something wrong, sir?" a paramedic asked him, looking up from Phil's insensate body. The EMTs had originally objected to Tom riding along in the back of the ambulance, but his badge had silenced their protests. As a division of Homeland Security, NTAC carried a lot of weight these days. Now Tom sat alongside Phil as the stricken retiree occupied a stretcher a few inches away. An oxygen mask covered the old man's face. Diagnostic equipment monitored his vital signs. Unable to revive Phil, the paramedics had briskly loaded him into the ambulance, which was currently racing through Puyallup toward the nearest hospital. Flashing lights and a blaring siren cleared the early morning traffic out of their way.

"No. Yes. I don't know," Tom groused unhappily. Alana and Diana might be in danger at this very moment, and he had no idea what he should be doing. The last thing he wanted to do was risk killing Phil by breaking his psychic connection to his brother, but that left both his partner and his lover on their own against the murderous doppelganger. *I should be on that mountain with Diana,* he thought. *Not Alana.* "Just keep taking care of Phil."

The speeding ambulance hit a loose manhole. The sudden clang made his heart skip a beat, and he realized that he had been unconsciously bracing himself for a thunderous explosion from Rainier, just like the one that had rattled his bedroom windows when St. Helens blew twenty-six years ago. But if Rainier blew this morning, it would do a lot more than shake things up hundreds of miles away. Puyallup was right in the path of any potential lahars.

"C'mon, Diana!" He pressed the cell phone up against his ear. "What's going on up there?"

The worst part was, even if he got through to Diana, it might already be too late to do anything. Tom had heard recordings of the last transmission made by the geologist monitoring St. Helens right before it erupted. The doomed scientist had barely managed to shout a terse warning—"Vancouver! Vancouver! This is it!"—before an explosion greater than that of even the most powerful of atomic bombs cut off his voice forever.

Please, he prayed fervently. *Don't let me get a message like that from Diana.*

* * *

Crossing the narrow suspension bridge would have been frightening at the best of times. Doing so during an earthquake struck Alana as the height of insanity. How in the world had she ever let Diana talk her into this?

Because the lives of everyone we love are at stake.

The wooden floorboards bounced beneath her feet. The entire bridge swung back and forth like a carnival ride. Throwing caution to the wind, Alana scampered across the bridge as fast as she could, holding her breath until at last she set foot on the other side. Diana was already there, her gun drawn on a stocky red-haired young man. Like Alana, she wore an NTAC flak vest over her down parka. "That's enough, Gorinsky!" she hollered. "Get your hands off him!"

The helicopter had dropped them off on a snowy ledge a quarter mile below and they had sprinted up the trail following Simone's directions. The cuffed legal assistant had been left aboard the copter and had guided them the rest of the way by radio from above. The pilot was under orders to fly to safety, leaving Alana and Diana behind, if it looked like the mountain was on the verge of erupting. Feeling the ground vibrating beneath

her feet, Alana hoped that the pilot and Simone
were already putting Rainier far behind.

There's no need to risk their lives any further, she
thought. *Now it's up to Diana and me.*

"Stay out of this!" Gorinsky shouted back. He
fired a warning shot, or maybe the earth tremors
just threw his aim off. In any event, the shot went
wild, missing both women by yards. He kept a
tight grip on the other man, whom he seemed to
be subjecting to some sort of torture. Alana recognized Cooper DeMeers from the mug shots Diana
had shared with her. "It's too late. You can't stop
me now!" He sneered at Diana. "We both know
your gun can't hurt me!"

That's why I'm here, Alana thought. She knew
now what she was meant to do, if she could just get
through to Gorinsky. Catching up with Diana, she
gently placed her hand on the other woman's arm.
"Lower your weapon, Diana. Let me handle this."

A bone-jarring tremor threw her off balance and
she grabbed on to a nearby outcropping to support
herself. "Listen to me, William," she called out.
"We're not here to hurt you. We just want to help
you!"

"Who the hell are you?" he challenged her. "Another NTAC storm trooper?"

Alana shook her head. She lowered the hood of her parka so he could see her face better. "My name is Alana Mareva, and I believe I can give you what you want."

"It's too late for that!" he barked, his breath misting before his face. "I've already lost everything that matters. All I have left is revenge!"

"That's not true," she told him. "I have an ability. I can take you back to where you want to go, give you back what you lost." Doing her best to ignore the cold steel gun in his hand, she cautiously approached him. Her gloved hands were open to show him she was unarmed. "You just have to trust me."

"No, this is some sort of trick," he protested, but she heard a promising note of uncertainty in his voice. According to Tom and Diana, Gorinsky had returned repeatedly to Highland Beach in search of a way back to his own time. Now that she was offering him his heart's desire, the naked yearning on his face tore at her heart. "That's not possible!"

Alana stumbled nearer to him. She was close enough now that, should he fire the gun at her again, he was unlikely to miss. Her bulletproof vest would not protect her from being shot through the head. "Everything is possible now,

William. You should know that better than anyone." Ankle-deep in the snow, she stripped off
her gloves and held her bare hands out to him. A
frigid wind nipped at her fingers. "Please, William. Give me a chance to make things right for
you. Eleanor is waiting . . ."

"Eleanor?" His voice cracked on the name of his
long-lost sweetheart. His gun arm dipped toward the
ground. He let go of DeMeers, who collapsed onto
the snow beside him. "You know about Eleanor?"

She closed the distance between them. "Trust
me, William." Reaching out, she cradled his face
between her palms. A peculiar tingle, like static
electricity, raised goosebumps on her skin. "I know
what you need."

Closing her eyes, Alana experienced a moment
of trepidation. Would her ability even work with
the figure before her? According to Diana, Gorinsky wasn't really here in the flesh; this was just
some kind of projection composed of cerebral energy. Then again, so were the hallucinatory worlds
she created. Their abilities actually seemed to com-
plement each other. This was all about establishing
a psychic connection between the two of them. A
meeting of the minds, not flesh and blood.

I can do this.

Her mind reached out for his. For a heartbeat, she encountered resistance, as his wounded soul held on to the pain and anger that had been its only nourishment for so long. Then, with an almost palpable feeling of release, the barriers crumbled and his myriad hopes and dreams and fears poured into a safe place, a sanctuary she had brought into being on some other plane of reality. Her unconscious mind went to work, fashioning the life William Gorinsky should have had, if only the future had allowed it . . .

Eleanor is waiting for him when he gets out of the hospital. At first, he's afraid that the burns on his flesh, left over from that Nazi bomb, will repulse her, but her loving eyes and tender caresses soon assure him that nothing has changed between them. They marry soon after, in the same little Methodist church in Tacoma where he'd once attended Sunday School. Phil is his best man, of course. Eleanor jokes that she can barely tell them apart in their rented tuxes. Bill thinks she has never looked so beautiful.

They honeymoon in Yellowstone National Park, then move into a cozy bungalow not far from the university. He studies engineering on the GI

Bill, working weekends at the Midway Drive-In to make ends meet. Money's tight, but Eleanor never complains. Phil finds a girl of his own and they double-date sometimes. They play bridge and charades and croquet and badminton, and hold barbecues and New Year's parties for their friends and family. Among their acquaintances is an exotic foreign woman named Alana. Bill can never remember exactly where they'd met, but she's usually somewhere in the background, with an enigmatic Mona Lisa smile on her face.

After college, he gets a good job at Boeing as an aerospace engineer. Business is booming, especially after the Russkies put Sputnik into orbit and the space race heats up. Raises and promotions follow, always one step ahead of their growing family. Little Margie comes first, then Nicky and the twins. The latter are named William Junior and Philip Junior, of course. Eleanor likes to joke that she knew what she was getting into, maternity-wise, when she married Bill in the first place. Alana agrees to be the babies' godmother.

It isn't all bliss, naturally. Succumbing to the seven-year-itch, he stupidly drifts into an affair with this sexy Japanese girl he meets at work. Things get pretty rocky for a while, but Eleanor eventually forgives him. They never mention Simone again.

Years speed by, faster than he could have ever imagined. In 1961 Seattle hosts the World's Fair and Bill feels a peculiar sense of déjà vu as he watches the Space Needle and the Monorail go up. Before he knows it, the kids grow up and move out on their own. Nick joins the Marines, just like his old man, while Margie goes into real estate. The twins go through a worrisome hippie phase, even running off to Woodstock at one point, but eventually settle down. Bill Junior becomes an architect. Phil Junior chooses geology and goes to work for the Forest Service in Alaska.

Margie gets married first and makes Bill a grandfather in the summer of '72. More grandchildren follow. Christmases and the Fourths of July become hectic affairs, especially when you add Uncle Phil's multiplying brood into the mix. Phil has gone into education and eventually becomes principal of his own high school. It seems to suit him.

Bill takes early retirement in '77, rewarded for his long years of service with a comfortable pension. He and Eleanor relocate into a little cottage up on Lake Ohop, where he can hunt and fish to his heart's content. Mount St. Helens gives them a

scare in 1980, but all they get is a light dusting of
volcanic ash. He keeps a jar of it on the mantel as
a souvenir.

Doctor Hoyt's warnings about his heart finally
catch up with him. Lying on his deathbed in Good
Samaritan Hospital, Bill can't complain. He survived Normandy and the war to live a good, full
life. Eleanor and Phil and the kids are with him at
the end, keeping vigil at his bedside. Alana is there,
too. He feels her gentle palms against his cheeks.
"Has it been everything you hoped for, William?"

"Yes," he whispers softly. "Thank you."

A glowing ball of light descends through the
ceiling. It's come for him, he realizes, but that's all
right. He's ready now.

Smiling, he lets the light carry him away.

Philip Gorinsky awoke in the back of the
ambulance. A single tear leaked from the corner of
his eye. He looked about in confusion. "What . . . ?
Where am I?"

An oxygen mask muffled his words, but they
caught the attention of a paramedic nonetheless.
A startled-looking EMT leaned over him, observing him carefully. Phil was surprised to see Agent
Baldwin staring down at him as well. Phil realized

that he was strapped into a stretcher inside an ambulance. *How did I get here?* The last thing he remembered was fixing himself a cup of tea after dinner.

The paramedic checked him out and seemed pleased with the results. He removed the oxygen mask to allow Phil to breathe normally. "We should probably check him into the hospital for observation," he informed Baldwin, "but I think he's going to be okay."

"Glad to hear it," the NTAC agent said. Leaning forward, he spoke gently to the old man. "Phil, I'm sorry to trouble you at a time like this, but I have to ask: do you know where your brother is right now?"

Somehow it didn't surprise Phil that Baldwin was inquiring about his dead brother. Hazy memories surfaced inside his mind, of a trembling mountain and a blazing ball of light. Somehow he knew the answer to the agent's question.

"Bill's at peace now. Finally."

TWENTY

Diana watched with amazement as Gorinsky faded away into the ether. One minute he was standing there on the ridge, looking just as solid and tangible as anybody else. The next, he evaporated into whatever dream world Alana had created for him. Remembering how close she herself had come to losing herself in that alternate reality with Maia, Diana knew exactly how enticing that prospect could be. She had left a comatose physical body behind during her immersion in the other realm, but Gorinsky was no longer encumbered with any corporeal baggage. His gun crashed down into the snow. Diana guessed that this time he was gone for good.

So much for Gorinsky, she thought. *Now I just have to deal with Cooper.*

The former hijacker was sprawled on the ridge beyond Alana. Fighting to keep her balance despite the trembling earth, Diana staggered past Alana toward the remaining fugitive. Was he still conscious? Diana couldn't tell, although the quakes continued unabated. A violent earthshock knocked her off her feet, only a few feet away from Cooper. A melting snowbank cushioned her fall, but the shaking ground made it almost impossible to stand up again. Was it just her imagination or could she actually feel the heat rising up from somewhere deep inside the mountain? Solid rock cracked loudly. A geyser of hot steam burst from the newly formed vent, startling Diana, who threw herself backward to avoid being scalded. Ice water puddled beneath her. Loose scree went tumbling off the ridge, raining down on the slopes below. The muffled rumbling became a roar. Fresh steam vents hissed all around her. A sulfurous stench suffused the atmosphere. She heard Alana scrambling for safety. Maia's nightmarish prophecy raced through Diana's brain.

It's happening, she realized. *Just like Maia saw.*

"Cooper!" she yelled at the prone figure. "You've got to stop this!"

He lifted his head from the slush. Swollen veins throbbed across his scalp and forehead. Broken capillaries streaked his eyes with red. "I can't!" he cried out in anguish. "It's too late!" He trembled in sync with the ground beneath him. "I can't control it!"

I was afraid of that, Diana thought. This time she decided to take a more aggressive approach to the crisis. Climbing up onto her knees, she slammed a cartridge of tranquilizer darts, laced with a heavy dose of promicin inhibitor, into her sidearm. Winter gloves made loading the weapon trickier than usual. Fumbling with the gun, she struggled to draw a bead on Cooper even though the mountain ridge felt like a bucking bronco trying to throw her over the side. *Steady,* she told herself as her target jerked up and down in her sights. She tried to aim for his body, not wanting to shoot Cooper in the eye, but aiming for anything was almost a lost cause under the circumstances. *Wait for the shot . . .*

Her finger tightened on the trigger.

CRACK! Steam jetted up from the rock right in front of her, scalding her hand right through her glove. Diana screamed in pain as her pistol went flying from her fingers. The gun clattered onto the thrashing ground not far from a crumbling ledge. *No!* Ignoring her burning hand, she dove for the weapon, but it was too late. Her heart sank as it bounced over the edge, plunging down the side of the mountain. It was gone.

"Damnit!" Diana cursed. She glanced behind her, hoping to spot Gorinsky's stolen pistol, but God only knew where the earthquake had tossed it. Odds were that it was buried under debris by now. She spied Alana lying in the slush a few yards back, hanging on to the rocky spine of the saddle for dear life. The other woman's face was pale; she seemed to be praying under her breath. Diana regretted dragging Tom's girlfriend into this. She deserved better than to die upon an irate mountain. *We all do.*

Heavy cables snapped and the swinging bridge broke free from its moorings. The bridge crashed down into the ravine below, stranding them upon the ridge. Diana looked in vain for the helicopter that had brought them to this remote location. She guessed that, per her instructions, Simone and the pilot were long gone.

Good for them.

She turned her gaze back toward Cooper. He was their only hope now, provided he could somehow reverse the powerful seismic forces he had set into motion. Sitting up amid the slush, he looked about in horror at his tectokinetic handiwork. Plumes of steam rose hundreds of feet in the air. Newborn waterfalls ran like tears from the mountain's frozen mantle. Frenzied paroxysms caused the earth to crack and buckle beneath them. Rainier seemed on the verge of erupting.

"Stop this, Cooper! You've got to try!" The reek of brimstone filled her nostrils. Her injured hand stung like the devil. "Do you want to be responsible for one of the biggest disasters in U.S. history? Thousands of homes and lives are depending on you!"

He stared back at her with wild, bloodshot eyes. "You don't understand! It's too late." He clutched his head in his hands. Pulsing veins writhed like worms beneath his scalp. "I can *feel* the magma rising, surging toward the surface." His florid face was as red as molten lava. "There's no turning back!"

Diana refused to accept that. Maia had never actually seen Rainier erupt all the way; there was still a chance they could avert the worst of the disaster. Shoving off from the ground, she lurched to her feet. "No!" she shouted. "You have to stop this!" Avalanches and landslides echoed across the mountain, adding to the din. Practically all the nearby snow was melted now, exposing slippery gray rock. Ice water streamed off the ridge. Turbid puddles began to bubble and boil . . .

"Think about it," Diana implored him, recalling Cooper's hidden stash of scrapbooks and memorabilia. "You don't want to be remembered this way." She clambered across the shuddering rocks until she was right up in his face. "D. B. Cooper never hurt anybody!"

That struck a nerve.

"No," he whispered hoarsely. "I never did."

A new look of determination came over his face. Closing his eyes, he grimaced in concentration. His fists clenched at his sides and his entire body stiffened as he visibly wrestled with the cataclysmic forces unleashed by his mind. Sweat dripped from his face. The veins in his neck stood out like garden hoses. His knuckles went white. Blood trickled from his nostrils. His face turned purple. "I won't let this happen," he muttered through clenched teeth. "I won't!"

Diana looked on, holding her breath. Maia's angelic face flashed across her memory as she mentally bid good-bye to her daughter. *Look after her, Tom.* She had already made arrangements for her partner to get custody of Maia should she be killed in the line of duty. Her throat tightened at the thought of never seeing either of them again. *Keep her safe . . . and take care of yourself, too.*

"Aggggh!" An inarticulate gasp erupted from Cooper's lips as one last titanic effort rocked him from head to toe. His back arched, his eyes snapped open, and he threw out his arms before toppling backward onto the slick black rocks. His body jerked spasmodically, his head thrashing from side to side, before going completely limp. He lay atop the quivering ridge like a discarded rag doll.

The mountain stopped shaking. Not all at once, of course, but the tremors quickly subsided, with only a few mild aftershocks. Snow and ice continued to crash down in the distance, but the worst of the landslides appeared to be over. Within moments, the dripping ridge felt solid as a rock once more. Peeling off one glove, Diana laid her hand against the ground. She could feel the volcanic heat slipping away, retreating back into Rainier's molten depths. The exposed earth was cooling noticeably.

"Oh my God," she realized. "He did it." Elated, she turned and hollered back at Alana. "We did it! We stopped it in time!"

There would be no catastrophic eruption today.

They were going to live.

"Cooper!" she called out jubilantly. She was

so happy to be alive she could have kissed him. "Thank God! I knew you could do it." The latter was a bald-faced lie, but why spoil the moment? Diana promised herself that she would do everything in her power to see that Cooper got a full pardon for whatever crimes he might have committed in the past. He had really come through for them in the end. "Cooper?"

He didn't answer her.

"Cooper?" A sinking feeling dampened her spirits. She scrambled over to his side. Cooper lay flat on his back. All the blood had drained from his face. Foam flecked his lips. A blown pupil indicated serious trauma to his brain. She checked his pulse and was only mildly relieved to discover that he was still breathing. From the looks of things, that final seizure had fried his synapses. "Oh, Cooper . . . I'm so sorry."

Alana came up behind her. She appeared to have come through the earthquake with only a few minor scrapes and bumps. "Is he all right?"

"No," Diana said sadly. Spotting a lingering patch of wet snow, she pressed a handful of icy whiteness against her scalded hand. It helped . . . a little. "I don't think so."

TWENTY-ONE

"SO HE'S A VEGETABLE?"

Diana winced at Nina's choice of words. She and Marco were briefing their boss in Nina's office. Tom was elsewhere, taking care of some unfinished business of his own.

"Essentially," Diana admitted. "Doctor Clayton at Abendson doesn't hold out much hope for his recovery." A bitter smile tweaked her lips. "Chances are, he'll get Gorinsky's old room."

"Wow," Marco said. "Talk about irony."

Diana found it more tragic than ironic. No one would ever know how much Cooper DeMeers had sacrificed for the sake of Seattle and the entire Pacific Northwest. To avoid panicking the public with the knowledge of just how close a 4400 had come to triggering a major volcanic eruption, the entire case file, codenamed "Vesuvius," had been declared classified information. *Probably not a bad move,* she admitted. *People are scared enough of the 4400 as is.*

"What about the D. B. Cooper angle?" Nina asked. "The FBI would love to close that case at long last."

Diana thought long and hard before answering. She remembered what Cooper had said to her and Tom once, that it was the *mystery* of D. B. Cooper that kept people talking about the celebrated sky-jacker so many years later. "We never conclusively settled that issue, one way or another," she told Nina, neglecting to mention Cooper's final remarks atop Mount Rainier. "There's no real proof either way."

Let Cooper keep his legend, she resolved. *It's the least I can do for him.*

Marco gave her a funny look, but kept his mouth shut.

"Too bad," Nina said, scribbling a note onto the file. She shrugged and moved on to more pressing matters. "What about Aziz and Tanaka?"

"Looks like they were both in deep with the Nova Group. Besides their involvement in the 'Vesuvius' affair, we have reason to believe that it was Aziz who notified Jamie Skysinger that

Shawn and Isabelle would be at the Space Needle last Wednesday." Phone records had revealed that Jamie had received a call from Aziz's office earlier that morning. Confronted with this evidence, Simone and Aziz had wasted no time implicating each other. "We're not charging Simone with the assassination attempt, though, in exchange for her assistance in locating Cooper and Gorinsky."

"That may not help her much," Nina said grimly. "The NSA has expressed interest in both of them. Needless to say, the intelligence community can't wait to get their hands on a man who can detect liars and a woman who can see through walls."

Diana's conscience tweaked her a bit. This was Gary Navarro all over again. Not that Aziz and Simone didn't have it coming; their misguided attempts to recruit Cooper had nearly led to a disaster.

"Well," Marco quipped, "wherever they ship her, I hope it has a nice view."

Diana didn't like the idea that Simone would still be able to spy on people without restriction. *How long was she watching me and Tom?* She wondered if she would ever feel a true sense of privacy again.

"Still, that's two more Nova members down," Nina commented, looking on the bright side. "We think we've rounded up pretty much all of them now, except for a few stragglers."

Like Gary Navarro, Diana thought. She wasn't looking forward to bringing him in, which was only a matter of time. *He was our responsibility and we let him down.*

Nina closed the file. "Good work, people. I've already discreetly informed the emergency response folks that Rainier no longer poses an imminent threat."

"At least no more than it usually does," Marco added ominously. He scratched his head. "There's just one thing that still bothers me. You got to wonder what kind of ripple effect the Far Future People had in mind when they sent Cooper back to the twenty-first century with the power to trigger earthquakes and volcanoes?"

"Maybe we don't want to know," Diana said.

"Thanks for updating me in person about Aziz and Tanaka," Shawn said to his uncle. "Better I hear about it from you than on the evening news." He shook his head, appalled that the Center was linked once again to violence and terrorism. "I swear, I had absolutely no idea that Aziz was mixed up with Nova."

"That's kind of why I'm here, Shawn." His stern tone caught Shawn by surprise. Looking up from his desk, he saw that Tom Baldwin wasn't smiling. "This isn't the first time you've lost control of the people around you." Shawn realized belatedly that his uncle had requested this closed-door meeting at the Center in order to read him the riot act. "Maybe you need to run a tighter ship."

Shawn couldn't deny the accusation. He still blamed himself for naively funding the Nova Group's early operations, before he realized Daniel Armand's murderous intentions. "I know," he admitted guiltily, taking his uncle's words to heart. "I've been distracted lately. I'll try to do better."

"That's what I wanted to hear." Tom lightened up, sounding more like a concerned relative than a hard-ass federal agent. "Sorry to come down on you so hard, but I thought we needed to talk." He peeked at his wristwatch. "Gotta run. I promised Alana a night out. I figure I owe her one." He headed for the door. "Say hi to your mom and Danny for me."

Like I ever see them anymore, Shawn thought as his uncle left. The demands of running the Center, and keeping Isabelle happy, left him little or no time to spend with his own family. He couldn't remember the last time he'd talked to his mom. Maybe once this whole Nova business was history . . .

"Another hush-hush private meeting?" Isabelle

asked sarcastically as she barged into his office uninvited. Her exquisite face was flushed with indignation. She tossed a top-secret file on Cooper DeMeers onto his desk. "I can't believe you didn't tell me about this. A dormant volcano is about to blow up in our own backyard and you didn't think I needed to know about that?"

Shawn flicked through the folder in shock. There were details here even he didn't know. William Gorinsky had leeched energy from his own twin brother? "Where the hell did you get this?"

"That doesn't matter," Isabelle replied. "The point is you withheld vital information from me. I expect that of my father, but you're my boyfriend. You should know better than that." Resting her hands on the desktop, she leaned toward him until their faces were only inches apart. He nearly choked on the cloying aroma of her perfume. "We could have all been killed, Shawn. The entire Center could have been buried in a mudslide. Why didn't you tell me about this D. B. Cooper creep? I could have taken care of him in no time."

"That's what I was afraid of!" Shawn blurted.

Isabelle recoiled from his words. Her brown eyes narrowed suspiciously. "What's that supposed to mean?"

"Nothing," Shawn lied. He didn't want to fight this battle yet, not before he was ready. *If Uncle Tommy wants to know why I've lost focus,* he steamed, *here's a big part of the explanation.* There was no way around it: he had to break up with Isabelle for good, before she drove him to a complete nervous breakdown. But how could he do that without setting her off on another bloodthirsty rampage? What was that old saying about Hell having no fury like a woman scorned? Whoever coined that quote had probably never envisioned a woman like Isabelle, who could take that fury to a whole new level. He was going to have to handle this breakup *very* carefully.

But not right now.

"That didn't sound like 'nothing' to me," she accused him. "If you've got something to say, tell me."

"Forget I said anything," he said apologetically. Taking the folder off his desk, he tucked it into one of the attached file drawers. "I'm just buried under right now. Seems our chief legal counsel was in cahoots with the people trying to kill us." He gave her a sheepish grin, hoping to buy himself some time. "Maybe we can have this conversation later? Pretty please?"

His lame excuse did little to mollify her. "Fine,"

she said icily. "Come to think of it, I have some-where I need to go, too."

She stormed out of the office in a huff.

Dennis Ryland immediately cleared his schedule when Isabelle dropped in at Haspelcorp without an appointment.

"You know those experiments we talked about before?" She sat down across from him. Although her manner was cool and composed, he got a sense that she was seriously mad at someone. "The tests your scientists want to run on me?"

Ryland's eyes gleamed avidly. Doctor MacKay and his people had been chomping at the bit to get Isabelle into their labs. They believed that her unique physiology held the key to replicating the 4400s abilities. Doctor Ellsworth in Neuro was particularly keen to monitor her promicin levels, but so far Isabelle had resisted the idea of playing guinea pig for the scientists.

Was that about to change?

"Yes." He tried to conceal his eagerness. You didn't pressure someone like Isabelle. You let her come to you. "What about them?"

"Let's get started," she said decisively. Standing up, she turned toward the door. "Which way is the lab?"

EPILOGUE

IT WAS A beautiful spring day as Diana drove Maia through the large log gateway that served as the entrance to Mount Rainier National Park. Frankly, she had been in no hurry to return to the mountain anytime soon, but she thought it best to show Maia that there was no longer anything to be afraid of. She didn't want her daughter to grow up in the shadow of Rainier with that dreadful field trip still lingering in her mind. The goal today was to give Maia some happier memories of visiting the mountain.

Plus, if Diana was completely honest with herself, she wanted to see for herself that the frightening events Maia had foreseen had indeed come and gone.

The last time Maia had set foot on Rainier, she had been struck by a vision right away. Would the same thing happen today?

Please, no, Diana prayed. *I've had enough earthquakes to last a lifetime.*

Ever the scientist, she drove all the way up to Paradise to better duplicate Maia's original experience. Brightly colored lilies, bluebells, and heather beautified the grassy meadows overlooking the parking lot. Fields of flowers sprouted amid the retreating snow. Diana was glad to see the looming glaciers staying right where they belonged at the higher elevations. No steam or ash spewed from the snowcapped summit towering above them. Rainier was on its best behavior today.

Let's keep it that way, Diana thought.

"Here we are, honey." She parked the car a few yards away from the saucer-shaped visitor center. Doing her best to mask her own anxiety, she stepped around the car to open the door on the passenger side. "Let's go check out the snow."

Maia swung around in her seat, but hesitated before stepping out onto the pavement. The soles of her cute pink snow boots hovered above the blacktop. Diana knew she had to be remembering exiting the school bus over a week ago. Having recently lived through the real-life version of that vision, Diana couldn't blame her for stalling.

"It's okay, honey," she said soothingly. "Mommy's here for you."

Maia took a deep breath and bravely stepped down onto the asphalt. Diana watched her daughter's face carefully, alert for the signs of a scary vision coming on. She mentally crossed her fingers. *Here we go . . .*

Nothing happened.

Maia let out a sigh and smiled up at her mother.

"Better this time?" Diana asked.

"Yes," Maia said calmly. "But it's still going to erupt someday."

ACKNOWLEDGMENTS

As a devoted fan of the TV series, and an expatriate Seattleite, I jumped at the chance to write a novel about "The 4400." I owe a debt of gratitude to my editor, Margaret Clark, for thinking of me for this assignment; to my agents, Russ Galen and Ann Behar, for handling the legal end of things; and to Paula Block at CBS for approving the outline and manuscript. I also have to thank Michael Burstein and Inge Heyer for supplying me with the floor plan of the Science Fiction Museum in Seattle, the folks at TV.com's "4400" forum for helping me with obscure points of trivia, and the 4400 Wiki for being an incredibly useful reference source while writing this book, as was *The 4400: The Official Companion,* by Terry J. Erdmann.

And, as always, thanks to Karen, Alex, Churchill, Henry, Sophie, and Lyla for putting up with me while I obsessed over the 4400 for weeks at a time.

ABOUT THE AUTHOR

GREG COX is the *New York Times* bestselling author of numerous books and short stories. He has written the official movie novelizations of *Daredevil, Death Defying Acts, Ghost Rider, Underworld,* and *Underworld: Evolution,* as well as the novelizations of two popular DC Comics miniseries, *Infinite Crisis* and *52.* In addition, he has authored original novels and stories based on such popular series as *Alias, Batman, Buffy, Fantastic Four, Farscape, Iron Man, Roswell, Spider-Man, Star Trek, Underworld, Xena, X-Men,* and *Zorro.* His official website is www.gregcox-author.com.

A former resident of "Promise City," Greg now lives in Oxford, Pennsylvania.

Not sure what to read next?

Visit Pocket Books online at
www.simonsays.com

Reading suggestions for
you and your reading group
New release news
Author appearances
Online chats with your favorite writers
Special offers
Order books online
And much, much more!